LOVEBOMBING

How to Avoid Narcissists and Scammers and Unlock the Treasures of Self-Love

Mara Hall

First Edition July 2022

Book cover design by Fyra

ISBN 979-8-218-03615-7

www.marahall.com
www.lovebombingthebook.com

Dedication

This book is dedicated to my pride and joy, my "Tasmanian Toddler" Marley Nicole. I love you endlessly, and all I do is for you.

Preface

This story is a true testament of pain, struggle, and not acknowledging unhealed childhood trauma. This story is loosely based on true life experiences that happened during a global pandemic. This story is not meant to showcase but shed light on people who take advantage of empaths and get away with it. This book is entertaining, jaw dropping, and is meant to warn while also inspiring and providing education on new terminology and topics that most have never heard of.

This book is not meant to pass judgment or bash a certain sector of society. It is meant to showcase what happens when someone falls for the wrong person, gets taken advantage of, and can't let go of the detrimental grips of love and lust, which leads them to succumb to desperation.

Although I had my own horrifying experience with an actual sociopathic narcissist, the following story is loosely based on these real events. Certain parts have been fictionalized solely for dramatic purposes and are not intended to reflect on any actual person, place, event, or entity.

Mara Hall

September 2022

Table of Contents

Acknowledgments

Thank you, FATHER, for creating me and making me into the BLACK UNICORN that I am.

Thank you to my MOM and DAD for providing an amazing foundation for all of my creative endeavors and raising me to be the woman I am today.

MARLEY NICOLE, THIS BOOK IS DEDICATED TO YOU, TO NEVER MAKE THE SAME MISTAKES THAT I MADE.

THANK YOU TO: CARL, my best friend in the whole wide world who has put up with me since 1994; NATALIE for the inspiration for this book and for the months and months of listening to me vent and hash out all of my emotions; TRIANA for being the sister I never knew I needed; KAYCEE for inspiring me daily to keep going; NICOLE ANN, thank you for loving me and Poohder through this turbulent roller coaster ride; KOKO, from student to good friend, you have helped me tremendously; GINGER for always having my back and front; GIGI, my main girl forever; SPREES, my sister from another mister! DDE, I love you to the moon and back. TASHA, I can always count on you for help and support. NIKEA, thank you for always giving me the hard facts and tough love that I need. GRANDADDY, you've seen it all and love you for being here for me at my time of need and pulling me through with positive words of encouragement.

Thank you Alana, Allison, Charita, Talora, Miss Janet, T. Leake, Chad, Jocelyn, Deeran, Maieka, Mario, Josh, Tracey, Malika, Stu, and Coley Cole for being my village and holding me down.

My Bigo Tribe, you rock for helping me through this all. Jarhonda, Millie, JJ, Ari, Nicki G, Stevie, Mila, Jerri Reid, Shalik, and Boogie.

I'd also like to give a huge thank you to A.J. Joiner of Blooksy Books/Blooksy Publishing for all of his help and guidance on this writing journey.

Introduction

In *Lovebombing: How to Avoid Narcissists and Scammers and Unlock the Treasures of Self-Love*, author Mara Hall takes readers on a journey through the dark levels of narcissism and how to see the signs when they first arise. Because of the twisted nature of narcissism, Mara reveals alternative lifestyles to the average person and how this can affect your psyche. Welcome to *Fifty Shades of Grey* meets *Zane's Sex Chronicles*—with a little self-help sprinkled in!

Let's meet Heather Moore, an accomplished reality TV entertainer and recently divorced single mother. During the global COVID-19 pandemic, Heather was introduced to a live streaming platform called EGO Live, where she found comfort, solace, and a social life outside of herself. It was there she meets Kyrie, a young sculptor who sweeps her off her feet instantly and cures her lonely woes and pandemic blues. He is a dream come true—or so Heather thinks.

LOVEBOMBING takes us through love at first sight gone wrong: the dark and twisted mind of a narcissist and a loving, unsuspecting victim.

STORY 1
Welcome to EGO Live

I hate COVID. The toll that this pandemic has taken on society is unparalleled. I was completely losing my mind in the house with a Tasmanian Toddler. For months, she was my only company and companion. By the end of summer of 2020, four months into the global pandemic, my parents promised me that they were going to drive all the way down to Atlanta from Cincinnati to pick me and my daughter Morgan up and take us back to Cincinnati for a few months. They knew how miserable I was and how hard it was to be by myself with my daughter. Only problem was they had to wait for the worst part of the pandemic to pass. It seemed that we were already through the bad times, and it was safer to travel the mean streets of Cincinnati and brave the wonderful highway of Interstate 75 South to Atlanta, Georgia.

On that wonderful day in June, they packed up my mom's Ford Fusion to *rescue* us. They came down to the ATL like saviors! We packed up all of our things, and we went traveling as a family to the Queen City. This was great because now I had help with my daughter who was around fifteen months old. In Cincinnati, I was at home. It was now time to rejuvenate my mind, body, and soul by spending lots of quality time with my family, as much as we could during a global pandemic.

My friend, Ray, who I met in Los Angeles, dated one of the writers on a TV show that I worked on. She hit me up on Facebook Messenger saying that she had an opportunity for me that I should know about. I looked through and read the message that she sent. She also gave me an Exhibit B sheet, where it had the payout for what was going on. At the time, I didn't realize what it was or what she was giving me.

"I have this business opportunity for you, and you can make a lot of money on a live streaming app that I am on called EGO Live," Ray said. "I'm trying to bring real entertainment to the app and people who are actually entertainers versus people who are just live streaming on here for no reason."

"Cool. What do I have to do?" I asked.

She said that I would have to download the app and audition for thirty minutes to show my talents, skills, and prospective content for the app.

"I can do that."

Ray set up an appointment and told me to download the app and gave me additional instructions on what to do. She set up the time for my audition, and BAM, I went live! During the audition, I was myself—talking, dancing, turning on music to perform an HBCU majorette dance; I was just being my vivacious, effervescent, amazing self. It wasn't anything extra for me. It was just me being me, and I thought that I killed the audition.

I did. The EGO admins accepted me, and I became a host.

After this, Ray told me that I had to do a maximum of two hours a day for thirty hours a month. This was the first requirement in being an EGO Live TV Host. This had to be completed within thirty days to fulfill the quota requirement. The second requirement was to acquire or receive forty thousand "Mean green" or gifts during the month. Forty thousand Mean green was equivalent to around six hundred cash. This was not an easy task I soon found out.

I got started right away doing my hours, sitting on my phone, talking, and thinking somebody was watching me live. But actually nobody was in my room. It would just be a lot of bots. They have bots looking at the broadcasters on the app. This is the way they monitor the live broadcast. At first, it was very hard for me to be on there talking to bots or basically talking to myself. To make it interesting, I would try to incorporate the app into my day-to-day activities. I would play with my daughter live and exercise during my broadcast.

Whenever I would do my hair, I would wash my hair and twist it on live. I didn't have an audience. Nobody was checking me out—until one day, somebody found me. It was a guy from London who saw me working out on the app. He liked my energy and vibes. He said there was something about me that intrigued him. He introduced me to his friend on the app, and they showed me a few things, like how you give the gifts and what happens with the gifts. That was my first interaction with people on the app where somebody was actually talking to me in my live broadcast.

I told Ray that the app was okay, but I felt like I was on there most of the time by myself, not doing anything, talking to these bots. I told her that I thought that it was a waste of time. In fact, I really didn't like it, and I wanted to quit. I was tapping out. This was not for me. She reassured me three to four times to not quit, that I could do this.

"Quite honestly, people are making a killing," Ray said. "They're making so much money on this app. You do not want to stop."

I didn't get what she was saying and how much money you could make on the app. At the time, I thought that it was a waste of time. But she said it wasn't. After a week or so of thinking about the pros and cons of the app, it finally clicked. She had introduced me to an app that could change my financial status and definitely supplement my income. I could literally make up to twenty-four thousand dollars a month on this app live streaming because there were regular people on this app that didn't have as much talent as I did, Regular Joe Schmoes from Cleveland, Ohio, who were making a killing just by sitting there talking to people.

I stuck it out, and I started spending more time on the app, looking at everybody's profiles and going through, seeing people's lives, and seeing what people were talking about. Then I found that there was a lot of negativity all around the app. A lot of the people on the app were low vibrational people who cussed out other people and started fighting. Now, don't get me wrong; it was very entertaining, but it was also kind of too much as well. The app reminded you of people basically having their own personal reality show for their live broadcast. I kept scrolling through people's live broadcasts, and many nights, I would go down a rabbit hole and end up watching broadcasts into the wee hours of the night.

The rabbit holes are where the story began.

STORY 2
Getting to Know EGO

As August came to a close, I was at the end of my summer vacation in Cincinnati with Mom, Dad, and my daughter Morgan. Because of COVID-19's strict guidelines, we were basically confined to the house. The only places that we could go were to grocery stores and restaurants for carry out.

I was still on the EGO Live App until three and four o'clock in the morning night after night.

Addicted.

"Scrolling the EGO streets" is a term used for when we felt like we were eternally swiping. It took you down a rabbit hole because the entertainment sucked you in. While scrolling, I came across Connie O, a full figured, African American woman with a raspy New York accent who had a tremendous following, was doing a live broadcast.

My goal was to enter her EGO room and take notes. In the app, a broadcaster has a room and a box; in the box, another host or person on the app can join the broadcaster and talk to them live. Just as I entered, a man named Woodie was in Connie O's box, and the pair was talking.

Woodie was a very articulate, attractive African American gay male. His voice was smooth as silk and comforting. He seemed very knowledgeable about the app. He was also very happy to give information about EGO. I was drawn to them because they felt like people that I could relate to. They also gave me the impression that they were kind and not messy, like everyone else on the app. I started talking to them in the comments and saying that I was new to the app. I told them that I was a public figure who worked on many reality TV shows, which they didn't believe.

"No, you're not," Connie O said. "Come up here and let me see your face because people like to catfish on this app."

After joining them in the box, I said, "No, I'm really on a lot of reality shows. Google my name."

"Oh my God, you're famous," Woodie said.

I came on the stream with my head scarf on, lying in the bed with my comfy pajamas. We immediately clicked, and they gave me a wonderful introduction to the EGO Live App.

Connie O and Woodie seemed to be really good people. They told me that they would help show me the ropes, get my name out there, and highlight my platform.

After that night, I continued to frequent Connie and Woodie's lives. I found myself resonating more with Woodie. He had a fantastic personality and an amazing voice. He was very personable, engaging, kind, and he was very giving. Because of this, I would frequent his live broadcast all the time. Every time I would come to one, he would be so kind and so nice to me and impart vital information about the app. He would also have panels, which were forums for four to nine individuals to participate in discussion at one time. I loved participating on his panels because they were very entertaining. Coming on his panels and live broadcasts made me feel like I had found someone on the app that I could relate to. I felt at home and welcomed. This was important because during the pandemic, I felt like I was losing myself with depression and loneliness. This helped me tremendously.

Soon after I befriended Woodie, he stopped by my live broadcast. Whenever I went live, he would give me wonderful gifts called "Mean green" on the app. I saw that he was a giving person. So in my eyes, if he was giving me gifts, then I could trust him. He was the kind of person that I could work with or collaborate with on the app. From there, we just created such an amazing relationship going to one another's lives. He was always teaching me something new about the app.

On Sundays at one o'clock, he offered Wood Lessons where he would teach people about the app, explaining the ins and outs about the app, how to make money on the app, who to talk to, and who to connect with. Every time I would come to his live broadcast, he would connect me with different people that I needed to know. The first person that he connected me with was a guy named Bamm. Bamm was the founder of the Live Thrive family, which was a popular family on the app.

Bamm was extremely ambitious and took pride at being the number one entertainment family on EGO. I would see their members often as I scrolled the EGO streets. I remembered him mentioning that he taught EGO Lessons in Woodie's live streams. So when Woodie connected me with Bamm, I immediately contacted Bamm via Instagram about taking the class that he offered to learn about the EGO Live App. I paid $100 to sign up for the class, and I was excited with my first foray into EGO and about learning the app from Woodie and from Bamm.

After becoming Bamm's client, I noticed that it was difficult to get in contact with him so that I could get on his schedule. I soon realized that he did business in a "millennial" type of way. That didn't sit well with me because it lacked professionalism.

Examples of this were having to contact him for sessions and him being late for calls or making calls and not being available when I would call him. I indicated this to him, and he was very responsive to constructive criticism. Moving forward and working with him more, he changed for the better and became a valuable ally and asset to me on the app and in real life.

Like Woodie, Bamm also introduced me to other people. Most of Bamm's friends, like Temi, Louie, Blaze, and Kyrie, were in the LGBTQI community. Most of the host on the platform were from the LGBTQI community. I enjoyed watching and participating because, for the most part, they were a hoot! EGO was becoming a mainstay for me. It really provided a new avenue to escape the reality of the pandemic that we were in. Meeting new people on the app was a great substitution for the real world—at the time.

STORY 3
EGO Joy

September 2020 was the seventh month of the global pandemic. I was truly enjoying the EGO live app, spending more time on the app every day, watching people's live broadcasts. I was going into people's rooms on the app and making friends and alliances. The app was truly bringing me joy. I loved being live in my broadcast. I loved meeting people. I loved talking to people. I loved people coming into my room and just sharing with me their hopes, dreams, aspirations, and then doing the same thing. I found so much peace, so much joy, and it was getting me through the uncertainty and turbulence of the pandemic.

During this time, my friend Natricia came into town from LA with her sister Latrese, and they spent time with me and Morgan. We had a really good time. I had her on my live broadcast. I taught her about EGO. She spent lots of quality Auntie Time with

Morgan, and they had a great time. I was still substitute teaching virtually, and I absolutely hated it. I was teaching elementary school, fourth grade to be exact. It really got on my everlasting nerve. Morgan was still in a home daycare, and she was learning a lot at school. The activities that she learned were amazing. She was really doing well. Every day, I enjoyed my daughter being creative, energetic, and full of life.

On EGO, I hung out in Woodie's room and loved every minute of it. I was always around him in his solo lives, in his box, or also on his live panels. I found new hosts and new people to hang around and people who were just making my time on the app better. I also met several characters on EGO Live through Woodie. These were the people that frequent his room that he was close with. I started to develop EGO bonds or friendships with them. The first person was Woodie's best friend Temi, who worked in human resources for a retail company and was an aspiring podcaster.

Temi was a tall African American gay male that had extremely feminine mannerisms. He had a very condescending and negative tone and spirit. His voice was very distinctive, and the timbre was very annoying. His demeanor was quiet at first, but he was not a nice person. My first impression of him was that he was very fake, and he seemed to be an opportunist.

Ramel was African American—with *a little more* as he would say. A gay man, Ramel was mild mannered, very nice, and very pleasant. He was short in stature and fair skinned. From the very start, Ramel seemed cool. He was also a great listener and sound individual.

Louie, a light skinned African American gay male who was very vibrant, positive, and supportive, was best friends with Blaze, an African American gay man who had the warmest personality. Louie was very much so the life of the party, very jovial and very loud at times, but had an infectious personality. His personality meshed well with Blaze's, who was good-hearted and often appeared to be the three C's: cool, calm, and collected. Like their meshing personalities, their Louie and Blaze's different appearances complemented their friendship as Blaze's chocolate complexion, beautiful skin, and enough hair waves to fill an ocean was the yin to Louie's light-skinned yang.

I also met Kyrie, who said he was pansexual. Quiet and reserved, he was always doing something artistic like sculpting, painting, or designing art pieces in his live broadcast. He was an attractive guy but seemed to have a dark cloud around him. He also smoked a lot and was always high. He seemed very nice and pleasant in his live broadcast as well.

One day as I was scrolling through the EGO streets, I came across a host named Fresh Live.

Fresh Live was a fun, cool, hip Southern and intelligent guy. From what I gathered, he was an engineer by trade, college educated, from Louisiana with a wonderful Louisiana Southern accent. I loved being in his room, which was very energetic and drama free. He was very helpful with teaching about the app and letting me know things about it. Fresh Live was very easy on the eyes, a very handsome man and someone whom I would love to date. When I visited his live broadcast, I was having a good time meeting all the people that he knew.

Fresh Live started introducing me to all of his people. They followed me, and I followed them. After a while, I grew to have a crush on him. The crush I developed made me go to his room all the time. Every time he went live, I was there watching him. He also flirted with me in his live broadcasts. It sparked something in me. It actually let me know that my woman parts were working just fine because I thought they were expired and out of commission forever!

Going through a divorce created a belief that I never wanted to be with men ever again. During my marriage, and after my libido was very low, I wasn't even interested in being intimate, nor did I have the desire to ever be so again.

Fresh Live was the first guy to excite my spirit and my soul. He was very attractive and my type. This secret crush made the app even more fun. I told Woodie about him, and we both tried to get some more intel and hang out with him in his room. As we watched him, we figured out that he had an affinity for Caucasian girls. This was a bummer for me because I really wanted to date him.

As I tried to show him that I was interested in him, I sent him a Unicorn during his PK. A PK was an event that hosts used to get a lot of Mean green at one time, and a Unicorn was a very expensive gift on the app worth two hundred fifty dollars. I knew or thought that I was ok in doing this because he taught me that whatever you give in a PK, the other host should give it back.

Well, Fresh Live would come through my live broadcast from time to time, but he never returned the Unicorn. I actually had to ask him flat out for it back. He didn't return it until a few months later. I also realized that people flirted on this app so that people would give them Mean green. That's exactly what he was doing with all of the guests in his live room. This was basically the end of our friendship on EGO. When he showed me his true colors, that was a wrap.

The next person I met on the app was a girl named Easy Lay. Her name was Easy Lay because she was very promiscuous and as old folks say, 'loose as a goose!' I met her after she came into my room. She said that she liked my energy, spirit, and personality; she came by my room all the time and always threw different gifts at me.

We started to develop a friendship because of that. I would go to her room and show love to her, and she would do the same. She would also spend time in my room and be in the comments. She was African American, had a light skin complexion and beautiful sisterlocs down to her backside. She was a beautiful young lady, stunning actually and the life of the party, but very aggressive.

As me and Easy Lay started to develop our friendship, we decided to exchange information off of the app and talk via the That's That app. As this relationship started building, we enjoyed talking about different EGO relationships and different things happening on the app. She started telling me about a guy on the app who was the founder of a family called Denied Access; his name was Reimo. Reimo really took a liking to her and started gifting her many gifts and showed her attention and came into her live broadcast. They started talking and dating on and off the app. The only thing about Reimo was that several girls on the app liked him as well. They actually started to hate on Easy Lay and got her account banned often because of how jealous they were of her and Reimo. Through her telling me about her relationship with Reimo, our relationship continue to build. She became one of my biggest supporters on the app. She enjoyed telling me how to make more money on EGO.

As time progressed, I started developing my own programming on the app. I had different events day to day that would bring people into my lives. The first event that I did was Grown Woman Wednesdays, "where we would drink our wine and we feel oh so fine." So every Wednesday, I had Grown Woman Wednesday, either a solo live, or sometimes I had panels where we talked about different topics. At first, it really moved very slowly. But after a while, it picked up, and all of the people that I met on the app started coming to support me. It became a really joyous occasion and event on EGO LIVE.

Through all of this, I was creating a community on the app, and I so loved what I was building.

STORY 4
EGO Is Life

By October 2020, I was still teaching school, and I began to really enjoy the kids because I taught music to them, and they loved my lessons. However, the stress of everything that we were doing in the class made it very, very difficult. Being on Zoom for six hours a day and sitting in front of the computer was taxing on my eyes, mind, body, and soul.

So my outlet for that was getting on EGO. I spent a lot of time on EGO. I found a community and a tribe there. I spent time on Temi's panels. Temi, who seemed to be the ringleader of all of the gay guys, usually coordinated everything that they participated in and did. They usually had night panels every day. The panels were a good substitute for not being able to go out. It was like a social hour or social party, and I was having a blast. Usually Louie, Blaze, Kyrie, and sometimes Woodie and Ramel, were there.

The panels were so much fun. Hanging out helped me forget about the pandemic and how miserable I was. All of the guys on the panel were from the LGBTQI community, so a lot of the verbiage that they talked about had to do with the gay lifestyle and gay colloquialisms, which was fun to be around. I enjoyed it because I loved hanging around gay dudes and always had. I'm what the gays call a "good Judy." I spent a lot of time getting to know all of them. It was really an outlet for me to just let go, let loose, and get my mind off of the fact that we were in a global pandemic. It also gave me a lot of time to have a social life. A social life inside of my home without leaving my home. On the panels, I would banter with Louie or Blaze. They really took a kind and genuine interest in me.

Louie was usually the one who was cracking jokes and singing. Blaze was real chill and laid back. Woodie was always giving information and trying to teach people about the app. Temi was usually playing video games while he was on the panel. Then we had Kyrie.

Kyrie was always doing something artistic on the panel because he was a self-proclaimed artist. He was always painting, drawing, and making sculptures. He was always at his artistic workstation. One day, he began flirting with me, which was so confusing to me. I thought that he was gay. He had feminine mannerisms, and the tone of his voice was a dead giveaway for his sexual orientation.

The way that he interacted with the others in the group also pointed at the homosexual direction for him. He used all of the terms that they did and laughed at all of the jokes they told. I thought that it was flattering and really cute that he was flirting with me, but I didn't pay it any mind because one: aesthetically he wasn't my type; and two, he was gay. I don't date gay men. Kyrie wasn't my type also because he looked very mangy. He would often wear do-rags and clothes that were not flattering. He reminded me of a thug or a street dude. I hated when guys wore do-rags. It was like "school on Saturday" with no class. He also seemed as if he was sad. There was always a look in his eyes like he was hurting deep down inside.

At the end of the month, my cousins Mecole and Myra came into town for Halloween. I was so excited because we had things planned for Halloween. We went to a drive-thru trick or treat situation and different parties. We went to Six Flags, which was exciting for Morgan. I was excited, too, because we had an amazing time.

On Halloween, I dressed up as a pumpkin and so did Morgan. Mecole dressed up as the Bride of Chucky, and her daughter was Chucky. We got a lot of candy, and we all had a blast. Later on that night, there was a

Halloween panel on EGO for one of my agency members. At this Halloween panel/Halloween variety show, I dressed up as Lizzo. I wore a risqué leotard/bodysuit. I also had my flute and played it just like Lizzo. You couldn't be Lizzo without a great twerk session. It was so much fun impersonating her! I received a lot of "Mean green" that night for my performance. This was the first time where I saw a return in my investment on the app. I actually made a lot of "Mean green" on the app because I had good content, and I built great relationships.

I met a wonderful friend on the app, John Mississippi. I met John the first week that I was on an app by "Matching." "Matching" was a way for hosts and users on the app to meet and possibly network and build alliances. I met a lot of good people this way. John was a really nice guy and very, very attractive. He had an amazing energy and wonderful light and spirit. We frequented each other's rooms and helped each other out and supported one another.

John invited me to an auction panel that he was participating in. At this auction, Kyrie and Bamm were also participating. At the time, I didn't realize that they were all in the Live Thrive family. At the auction, John was doing very well because he had a lot of organic, genuine support. People really loved him. Kyrie and Bamm were not doing as well as John on the panel. No one was really there to support them and hadn't really given them any "Mean green." So I texted Bamm and asked him if he was participating, and he said, yes. When he told me that, I sent Bamm a Unicorn, and I also sent Kyrie a Unicorn to help them out.

They couldn't believe that I sent them those Unicorns, but I was just a helpful person. Remember, a Unicorn is worth two hundred fifty dollars on the app. Very expensive! It's EGO protocol that if someone sends you a Unicorn, you should reciprocate that and send it back. Well that's what you were supposed to do. Two days later, Temi decided that I should have a PK so that I can get the Unicorns back from the people that I sent them to. He wanted to do a PK with me. But I also felt like he had an ulterior motive in doing so because he said he also wanted to interview me. My Spidey-sense kicked in because I really felt that Temi was an opportunist. So we had the Impossible PK, and Kyrie threw the Unicorns back to me, but Bamm only trickled "Mean green" back to me in the form of bells.

I was really taken aback that Bamm didn't give me the Unicorn back that I gave him and that he trickled the "Mean green" back to me. I was surprised because I told him about the situation with Fresh Live and how he never came back to give me the Unicorn that I gave him in his PK a month earlier.

When Bamm didn't give me the Unicorn back, I asked Woodie what I should do. He told me to ask Temi because they were both in the Live Thrive family. I ended up asking Kyrie about Bamm, and he asked that we talk about that off of the app. We exchanged information and talked for like maybe thirty minutes on the phone. He told me that this was his real number. He seemed to be a very kind and caring young man. He was super-duper nice to me and gave me his opinion on Bamm and told me that he really didn't want people to take advantage of me. He also wanted to be my alliance on the app and do EGO business.

This meant that we would come by each other's lives and tap the screen, share the live and gift each other as host. As he spoke negatively about Bamm, like he was throwing shade at him. I thought that was interesting, but I was also happy that he gave me an outlook into who Bamm was. This was one of the first signs of what Kyrie's personality was. Kyrie told me that he would like to keep in contact with me, and I told him that was ok. He also told me that he would come into my live broadcast and support me in any way that he could. I was happy to have another alliance on the app to push me toward reaching my quota and goals. Now I was also side eyeing a few folks on this app. Bamm seemed nice at the heart of it all and later proved to be a great friend, but he was definitely driven by his ambition. Temi, on the other hand, was a low down dirty snake, and I should have followed my intuition and discernment when it was tingling in my spine. Note to self: go with your gut!

STORY 5
EGO Boo

The global pandemic was still in full swing in Nov 2020, and the country was in the midst of an extremely important presidential election. Kamala Harris, my sorority sister, was penned for the VP. Joe Biden was running for President of the United States against Donald Trump. I was still teaching, and EGO was giving me relief from *all the things*. I went live when I was teaching, multitasking because I was also teaching Music Appreciation at a local HBCU. Things felt like the new normal.

On November fifth, I texted Kyrie, asking him to support me on the app. We made small talk about how he would send me a shield or two during my next PK. He was always polite and asked how my day was going.

A few days later, he sent me a picture of him from an LGBTQI Ball. He looked very handsome.

"You cleaned up nicely," I said.

"I was thinking about you."

Now I wondered why he was telling me that he was thinking about me.

"That was sweet for thinking about me," I replied.

"Did you have a good weekend?"

"Yes, I'm tired from wrangling with Morgan."

"She's adorable."

We kept having small talk via text on that day. He texted me again a couple of days later to ask how I was doing.

"I'm thinking about you," he answered simply. "I hope I'm not bothering you."

"You're too sweet. You're not bothering me. I'm about to teach my college class."

He told me that he was making a new sculpture, and I invited him to Grown Folk Wednesday, which was the name for my live show on Wednesdays. He said he would come and do anything for his "EGO Boo." I told him that I liked the sound of that "EGO Boo."

"I think you're so beautiful."

"Thank you," I cooed. "You really know how to make a girl feel good."

I also invited him to my Impossible Star PK. He said he would come and told me that he just loved my personality and my smile.

"Yay! I'm blushing."

"You should be blushing."

With that, I could only respond with *LOL*.

"I know I'm not your type," he said, "so it would be just an EGO crush."

I lifted an eyebrow and texted, "How do you know you are not my type?"

"I guess I don't."

"Why would you say that? Are you just trying to put your feelers out there?"

"Just making a statement. Not too many women would date a pansexual."

I thought he was talking about his looks.

He told me that he was attracted to personalities, not limited in sexual choice with regard to biological sex, gender, or gender identity. However, he was attracted to mostly women. He had dated men, but he never slept with a man. He had also dated transgender women. I was like wow! I had never heard of Pan Sexual until now. I also told him that he was actually too young for me. He was twenty-nine, and I was forty-four. I was old enough to be his teenage mother. But I was so flattered, and my heart was giddy.

"Trust me, you're actually younger than the women I usually date.

But he understood, and that's why he didn't really want to say anything. I asked him how old were the women that he usually dated? He told me that his ex was forty-four and they dealt with each other for five years. Before her, his ex may have been almost fifty now.

I told him that I was in that age group and that he thought that I was actually younger than I was. I asked him did they know he was Pan Sexual?

"Yea I'm honest about who I am; some people get it, some don't," he said. "I have never cheated.

"I told him that I love your honesty."

He also said that he was attracted to men but had never been with a man. On EGO, there was a lot of LGBTQI talk, so I asked him would he be a top or a bottom because that's what they ask all the time.

"Oh I'm sorry, I ain't taking no penis, to each his own," he said. "They always say I'm not really gay because I love women. Everything about a woman, there's not a man can do to compare. I would most likely talk to a trans woman before a man and even that's not likely. I don't know; I'm weird, I just like what I like. I guess I'm just complicated.

"Do trans-women have penises?" I asked.

" Some do, some don't."

Oh wow I was learning.

Kyrie said, "I like ass and breasts; penis doesn't do it for me."

"What about men attracts you?" I asked.

"I used to think I was a lesbian until I had oral sex with a woman and saw it wasn't for me. The appearance of a man attracts him. See, I love eating pussy. Really love it. Something about that statement excited me."

Maybe it was the fact that I hadn't had sex in two years. Or I thought that I couldn't be aroused in that way again. This intrigued me, so that's when I called him.

And we talked for hours.

Is This Too Good to Be True?

Almost immediately, Kyrie started lovebombing me.

Lovebombing occurs when a person bombards their partner with excessive attention, grand gestures, and lavish signs of affection often in the beginning of a relationship. While this may sound great and like a normal part of the "honeymoon phase," lovebombing has dangerous ulterior motives rooted in manipulation and control. Lovebombing is not a genuine attempt to build a healthy, loving relationship; it is a tool of emotional abuse and creates toxic relationship dynamics. It is characterized by excessive attention and affection with the goal of making the recipient feel dependent and obligated to that person. Another way a lovebomber hooks you in is by mirroring all of the things that you are into.

Kyrie called and texted me several times a day and spoke only sweet nothings into my ears. This was a dream come true for a girl like me or any girl. Who wouldn't want affection and attention from an attractive, talented young man?

With a narcissist, they use this tactic to put you under their web of lies and deception all in an effort to use you for their narcissistic supply.

Because of what I saw as an overflow of love, attention, and mutual interests, I fell for Kyrie quickly.

The beginning of our relationship began after he texted me one night, telling me how much he enjoyed giving cunnilingus.

After that, I called him. We spoke on the phone for hours and enjoyed each other's company on the phone for the rest of the evening. There was an instant attraction emotionally, physically, and mentally. We didn't have phone sex on that first conversation, but I was definitely aroused.

There was something about Kyrie that was soothing. He made me feel at ease and put me on a high level of comfort. He was charismatic, engaging, thoughtful, fun, youthful, and highly intelligent. Speaking to him on the phone that day gave me a certain level of energy that I needed but didn't know I needed.

He spoke love, confidence, and encouragement to me. He spoke to my ego by showing me with words that complemented my other features. He said that I was beautiful, loved my personality, and that I had an amazing smile. The words that he spoke were electric and even more so on how he said them to me. I was literally on cloud twenty-five while talking to him.

We spoke about EGO Live, art, fashion, music, and our careers. We seemed very compatible. I was immediately smitten by his charm, his wit, and his intellect. He was very smooth and thoughtful. He asked about my relationship with my soon-to-be ex-husband and was very caring in his responses and advice he gave me on how to get through it.

I was so happy that I gave him a chance because I was really enjoying his company. The first day that we spoke on the phone, we spoke for hours; it was like I was speaking to my best friend or a person I had known for a very long time. There was a high level of comfort and familiarity with Kyrie, and I felt at home. Everything that I liked, he liked—from my musical choices, to art, to clothes, to fashion.

We spoke about where we came from. He told me that he was raised in the Cabrini Green projects of Chicago, Illinois, and that he was raised by his aunt because his mother was bi-polar schizophrenic. He also told me that his father was a career criminal and was incarcerated. He went to college for art and went for his master's degree in design. I was impressed by the life that he had made for himself. He was twenty-nine, had a career, was college educated and driven. All of those characteristics were very attractive to me.

I was immediately smitten by Kyrie, so much so that I called Woodie to see what the scoop on him was.

"I just got off the phone talking to him for hours, and I like him," I said. "But is he gay?"

"No," Woodie said, "he's Pan."

In the end, it really didn't matter what Woodie had to say about him. I was hooked from the very start. I also admired him for his honesty with his sexuality. If he was this honest about his sexual orientation, I could accept him for who he was because he bared his soul with me.

Kyrie and I talked on the phone every day and night. When we weren't on the phone, we were in each other's rooms on EGO, gifting each other. He even came to my Grown Folk Wednesday Panel and said that he enjoyed it. After the panel, I thanked him for coming, and we FaceTimed each other for the rest of the night. The overwhelming sense of comfort and attraction was evident from the beginning.

The next morning and every morning after, he would either call or text me "Good Morning, Beautiful. Hope you have a good day!" Then he would add something sexual like, "I want your lips."

This would excite me because I literally hadn't had sex in two years. I tried to keep it casual, but it didn't work. In between casual conversation and pleasantries, he would lead the conversation to the sexual lane. I tried to steer clear from it, but I couldn't. Since I hadn't had sex in so long, I thought that my lady parts expired to never work again. I told him that my check engine light was on, and I needed a tune up. That was a hint to him if he was paying attention. Talking to and videoing with him brought up so much pent-up sexual desires that I didn't know existed in me anymore.

He moved fast. Very fast. We began our conversation at eight a.m., and by ten-thirty, keep in mind this was the first week of us talking on the phone, he was sending dick pics to me, but I didn't need them because I had a very vivid imagination.

"I guess your check engine light is off," he said. He wanted me next to him. We masturbated on the phone with each other. I didn't let him see my body, but it was a euphoric feeling. I didn't know that I could be that aroused by a man anymore. I loved the way I felt: Alive again.

He gave me a sexual rebirth.

During our time on the phone, he told me that I was gonna make him come to Atlanta. He asked if it was ok if he came to visit me. I said yes. I don't know why I did. This was gonna be the biggest mistake of my life. He started looking for flights on Expedia. I told him to see if he could come the weekend before Thanksgiving because I was off work. He checked the dates to see if there were any flights. I checked in with my nanny to see if she could watch Morgan. As we continued talking, I told Kyrie about my anger toward Fresh Live because he wouldn't return the Unicorn I gave him. I got very upset, but Kyrie comforted me by saying he didn't want me worrying about him anymore, and I let his calm demeanor wash right over me, calming me as well.

By three o' clock, he told me that he really wished I was in the shower with him. I called him and then afterwards, sent him a video that said I was smiling over here for real, for real. He told me that all he wanted to do was help keep that beautiful smile on my life. By the end of the night, he asked if I still wanted him to look for flights.

"I sure do, Boo!"

The next day I texted him, "Good Morning, Handsome!"

I woke up that day with so much joy, thanking him for making my heart smile.

"Anything for you, Beautiful. Thank you for giving me a chance," he said. He also told me that he couldn't get me off his mind.

"The feeling is mutual," I shared.

"I'm seriously sprung over here."

For the next couple of days, we spoke every day and every night. He would tell me things like he couldn't get my voice out of his mind, he adored me and that he should be here holding me.

Very sweet things that a girl wanted to hear from the guy that she was dating. Each day, I was falling for him more and more. I would watch his lives more and more and give him strategies on how to win with his contributors. We were building a solid foundation, and I was truly smitten by his every word, thought, and movement.

He had booked his flight to Atlanta, and we both scheduled COVID and STD tests.

He was coming to visit me.

And I was *so* happy.

STORY 7
I Found Love on EGO

I was falling deep for Kyrie. But with a narcissist, the person that I thought that I was falling in love with didn't exist. This person that Kyrie was presenting was a mask. He was showing me a reflection of what I wanted and what I was, so I was essentially falling in love with myself. Kyrie got to know me very well. He wanted to know everything about me: my likes, wants, dreams, hopes, and most importantly my fears. He wanted to know my hurts, my embarrassing secrets, and the things I would give my life to protect. He was so easy to talk to. In fact, I had never met anyone like him in my life. I was truly open to sharing everything with him, not knowing what was in store for me.

The amount of passion, love, and desire that we shared on the phone was unparalleled. His words were very endearing, almost to a sense where his words were touchy feely. The words that he spoke were very descriptive.

"I just wish you were right here next to me," he would say, or, "I just want to feel you."

When he spoke to me, it was like I could literally feel, see, and touch him. Every day, I was thinking about him. When I woke up, I thought about him. I checked my phone to see if he had texted me. I thought about how wonderful he made me feel. The level of euphoria was equal to taking a drug. The way my body reacted to his voice speaking to me sexually? I had never experienced anything like it in my lifetime.

As I drove my daughter to school, I eagerly anticipated receiving calls to tell me sweet nothings in my ear. To tell me how much he loved talking to me and loved spending time with me.

The amount of passion, the amount of lust, the amount of excitement that I felt when I talked to him, I was truly falling for this man. Every day, my heart grew fonder for him. I loved going on EGO to see his live broadcast. My heart jumped because I was always so giddy when he came by my live broadcast, and he threw me gifts. I couldn't believe I really had an EGO Boo. He really cared about me, and I cared about him. I absolutely loved and adored spending time with him on the app and off the app. This man was truly winning my heart. My heart was swelling with passion, with desire for this man. I hadn't even met him yet, but it was like I'd known him for years.

I was eager to tell my friends about my EGO Boo. Every friend gave cautious advice, telling me to slow down, that I was moving too fast, and they didn't think him coming was a good idea.

"Heather," my girl Kelly began, "you don't know this man from a can of paint. He could be a serial killer. What are you doing?"

"Well, I don't think he's a serial killer."

I truly thought everything was going to be okay. Because even if he was a serial killer, there was this unrelenting need to learn what was going on with him. I *had* to experience this, I had to. I had to sow my royal oats. I had to feel and see what this was really about. If it wasn't good, then it wasn't. I was willing to let the chips fall where they may. I had to experience it.

I talked to Ray, my agent on the app. She told me just to have fun and be careful, and my mentee Jack echoed Ray's opinion.

I decided that's what I was going to do. I was just going to have fun. I was just going to take everything day by day and enjoy myself and enjoy the ride.

That decision began to eras as worry and then doubt set in.

I would go to Kyrie, asking, "Do you think we're moving too fast?"

I was trying to make sure all of the checks and balances added up.

"No, but if you aren't ready for this, then move on," he replied.

If he didn't say that, he would immediately catch an attitude.

I saw these reactions, but I kept going because deep down I didn't want to lose him. I needed to explore what this *new* thing was.

Whenever I talked to my friends about everything, I would give Kyrie summaries of our chats. He did *not* like or appreciate it.

"Your… *friends*… don't got shit to do with this," he said.

The way that he responded to me gave me pause. I had these doubts, and hindsight being 20-20, this was one of the first red flags. Attitudes would flare from him when I asked any kind of question, but then he would immediately change his demeanor and posture.

I was trying to set up some boundaries, but he didn't want those boundaries to be set up. I felt like I couldn't ask certain questions. Because if I asked those questions, then things wouldn't go in the direction that he wanted them to go in. So I just didn't say anything.

I got my COVID test. He got his COVID test. We both got our STD tests, and he was coming to visit me.

STORY 8
The Visit

In the last story, I noticed some red flags and ignored them.

When I questioned Kyrie about creating some boundaries, I was met with opposition, and I blew things off. This is where I knew in my spirit that my friends were right. We were moving very fast, and that wasn't normal. He was upset at me for trying to implement a boundary.

He would use this to say that I was declaring I didn't care about him and that I didn't love him. At the same time, Kyrie began to use another tactic on me called "Future Faking." This was where a narcissist will tell you things like they are going to marry you, take you on a vacation, retire with you in Florida and a number of things that will lead you to believe you have a future together, while never actually intending to follow though.

Kyrie lovebombed me to hook me and used "Future Faking" to reel me in.

Kyrie and I spoke on the phone every day, several times a day. We texted continuously every day, and we spent so much time together on EGO. Kyrie spoke so much joy into my heart and told me many things that made me think that he was really, really, really into me. He told me that he wanted to spend the rest of his life with me. He told me that he wanted to travel the world with me, that he wanted to marry me. He told me that he wanted to have children with me and wanted to be a stepdad to Morgan. By the words that he spoke to me, I thought that he liked me just as much as I liked him. I thought all of it was true. It seemed real, and it felt great.

I was still very nervous about him coming to visit me in Atlanta. What if my friends were right? What if he was crazy? What if he was a serial killer? What if he was a bad person? What if he was trying to do bad things to me?

There was no way I could have known, but I was willing to take that chance. I was so excited about taking that chance. I knew in my heart of hearts that I really liked this guy, and he really liked me. Our attraction to each other was undeniable.

The day he was scheduled to arrive, I was so nervous as I made sure that the house was clean, and everything was in order. I also got my cousin's macaroni and cheese recipe to make dinner for him, complete with cabbage with turkey sausage, hot water cornbread (my dad's recipe), and the macaroni and cheese. I was really trying to impress him. I really wanted him to feel at home and be comfortable with me because that's how I felt with him.

I went to the airport to pick him up, and when I saw him come out of the airport doors, I was mesmerized. I had never seen a more beautiful man than Kyrie Jenkins Dubois. He was so attractive. He was fine.

Y'all, it was like his skin was as smooth as butter. He was fly AF, and he was dressed to the nines. He looked so good and smelled even better. I couldn't believe it. He looked so much better in person than he did on EGO and through FaceTime. His swag was unparalleled. He rocked a white sweatshirt, velour black pants and some black Jordans. His haircut was immaculate, like he just came out of the chair. I'd never seen a haircut that looked that good. I was immediately star struck by looking at him. He was so attractive, and it made my heart palpitate and beat so fast. I was so nervous because he was so delicious looking. When he got to my car, I gave him a hug, and we kissed. I was so happy.

Then we went over to my mentee Jack's house because Kyrie liked to smoke weed. I knew that Jack smoked as well. So we went over there and just had a good time talking to his family members. We took pictures and just had an amazing time getting to know one another in person.

When we got to my house in Atlanta, we ate the dinner that I prepared. But as I could see, the macaroni and cheese wasn't a hit. I used Velveeta cheese, and the consistency of it was off. So that was a bust, but I got an A for effort! After we were just chilling around the house, we took separate showers. I had really wanted to set up some boundaries for us: he would sleep in the second bedroom the first night, and I would sleep in my room because I wanted to try to take it as slow as we could, even though we knew what we wanted to do. The want to set up boundaries failed because I couldn't resist. I got in the bed with him, and immediately, I was aroused. So was he. There was nothing I could do but fall into the temptation of what Kyrie was. The sensuality of what and who he was.

The next six days were blissful. We really enjoyed each other's company. We went out to restaurants. We went to the mall. He had a very good fashion sense, so much so that he didn't bring any clothes to just be "regular" in. He wanted to help shape my wardrobe and style me in designer clothes. I felt like Cinderella. We also went on a Sound Bowl Meditation.

We had meditation at a park and had to hike or walk a little ways to get to the river. This immediately upset him because he had on expensive shoes. Actually, he was wearing five hundred dollars Air Jordans. As we were walking, Kyrie was fuming mad. He had a major attitude. If there was such a thing as fire coming from someone's head, that is what was happening to Kyrie. Step by step, he was going to explode. I was just trying my best to get through the Forrest that we were walking. I found my equilibrium off often as we walked the unleveled terrain. It made it so hard for me to get to our location.

Did Kyrie care?

Not in the least because he was only concerned with his shoes getting messed up. When we got to the location, I tried to calm him down so that we could enjoy the meditation. But it did not work. He was furious and stayed in that space for the rest of the meditation. We were surrounded by waterfalls and beautiful glistening water. The sounds were soothing to our souls. This was the perfect environment to recharge and regroup. I wanted Kyrie to enjoy this experience, and I said to him several times, "Let's just enjoy the meditation and the beautiful scenery." He couldn't. The sound specialist also tried to chime in, but it didn't work. Kyrie was in a FUNK, and he was NOT going to let it go.

This scared me. I didn't know what was going on. Was he a divo? Was he just having a bad day? This was another red flag. This really bothered me, so much so I knew that he wasn't the one for me.

When we got back home, I expressed this with him, that he wasn't gentlemanly enough for me. I told him that he didn't open the door for me. He didn't hold my chair out and let me sit down before him. He didn't say anything. The next day when I woke up I found him putting things together for Morgan and helping me around my house. He put together my two end tables and Morgan's new potty. I was impressed. What I didn't know then, but I definitely knew now, this is how a narcissist traps their prey. They change on a drop of a dime, confusing you when they are angry and mean, and makes you think it's "just you" when he becomes endearing again.

And this is what he did to get me tangled in his web.

STORY 9
The Passion of Everything

The first night that we made love, I tried my best to hold back. But I couldn't stop myself. There was an immense amount of passion radiating from my body: from the top of my head down to the bottom of my toes. I was so sexually aroused by him that I couldn't control or contain myself.

In fact, I initiated kissing him, rubbing on him, and loving up on him. I kissed every part of his body. I marveled at how beautiful his body was adorned with tattoos.

He was thin in stature but very much so attractive. His skin was smooth as silk and felt like butter to the touch. You could tell that he was a hairy individual, but he did his job to manscape appropriately. His chest was manscaped to perfection. He didn't have any hair that my eyes could see. But I could feel a little stubble. His private parts were very nice looking as well. When we started to kiss and caress one another, it was like I was in heaven. He was very sensual. He was very sensitive and very caring with the way that he kissed me. I loved every minute of it.

After we finished kissing one another, we engaged in heavy foreplay where I caressed his penis in a very seductive way to make sure that he knew that I cared about his member and wanted to take care of him. After I caressed his penis with my hands, I had no problem tasting it as well. I enjoy the art of good fellatio because it just really does something to a person, and it can get them in the mood. After I gave him fellatio, he gave me cunnilingus. You could tell that this wasn't his forte because he didn't know my angles and pressure points. I knew he didn't do it often because he didn't know how to do it right for me. I saw that right from the beginning.

After we finished, he entered into me, and it was painful because I hadn't had sex in two years, but he took his time. He stroked me very gently and softly, as if he was making love to me. You could tell that the passion was so radiant, so vibrant, so electric and you could feel it in the air. The way that he looked at me while he was making love to me made me feel like he was looking inside of my soul and that he was making love to my soul. This was probably why I stayed addicted to him for so long.

After a while, the pain subsided, and my lady parts got accustomed to his wonderful love stick. We kept going and going and going until we couldn't go anymore. We started in our regular position, which was missionary. This was the best position for me because it was the only way that I was going to climax by playing with my clitoris. So after I got used to him and his amazing stroke, I got comfortable enough to start stimulating my clitoris so that I could climax. I couldn't remember if I climaxed the first time; but after we got comfortable with one another, he flipped me over and we started doing it doggy style. This was his favorite position. You could tell that he took pride and passion in doing it doggy style because of the way that his stroke would feel entering me over and over and over and over again.

The first time that we made love was okay, but the best parts were yet to come. Each and every time we did it, it got better and better.

I'd never been that aroused by a person in my life. The entire six days that he was at my house, my vagina was consistently moist, ready to go, and ready to be penetrated the entire time. Making love with Kyrie because of all of the emotion and all of the passion that he and I shared was on another level. The electricity that we shared was one of the best sexual experiences of my life. We would have sex five to six times a day, the entire six days that he was there. We would do it one time, then we'd do it again. We did it on the couch. We did it in my bedroom, did it in the guest bedroom.

We would go to sleep. He'd wake me up in the morning, and we'd do it again. It was amazing. It was an experience that I'd never forget.

STORY 10
Red Flags

Kyrie came to Atlanta to sex me crazy and make sure he sealed the deal. He wanted me to be committed to him, addicted to him as soon as possible so he could gain his narcissistic supply. His supply was the goal, not me as a person. I was merely an object that Kyrie used to reach his goal.

And once his initial goal was met, Kyrie moved into the next narcissistic phase: DEVALUE and DISCARD.

The day before Thanksgiving, I dropped Kyrie off at the airport. I felt awkward during the time because he wasn't very affectionate with me. As he got ready to depart, he didn't speak much to me, barely one-syllable words. He seemed distant, but I ignored it—perhaps he was sad to be leaving, I thought. I knew, based on the time we had spent together, that everything was okay.

The night before we concluded our time with a wonderful dinner I made: chicken with quinoa and broccoli, and we had mimosas. Kyrie really enjoyed the meal. He liked the quinoa because he had never tasted it before. He was very happy about that. We had a magnificent time. We rested together. We slept together. As we fell asleep on our last night together, I felt at peace. Happy.

That's not to say that I didn't notice some red flags. First one was being at the outing that we did with the sound bowl meditation. The way that he acted, the fury and the rage that he showed really scared me. When we were at the sound bowl meditation he looked like he wanted to kill someone. That is how mad he was. There was no talking him down off the ledge, he was ready, or he looked ready to fuck someone up. Just because he messed up his shoes-lol.

Second, Kyrie wasn't gentlemanly; when we went out, he wouldn't open the door for me or pull out my chair to be seated. I chalked it up to his upbringing and how he was raised in the projects of Chicago. He told me that they didn't do stuff like that. But it definitely was something that I didn't like, and I communicated my thoughts to him about it.

A few times, I became very emotional about all of the things that I didn't like about him. I didn't think we were going to be a good couple for each other. Each time, I would cry because I truly liked him. I showed a very vulnerable, emotional side of me, but I didn't really care because I wanted to be transparent. I liked to be honest and liked to let people know where I was coming from in the beginning of any relationship. Every time I expressed a concern to him, he tried to change it immediately, which was very impressive to me. I thought it was really a great gesture for him to do better and try to be a better man for me.

Unbeknownst to me, this was a narcissistic trait. They try to do everything they can do to win you over and get you under their web so they have control over you.

During Thanksgiving, I really didn't talk to Kyrie a lot. He told me that he was cooking and preparing food for his family because he cooked for his aunt and his sister. I was okay with it because I thought he was actually busy cooking for his family. We just spent six days together, and I had stuff that I had to do. I went over to my friends and family's house for dinner.

After the holiday, it became as quiet as a ghost town between me and Kyrie. We weren't talking on the phone as much as we were before. Our text messages were few and far between, and our conversation was very limited that next week.

Even with the strangeness of not communicating like we had been doing, my love for Kyrie grew. I thought that we were building what we had with each other, and that it was going to grow into something great because of all of the history that we had.

But I was wrong.

We both stayed on the EGO Live App, however, going into each other's rooms, gifting each other. I found myself gifting him more because I loved to see him smile and loved to see him happy. Every time I would give him a gift, he would smile and dance. As much as I loved our time on the app, I did feel hurt by the decrease of "Good morning, Beautiful" texts.

Over time, it seemed like I was reaching out to him more than he was reaching out to me. On EGO, we made it known that we were a couple on an audio live that his friend Temi held; well, I made it known when I said aloud, "Kyrie is my boo."

Nobody really said anything about it except for Temi. It seemed like Temi was mad at the fact that I announced our relationship. That was really, really interesting. When Kyrie was here in Atlanta, we went live, Kyrie was sitting next to me in the car, and Temi saw Kyrie's ring in the camera, and he had a lot of commentary about Kyrie calling him. Temi was mad because Kyrie didn't tell him that he was coming to Georgia.

This was the first time that I believed that their friendship was questionable. He acted like a jealous girlfriend with the words that he spoke. When I made mention of it, Kyrie's response about him was even more weird. He would say that Temi acts like he's his dad or mom and that he has to tell him everything. Temi seemed to have a crush on Kyrie and needed to know whatever Kyrie was doing.

As much as Kyrie had me wondering about his feelings for Temi, he also had me wondering if he hated Temi because he talked about him like a dog every chance he got--especially when Temi did something Kyrie didn't like. He made it seem like they weren't very close. He told me that they went to undergraduate school together but hadn't spoken in a very long time and reconnected on EGO.

I would later find out that Kyrie, in true narcissistic fashion, applying another technique to keep those close closer: setting up *competition* between me and Temi.

STORY 11
The Switch Up

Narcissists lie about everything. In the last chapter, we learned about Temi and Kyrie's friendship, which Kyrie would change and lie about all the time. He also created a separate narrative with Temi so that Temi wouldn't like me.

Kyrie was beginning the devalue stage of our relationship as he began to step away from me. The quality time was now gone, and I didn't know why.

And despite that knowledge, I still did more for him, as if in doing so, things would be right again. As we moved forward in our relationship, I began pouring into Kyrie financially on the app. When I started this, usually Temi was around on his live broadcast. After a while, Temi's jealousy rose as he always made little remarks about what I was giving Kyrie *all the time*. I felt sorry for him, so sometimes I gave him Mean green as well.

When I would try to talk to Kyrie about how Temi was acting, he'd tell me that he didn't care what Temi thought and that he would go broke supporting me. He had me thinking that we were on the same page. Whatever "mean green" that I would give him, he would give back to me and then some.

After a lull in our daily interactions, they picked up again. We shared cute text messages back and forth, and I sometimes sent him videos and pictures of me blowing kisses at him. He began repeating how much he missed me. At the end of November, we discussed how much we missed one another and that he should come back to Atlanta.

He also told me that his unemployment hadn't come through yet, and he didn't have the funds to get the ticket. I told him that I could get a ticket for him just as long as he paid me back. He agreed, so I booked his ticket on Southwest Airlines to come back to Atlanta in December. I was sooooo excited. I couldn't wait for him to come back to me.

As the days/weeks progressed, I loved sending him pictures and videos of me throughout my days so that he could get to know me better. But as I was sending them, he always seemed busy or preoccupied with work. He would respond with, "I'm not ignoring you; I'm with a client," or he would say, "I'm in a meeting." I didn't make anything of it. I loved that he was working in his passion with his craft.

I was always watching his lives, and as I did so, I began to notice a few common denominators. Kyrie got into disagreements with his contributors a lot. One in particular was T-Ross. When this happened, he always texted me immediately and said that he would tell me about it later. He never told me though.

Kyrie and I told each other that we loved each other often via text message and on the phone through talk and FaceTime. But every day, it seemed like he was on EGO all day long—at least more than four hours at a time.

One day, I told him, "I'm gonna need some personal time with my man." He promised me that he would after his time on his live broadcast. Something in my spirit didn't sit right with me about that, but I stayed patient with him.

A few days later, I asked Kyrie if he received his unemployment money yet because I needed to be reimbursed for the plane ticket that I bought. Instantly, any positive feelings he had died. "No," he would say, his tone hard, "I didn't get it. Don't be on my ass about this all the time, Heather, damn."

Before I could even respond, each time, he would complain about how he didn't have the money. Each time in an angry, irritated tone as if he was dismissing me. He complained vigorously about not having any money. He started shouting at me because he wasn't going to make his quota. It was like I was witnessing Dr. Jekyll and Mr. Hyde. I hadn't seen this side of him. I couldn't understand why he was acting like this. Because I was so supportive all I was trying to do was help and be solution based in my approach to him. He continued to lose his mind via FaceTime.

He also started to complain that his number one contributor on the app was missing in action, and he didn't know how he was gonna make his quota. He complained about EGO being his only source of income at the time and that he was struggling and was scared. I told him not to worry about the ticket. He started to complain about his next art collection and how he didn't have the materials to continue and that he was forever making masks to make ends meet.

Me being a solution-based problem solver, I stepped in and tried to give suggestions on what he could do. He immediately got angry with me and said that I was trying to silence him.

"Stop telling me what to do, Heather," he yelled.

"I'm not, Kyrie, I'm only trying to help you, babe."

"I don't need your help, Heather, fuck!"

His words, his tone stung my heart. In my mind, I was only wanting the best for him and wanted to help in any way that I could. His anger, his shutdown of my help was one of my first glances of him devaluing me. I was literally trying to help but I was met with fury, anger, and aggression.

Every time I tried to give a suggestion, he bit my head off and made more excuses. This was very disturbing for me, and I didn't understand it. All I was trying to do was help my man be successful. I asked what could I do to help? That's when he told me that he didn't have any money to buy art supplies for his next art exhibit.

As a caring, loyal, and helpful partner, I asked for his Cash App, so that I could help him out. I sent him two thousand dollars for him to buy supplies for his next art exhibit. I told him that I supported him, and I wanted to help him out in any way that I could.

The mountain of thank-yous I got from him from this gesture. "I promise I'll pay you back," he said more than once.

"Don't rush if you don't have it. Consider it a loan with time to pay back. This is an investment into your company. I support you wholeheartedly," I said to him.

I learned later that I would regret that decision wholeheartedly! At the time, I didn't know that narcissist hate being helped.

After I sent the money, I asked him what else he needed help with. He told me to make flyers. So I asked him for his pictures, and I got to work. I made all of his flyers for all of his EGO events, and they were amazing! He was very happy about that. Before we got off FaceTime, his aunt called him and made a mistake with something regarding his business. Actually, she made a mistake and washed his Fendi sweater in the washing machine.

"You put my fucking sweater in the washing machine?" he screamed. "That's a $1,400 sweater! You don't put it in the motherfucking washer, stupid!"

She didn't say anything to him.

This act of disrespect that I witnessed scared the shit out of me! The way he chewed his aunt out in such a disrespectful manner was not warranted at all. I'd never seen a person be so mean to their elders in my life.

"You shouldn't talk to your aunt that way," I scolded him.

"She's more like my sister," he replied angrily. "This is how our relationship goes."

"It's still unacceptable."

The display of disrespect showed me how little respect he had for women in general. This was a major red flag.

After this, Kyrie continued to stay on EGO all day and night, and I never got to speak to him. I tried to spend time with him on his panels because it was the only way that I would see him and spend time with him. Oftentimes, when he was on panels, men and transgender women would flirt with him. He ignored them but didn't make a big scene about it.

One time, a dude asked if he could cuddle with him. I was so bothered by it I left the panel.

"Why did you leave?" he texted me.

"It was wrong for that guy to say that to you and for you to just let it slide."

"I didn't disrespect you. And I don't like him. I'm not even paying him any attention."

"Do you know that the only reason I'm on the panel is because I am fucking crazy about you and want to hear your voice and see your face?" My feelings caused my voice to go high. "Seeing you dance and smile brings joy to my heart."

"That's why I dropped the guy down and showed you how much I love you and didn't care about them." After a pause in texts, he added, "All I care about is you. I love you, Heather."

"I love you." I was conflicted at this point. I was really troubled by what I just witnessed. But when Kyrie said I love you, somehow, instantly it made it all better.

The next couple of days, we didn't talk much on the phone because he was preparing a sculpture for an art competition on EGO, and I gave him his space.

I would text to check in on him to see how the magic was coming, but we had little to no interaction. Eventually, he won the competition, and his sculpture was amazing.

During this time, I realized that I was head over heels crazy in love with this man. Day by day, the shit got more and more real. I wanted to do anything I could to be around him. These feelings and desires only heightened my emotions toward him.

STORY 12
He's Changing

In this story, Kyrie began to gaslight me. Gaslighting is a form of psychological abuse. Kyrie was manipulating my perception of reality for his own gain. When he started gaslighting me, I started to second guess my thoughts, feelings, and my memories.

I began questioning my own sanity.

The gaslighting developed subtly and gradually, making it difficult for me, the victim, to realize that I was being manipulated and abused. The gaslighting caused me to stop trusting my own judgment, where I began to live in constant self-doubt, developed trauma, anxiety, and depression. My self-esteem lowered tremendously. Kyrie was gaslighting to talk me out of my own experience in order to alleviate his shame and responsibility to the issues he created. This was his tool to control and manipulate me.

I noticed, yet again, that I was becoming more and more into him. I became more and more emotional, emotional to the point where I couldn't control my emotions. I kind of felt a little loopy and in love because something was different in him where we were not talking the same. We were not doing the same things that we used to do. Then I found myself getting off the phone with him because I often felt like I was about to cry for no reason.

"Getting off the phone with you has nothing to do with you," I said to him. "It all has to do with me. I just feel like my emotions are spiraling, not out of control, but they are very, very, very deep."

At that point, I continued making flyers for his and Ramel's programming on EGO. I also noticed that we were not getting along and had little arguments all the time. I would try to clear the air with him and try to make amends with him. But he didn't allow me to. He always avoided the topic or didn't answer my phone calls when I was trying to make up with him, which was troubling, and it bothered me.

So then I had a PK, and I got banned for fixing my bra strap on my live broadcast. I started talking to Kyrie, and I was talking to my friend Eddie. I was asking him to talk to Kyrie because we were getting into it and not getting along as much. I wanted my friend to talk to him about my personality and help Kyrie get a better grasp of who I was.

"I don't really want to talk to your friend," Kyrie said. "I don't feel like I should talk to your friend about our relationship. That's not really a good idea."

"You know what? I do think it's a good idea because it'll give you a better viewpoint of who I am and how to deal with me so that we can stop getting into all of these arguments. So when are you going to be able to talk to my friend?"

"I'll let you know, and I'll talk to him when I get finished working with my client."

"Okay," I said. But it really seemed like he was not trying to talk to my friend.

I couldn't understand why he didn't want to talk to Eddie. It didn't make any sense because I was really adamant about how important it was.

"Hey, babe. I just tried to call you," Kyrie texted me. "I'll reach out and text him. I was on the phone with the client."

I texted back, "okay."

After that I tried to connect the two of them, but he was avoiding my phone calls and text messages.

So then I called him. "Hey, like, if you really don't want to do something, you don't have to avoid me," I said. "You don't have to not call me or play any of those types of games. You can just tell me what's going on."

Boom! Then this was where the biggest fight ever happened with him. He started yelling at me at the top of his lungs, going off on me saying that I was insecure and that I wanted and needed people to talk for me.

He stated that he was a grown man and that he was not going to talk to another grown man about his relationship. He was literally yelling at me, so much so that I had to interject.

"Hey, I don't know who in the hell you think you are talking to, but you need to calm your tones down," I said. He was really out of pocket. When I said that, he hung up on me.

I called back; he kept yelling and hung up again.

He then sent me a text. "I just sent you a text saying I was on the phone with the client and had a meeting. You proceeded and scheduled this meeting with your friend. I'm a grown man. I'm not about to talk to another grown man to make you comfortable about handling you. You are clearly not ready to be with someone. If you yourself can't give me and trust me, I'm not introducing people into what I'm trying to build with. I've tried; I've altered. I've been open. I've given you honesty, but this has gone too far."

I texted him, "Goodbye, Kyrie. It was a pleasure meeting you and getting to know you. I wish you nothing but the best."

This was the pinnacle moment when I should have left him alone.

This was the point.

This was it.

This is where I knew something was wrong with him. Something was totally wrong with him for him to act like that and be that mad at me because I wanted him to talk to my friend. It made no sense at all. I couldn't believe that he acted like that and did that to me. I could not believe it. I was so hurt. I was so distraught. But at that moment, I knew that this was wrong, and he was wrong for me. But, I did not go with my first gut, and that was the biggest mistake I could have made in my life right now. He was gaslighting me.

After that pinnacle moment, the rest of my life changed for the worse. I should have stopped; I should have let him go. That should have been it, but I didn't leave. I listened to the gaslighting, and he showed me all of the tactics that narcissists use.

Right then, in that very moment, this was where he showed his true colors of being a total narcissist.

"The fact that you need me to talk to your friends about you and that's a make or break says a lot," he continued on his soap box. "I've never in my life heard of that. All this because you've never dealt with your hurt. And because I come along now, I get it. Thanks for being honest. Thanks for wasting my time. Thanks for allowing me to think that this was something different or maybe this was the difference."

"Stop projecting," I responded. "You hung up on me. I called you back to have a conversation. If you want to talk to me, then call me. I'm not going back and forth with you over text messages."

"I wonder why I hung up on you," he said. "You call me your 'niggah.' I have literally from day one gave you all of me, and it's not good enough. I gave you my time. Not good enough. My energy. Not good enough. You test me with situations, all of this. Then you come in my EGO room, and you give Temi a shield."

I did because I was being messy and petty.

So I wrote to him, "I apologize for getting loud with you and saying my 'niggah' to you. But I think you have a bad temper. It's not okay that I can't have a conversation with you without you getting loud and lit and not letting me say my piece. That's unacceptable, Kyrie."

"I wonder why, Heather, you don't trust me. You need approval of me from others to move forward."

"It has nothing to do with trust," I said. "I'm a difficult person to know, and I was trying to help guide you to avoid confusion. You immediately started getting loud with me, and that's not okay. I always try to stay calm when there's conflict, but I'm also about that life, as you saw."

"I don't talk like that in relationships, and I don't argue."

"You did to me tonight, sir. You were out of pocket from the start of the conversation, and I just met what you were giving me."

"Okay, not talking to a grown man to seek his approval and understanding of the woman I'm dealing with."

"Then that's what you say to me and tell me that. Don't avoid me and don't return phone calls because you don't want to do something. That's childish."

"I actually was going to, once again, do something I was going to do regardless of how I feel. But to please you. It's not fair that I keep altering myself to give to you."

"I'm not asking you to alter anything," I said. "I'm just telling you what my expectations are and trying to be open, honest, and transparent with you. But you won't let me speak my mind. That's not fair, Kyrie. I was trying to say my piece and be done with it. But you went in on me, and I don't deserve that."

"And you called me my 'Niggah.'"

"I especially don't deserve being hung up on twice. That's really childish."

"You call me my 'niggah' when I told you through texts that I had a client. So you want me to tell my client to wait to talk to your friend, not realistic. What's childish is that you want me to stop for you."

"I called you my 'Niggah' because you were yelling at the top of your lungs at me, and you were talking to me like I was someone you don't know and have no love for."

"Did I call you out of your name?" he asked.

"You yelling at me in my book is the equivalent of calling me out of my name where I come from. I just apologized to you for calling you that. Do you accept my apology or no?"

"Heather, I'm not going to lie to you. I need a minute."

"I can understand if you need a minute, but you have been non-stop texting me. Clearly, you want to come to a resolution, but take all the time you need. Because just like you, I have feelings, too, and I need a minute as well.

"I don't want you to be upset, and I can be the bigger person and apologize for any wrongdoings that you feel I put on you," I continued in true Heather fashion. "I hope you have a good night and rest peacefully, Kyrie."

"Thank you for putting the icing on my cake day in controlling the narrative to the ending. It's appreciated. You're unbanned. Maybe you should go on EGO."

"Kyrie, that was very mean. Can we talk? I'm not trying to control anything. I just don't want any bad blood. I'm going to call you. I hope you answer. I just FaceTimed you. I'm going to try to call you. I'm only going to try two more times.

"Maybe you're in the shower. Maybe you really don't want to resolve this tonight. I'm going to try one more time."

"I hate arguing with you," he said. "I just don't want to argue. I accept your apology. Tonight was a lot. I'm not ignoring you to disrespect you. I don't want any further disrespect. So I removed myself."

That was on December 9, 2020.

What the fuck is going on here? So we aren't going to talk? We aren't going to work this out? At this point, I feel like I'm in the Twilight Zone. I had never in my life met someone who would start a fight and then just leave it there not to resolve anything. I literally felt like I was losing my mind with no way to get it back.

All the Signs of Narcissism

The discard began because Kyrie would only be nice to me as long as I believed in the false version of him that he created. The discard phase began once I figured out that something was wrong with him. Once I saw the evil in him caused narcissistic injury, or questioned him, he had to discard me. It was a dangerous time when you know who and what they are. Kyrie showed me his true colors and began to discard me day by day, little by little.

Kyrie and I had the biggest fight ever in our relationship, but the next day, he texted me like nothing happened. Like we didn't just go at each other's throats. I apologized to him several times, but he did not reciprocate. I thought that this was very weird.

He texted me, "Good Morning" at 11:15 that morning. I didn't write him back until a couple of hours later.

"Good Afternoon. I hope your day is going well."

"It's not, but hopefully it will change," he said.

"I'm sorry to hear that, Kyrie. I'm sending positive light and energy your way."

"Thanks for dropping out of my event."

"I didn't drop out of your event. I just removed myself from the That's That App chat. Kyrie, you can call me if and when you feel comfortable to discuss. I would like to see you end your day on a positive note."

He texted me a love/heart symbol.

I didn't think we talked about what happened with the fight that day or the next day. It was like it never even happened. He just made small conversation on the phone, and we saw each other on EGO.

The day after, he was on EGO, and he spoke to me in his live: "I was talking to you."

"Oh, I must have missed it," I said. "I left your live because I'm cruising the EGO streets."

"I'm trying to talk to you, but I guess you're upset."

"I don't want to talk to you on the app, Kyrie. I called you earlier. You didn't answer. Enjoy your live, babe."

"I spoke to you. What do you mean? You called me after?"

"I FaceTimed you around eight, but you didn't answer."

"I didn't see that. If I did, I would've answered," he said. "I just got to finish my hours."

"Okay."

"I'm not sure what I did, but I did not ignore your call. I'm not sure why you don't want to speak but came to my live. I don't think that's cool, but okay. Heather, don't you want me to come see you? I have work I have to finish before I come. I'm literally doing the work on my live in front of you, SMDH."

"Hey. Yes, I do want to see you," I said. "But first we need to have a conversation, but not on EGO and between reasonable hours. I am free to FaceTime tomorrow between ten and two. If you want to talk, hit me then. If my hours are an issue, let me know when you are free."

"Heather, I really can't keep up with you. Like I can't."

"What did I do? Now? I'm trying to call you."

We talked for an hour, but it wasn't good. We just kept arguing and couldn't come to common ground. But everything seemed to point to me, like it was my fault. He didn't take responsibility for any of his actions, and he still didn't apologize.

After we got off the phone, I wrote a series of texts basically taking the blame for everything.

"I hate that this is happening between us," I said via text message. "I hate that this isn't working. I hate that you are mad at me and hate me. I hate that I'm distraught. I hate that I'm so sensitive and I can't control my emotions. I pray that we can heal and move forward. I hate that I love you so much that it's driving me crazy. I hate that I keep texting you. I love you."

At that point, we were preparing for the trip. He was coming back to my house on December 11th.

"I love you as well," he texted back. "I just think this trip, I should stay back. I think we both know arguing is just unhealthy, and we need to communicate. Right now, I don't want to give you this energy I feel. I hope you understand. I'm not removing myself. I just don't want to keep making this worse and see you cry or get upset."

Now this was from the argument that happened a day or so previously that we never talked about. We never reconciled the argument or made it better. He didn't apologize or anything. He just kept moving. Like nothing was wrong. Every time I asked him a question about it, he would avoid the topic and not talk to me about it or start another argument.

I really didn't understand what was going on. But as I looked into narcissism and what narcissism was, these were all classic signs of a narcissist deflecting and trying to make you feel like everything was your fault when in actuality, it's them and you'll find out later on in the story why he was doing all of this because he had another agenda.

After he said all of this, I kept texting him, and I was really at rock bottom. The things that I just said were really sad.

"No, let's start over," I suggested. "Can we be like we were the first time? I promise I won't argue or make you mad. I have to see you in my life. I really need you to come. Even if you're mad, I'll be okay. I'm desperate. At this point, I'm going to sign up for a counselor on Monday. Now I don't even care what I'm going to write every thought that comes to my mind. I'm leaving EGO because I can't look at you every day and know you aren't mine anymore. I'm deliriously in love, and you are the last person I'm ever going to talk to. I'm done with love. I gave it a try and fucked it up. I'm going to go take a shot of tequila FML. Ten years from now, we will look back at this and laugh. Can I please see your face before I go to bed? Pretty please with sugar on top."

"We can talk tomorrow," he simply wrote back.

"Okay."

"I will call you in the morning," he said. "I love you. Think of Morgan, you cannot lose it. I'm not worth that."

Then I sent him two videos, trying to see if we could work it out so that he would visit me in Atlanta.

"I hope you can see how crazy I am about you and how much you mean to me," I said. "I also will understand if you think that I'm bat shit crazy and want to run far away. I'll be okay."

With all of this was happening, I blamed me like I did something wrong, but I didn't do anything wrong to him. All I did was want him to talk to one of my friends, and then he switched that whole situation on me and made me feel like I was a crazy person.

I wasn't. That was typical narcissist behavior. I sent him a whole bunch of pictures showing the good times and stuff that we had.

Then he wrote me back the next day. "I'm happy with you, which is why I'm so upset."

"If you're happy with me, then I'll see you tomorrow."

On December 12th, I did a twenty-hour EGO marathon so I wouldn't have to look at him or think about him. I stayed on EGO all day playing my clarinet, talking to people, and a whole bunch of other things to get me through the day. This was all I knew to do. I was at a lost. I didn't realize it at the time, but I was dealing with a narcissist, and the next events signed, sealed, and delivered his true identity.

STORY 14
The Fights Begin

After a lovebombing stage, narcissists move into the devalue stage. During this stage, the narcissist tries to devalue you and diminish your self-esteem. Where you were the best, most handsome, beautiful, intelligent, and overall best person they ever met, suddenly, you are not good enough.

Kyrie began to shame me and made me feel like there was something innately wrong with me. He began to abandon and ghost me only to come back, charming me again like he did in the beginning. Sometimes, he would just continually make me feel like I was worse than yesterday's garbage. This is kind of a sudden switch, where the person completely changes into someone you don't know and treats you with such little regard, was extremely traumatizing and damaging to my wellbeing.

On December 12, I had a full twenty-four-hour session on EGO, where I was trying to occupy my mind and not think about Kyrie because at this point, we were fighting for no reason.

Now he decided that he was not going to come visit me again in Georgia. I was very distraught about this, and the night before I said a whole bunch of crazy stuff. It really made me look like a very emotional and out of control woman. I was literally losing my mind because I wanted to see him. I loved him so much at that point. I wanted to be with him. I wanted to be around him. I wanted to see him again. I wanted to experience all of the euphoria that I felt the first time that he visited me. Because he didn't call me that day on the twelfth, I was on EGO all day live.

I called him toward the end of the day to try to figure out what we were going to do regarding the plane ticket that I bought for him, the reimbursement of it, and to put it in his name. I called him three or four times, and he didn't answer the phone, which was really crazy to me because up to this point, he always answered my calls.

So I texted him.

"Kyrie, for the love of God, can you please call me back or text me and let me know when you're available to talk today about this ticket status?"

That was at 5 p.m. At eight, he still hadn't called me back. I texted him again.

"The worst possible thing in the world you can do to a person is ignore them when they are trying to contact you. This is very disrespectful, and it hurts me to infinity. I'm going to cancel the flight. I called Southwest and can't get a refund.

"The stand-up thing for you to do is to Cash App me the money for the ticket because originally you said you would reimburse me, and you are still free to use the funds to travel wherever you want to go. Please Cash App me the $137.96. The reservation number at Southwest Airlines is N Z 7 B R K. It's under your name Kyrie Jenkins Dubois."

He didn't call me back, and he didn't answer the phone when I called. I was just trying to get this ticket rectified. The only thing I thought to do was to FaceTime Temi, his friend and ask him if he could call him and tell him to please call me.

"I'm trying to get the information about this ticket for him so that we can cancel the ticket because he was coming back to Atlanta tomorrow," I told Temi. He looked totally shocked, like he didn't know what I was talking about. It was really weird. This was also a second look into the fact that Temi really liked Kyrie. He called Kyrie, and I guess Kyrie answered the phone. Then Kyrie called me screaming at the top of his lungs.

"You called Temi! You called Temi! You called Temi! Temi's not my father. He doesn't tell me what to do. Why would you call Temi and tell him to call me and tell him my business?"

Kyrie was absolutely livid. He proceeded to yell and go off on me.

"Yo, I'm not trying to get in an argument with you," I said. "I'm just trying to get this ticket done, and we can let the chips fall where they may from there. I just want to get the refund so that this money is not lost."

He continued to go off on me, calling me names and everything. Then he hung up on me.

He called me back, and it really got heated. I got upset and called him out of his name. I told him that he was acting like a gay ass bitch, and I did not like it. I was matching the negative energy that he gave me. I had to go off on him because he was going off on me, and then he hung up on me again.

I called him back, and he answered, but he kept yelling and kept cussing at me. That's when the texting started.

I wrote, "You're blocked, Bitch! Fuck you and everything you stand for. I tried to be nice, but fuck the day you were born. Fuck you. Stop texting me."

"Now, I'm done," he said. "I see why your husband left you. I had a relative who died, which is why I didn't answer the phone."

"You want the smoke? I'll give you the smoke. Don't deflect on me."

"You called me a niggah and now a faggot."

"I tried to be nice, but you trying it."

"You expect me to really give you my time. This is why. Be nice to yourself and your child."

"You pushed me to this point."

"I was busy, and I have other things to handle. You are not my number one."

"I tried to suppress my rage, but you want to talk crazy," I said. "Here it is. The trip is canceled. I don't ever want to see or talk to you ever again. You did this."

"You did this to yourself."

"I'm done."

"You and your lifestyle did this to you," he said. "So why are you losing weight and whatever, going through whatever?"

"See if you can find another woman who will accept you for who you truly are."

"Realize you fucked up. You're a grown child who was so selfish because you wanted an experience."

"Fuck you with your dysfunctional ass," I said.

"There's nothing you can say to hurt me."

"I'm not even reading what you're writing because I truly don't give a fuck anymore."

"But you will never have my time. You're not getting shit back from me."

"Fuck it and fuck you."

"I will call your husband."

"I knew you weren't going to give me anything back from rip."

"Fuck you."

"You like older bitches, so you can use them. You like being a sugar baby with your broke ass. Fuck the flight. Fuck the money. Get your punk ass materials. Make your punk ass pictures for your punk ass art exhibit and have an amazing life, weak ass niggah. And oh, please call my husband with his weak ass. Let me know when you want the number. I know you befriended me to be your supporter on EGO! Karma is going to bite you in the ass. I have been nothing but nice and kind to you. And you started this stupid shit by cussing and raising your voice at me, but I'm good. I didn't call you the F word. I called you a gay ass bitch. I called you a gay ass bitch because only bitches act the way you do."

This whole argument was because I called Temi and asked him to call him about a plane ticket. It made no sense at all that someone would get so mad with you over calling someone and asking for help.

It made no sense that they would treat you like this and talk to you like this. I couldn't understand it for the life of me, but as I researched and as I learned more about narcissism and narcissistic people, this is what they do.

He started an argument with me because he had other people that he was talking to.

I found out later that he had a whole girlfriend and that was probably who he was with when he wasn't answering my calls. That was why he was deflecting and doing all of this and putting it all on me. Like it was my fault. This was another instance when I should have exited stage left.

STORY 15

Phone Sex to Make Up

In Chapter 14, we spoke about how a narcissist will DEVALUE you. Let's continue the conversation. Devaluing occurs when the narcissist knows they have you under their control. They have done such a great job in lovebombing you that you have fallen for them and are emotionally involved in everything about them.

This was a very painful stage.

Once you have reached this stage, the narcissist switches up on you, getting you addicted to them. They trauma bond you, switching their technique, where they first adored you, and now they act like there is something wrong with you, and they start to devalue you by the negative things they say.

They start to judge you, and suddenly, everything about you is wrong. They act differently with you, and you are not only no longer special, but something is very wrong with you.

They shame you! This is one of the reasons why these relationships are so difficult to get over. They steal your self-esteem, your sense of worth, and the feeling that you are enough. Then when you feel broken and sad, they bounce back and are nice again. Thus, the pattern begins.

Then you become addicted to the moments they are nice to you. This is how they trauma bond with you. All narcissists follow this pattern.

I felt a sense of relief that we had this argument and that it was going to be over at that point. I really thought that after the argument we had and the things that we said to one another, there was no coming back from that.

Or so I thought.

He said some very mean things to me, and I said mean things to him. We were yelling and screaming at each other at the top of our lungs, disrespecting each other and disrespecting each other's boundaries. This was totally unacceptable.

Later on that night at maybe between twelve and two o'clock in the morning, Kyrie called me, and the first thing out of his mouth was, "You didn't think I was a faggot when I was inside of you. Are you gonna make me fuck another girl? Are you going to leave me?"

"You can't do this to me," he continued. "You can't leave me. I need you to cum on my dick. Don't do this to me. I need you in my life. Make love to me. Be with me. Don't leave me. Why are you doing this to me? I love you."

He was literally begging me to take him back. At that point, I had no clue what was going on. "How could you say all of those things to me a few hours earlier, and now you're trying to have phone sex with me saying, don't leave me?" I asked. "What are you talking about? You said all of those bad things to me, like, you don't want to deal with me. And now you do?"

This was beyond crazy behavior. At the time, I didn't know what was going on. I didn't know what he was doing. I had never experienced anything like that in my entire life, but he was exhibiting crazy, psychotic behavior. I didn't have phone sex with him that night.

He aroused himself. I just stayed on the phone, and he kept talking. But I didn't participate because I was so infuriated at what he was doing.

The next morning/afternoon, he texted me: "Hey, good morning."

"Good morning, King."

"I hope you got some sleep. I really can't stop thinking about my uncle."

I was working to try not think about it because he said his uncle passed away. He also had a habit of saying people in his family died when there was a struggle or strife or when we weren't getting along. So I didn't know if his uncle really died.

"I didn't sleep much because Morgan woke me up," I shared.

"Okay."

"I'm sorry to hear about your uncle. Three of my best friends passed away from cancer. So I know how you feel. Just remember the good times, and time will heal the pain. I'm driving, so I can't text much."

"I gave him a mask before I came to ATL."

"What type of cancer did he have? I asked.

"Prostate."

"Oh wow. I'm so sorry to hear that."

"Yeah, I just want a smooth day. I'm trying to grab hold and move forward and handle me. I feel like I'm ignoring myself to get things done."

"I want you to have an amazing smooth day as well," I said. "Please take care of yourself. I'm here for support. If you need it."

"I appreciate it."

At that point, I was shook. I couldn't understand this behavior. We would get into a big fight, he'd called me for phone sex, and then the next day, there would be a pity party for something bad going on in his life.

To add insult to injury, all this time, he was supposed to be in Atlanta with me.

When I got off the phone with Kyrie, I called Woodie to ask for help. He also included Temi in the conversation, and I told them everything from the beginning of our relationship to what was happening right now. They told me that I shouldn't be dealing with him because it was too toxic.

I told them that I was just trying to hang on because I needed him to catch up with me on my board as far as the mean green were concerned. So I was trying hard to just play nice and not get him mad so that he would trickle the mean green back to me. They told me to leave him alone all together.

After that, Kyrie and I kept texting, checking in with one another. A few days later, he told me that he wished he was holding me and that he was sorry that he messed everything up. I called him and tried to talk to him about what happened, but he would find a way to deflect and not solve the problem at hand. This was also a red flag.

The next day, I had excruciating pains in my side and had to go to the chiropractor to see what was wrong. I called and texted Kyrie for help with what to do about my back pain, but it didn't seem as if he really cared. The pain continued through the night, and I called and texted him to ask if I should go to the emergency room. He didn't respond until five the next morning, saying he was sorry that he fell asleep.

I told him that I wish he cared as much for me as I did for him. He called me and talked to me on my way to the emergency room. I knew something was wrong. That we were not healed and better from that fight. I knew in my gut that our relationship was over, but I was trying to ride it out.

We kept visiting each other on EGO and texting a lot. I asked if he could design artifacts for memory gifts for my sorority, and we were working on that as well. He would tell me that he wanted me so bad. I would blush, and he would add, "I'm serious."

"What are you gonna do about the fact that you want me so bad?"

"I need to come get you."

"You're not about that life."

"You know what I'm about, and you know what my dick is going to do when I'm inside you. I need you to cum on your dick."

"How is this gonna happen when I'm in Atlanta, and you are in Chicago?"

"I want to be where you are. You are touching it right now, aren't you? You need my dick, don't you?"

"Nope, I'm good. But I'm actually looking for a ticket to come see you."

"Oh really?"

I was really looking for a flight to come visit him. I was trying to find anyway to make things better between us because he was slipping away. I starting to see signs on EGO.

In particular was a girl that either visited his panel or was on the panel. Her name was Cloudy. She was a full figured, beautiful girl that would come around Kyrie's lives. I told him that she was cute. He told me that she was in his auction.

I asked how old she was and if she was his type. He told me that she was cute, but he never held a conversation with her like that. I would later find out that this was not the truth.

The next week or so was strange. We didn't talk on the phone as much, and when we did, we would get into arguments. Kyrie was having a BBW auction. At that point, I wasn't gifting him anymore because I was waiting for him to meet me halfway on my board. I would come by his live broadcast and talk in the comments and send hearts, but that was it.

Every day, there was something wrong with him. He would be in a bad mood and didn't want to talk. He wanted to cancel his auction, and I attempted to talk him out of it. Our relationship was changing drastically, and I didn't like it. I would later find out that he wasn't spending time with me anymore because he was talking to other women.

I made Kyrie a flyer for his first Big Box PK a few days before Christmas. He was trying to get ten boxes during this PK. I was excited for him, but unfortunately, no one showed up for him to help get him to ten boxes but me. I threw him two theophanies, which was the equivalent to two hundred fifty dollars each, so he could get the rebate from the PK. He was flaming mad that he didn't get to the ten boxes.

I tried to calm him down and tell him to look at the bright side: he got the rebate. He was very disrespectful and mean to me on the live because he was so mad. When I would try to comfort him, he would snap at me and say whatever he wanted because he thought no one was there for him in that moment. But I was . That hurt me. Before I gave him those gifts, I told him that I would need them back for my PK on Friday. He told me no problem.

The way that he was treating me would pose the biggest problem of the century. He used this as an out for what we had. For the next couple of days, he was in a consistently bad mood. We didn't talk, and I believe he was setting all of this up to get rid of me. This was the catalyst that changed the dynamics of our relationship.

STORY 16
Christmas Eve

For the life of me, I couldn't understand Kyrie's behavior. I thought that if I communicated effectively with him, everything would be ok. I was wrong. If it wasn't his way, it wouldn't happen. Narcissists are all about what they want.

"Christmas Eve morning," I texted Kyrie. "Good Morning-I hope you feel better... worried about u."

I didn't get a response. Later that day, I asked if he could send me a naughty video or voice memo so that I could engage in some self-love activities.

He didn't respond. So I texted him again a few hours later.

"I know you're busy, and I really appreciate this relationship. However, I need and require maximum amounts of communication. I was hoping that we could communicate more often, even if it's via text. Thank you for allowing me to talk about my needs and what makes me happy."

He responded an hour later with, "Heather, you really are killing me. You do not allow me to work, like you don't."

"Don't want to interrupt your work," I responded. "Just want a simple 'thinking of you.'"

"It's 4 p.m., and you keep calling. You are not allowing me to reach out. I just told you this morning, my mother is here. And because I'm not here to entertain the sexual stuff, I'm ignoring you. Like this has to stop, you have to stop."

"I know that your family is there, and by no means am I trying to get in the way. However, I'm just trying to navigate my feelings and communicate effectively."

"So why not give me a chance to call you back?"

"I understand."

"Like it's 4 p.m., it's Christmas Eve, and I have to work. And you're busy worried about me calling you all day. That's selfish, especially when you know what I have to do. You literally pick and choose."

"Ok."

All of that dialogue really troubled me. All I was asking for was a little communication from my man. Was I asking for too much? I almost never ask him for anything sexual, but the one time I did, it was too much? If you truly love a person and you want to be with them, then you try to make them happy. I wasn't happy, and I was trying to let him know that in the most respectful way I possibly could.

This was also the night that I needed the theophanies back for my PK at 8 p.m. Kyrie did not come to my PK.

"Wow," I texted him. "No support tonight. I guess you're mad."

"I have been waiting on my funds from that job all day. I have $3.43 to my name. I really do apologize. I can still drop them on you as soon as I get the money. But as you can see, I have three dollars."

I told him, "It's all good, Merry Xmas."

"See what I mean?"

"What? Huh? So not to be a party pooper, but I threw two 9999 gifts at you the other day. The Mean Green should be able to convert into at least one unicorn, right? Let me know if I'm wrong about that."

"Wrong. It would convert to one unicorn, and I converted those beans to pay another bill."

I knew this was a lie.

"Oh wow, interesting," I said. "So you knew that this was a loan, and I needed them back for Friday night? I'm trying to get on EGO so that I can pay my rent. I have a child that I am taking care of by myself. Bruh, you gotta do right by me. And if you don't, unfortunately the universe is gonna handle you. Maybe because you aren't a parent you don't understand that."

"I cannot control the bank. This check was supposed to be in my account."

"But you control you, and what you send and do."

"I just said you would have them before next week, and there is nothing else I can do."

"What would you have paid the bills with if I didn't send the gifts? Why didn't you use the two thousand dollars for bills and not art supplies? I'm not understanding at all. This is truly blowing me."

"Yeah, it's blowing me, too."

"Well, let's be blown together. Just do right by me, Mr. Kyrie. How can you be calling people out about what they owe you, and you owe me? That's crazy! For real for real; you should be taking care of me first. Actions speak louder than words."

And here came the bullshit!

"Moving forward, we need to be friends. I'm not going to be able to deal with you and you keep bringing me down. And I'm being one hundred with you. I can't ever win. I have three fucking dollars in my account. I never in my life asked you to take from your child and give me anything, so please with respect, do not put that on me. I have my parents here, and I can't have anything. I have no Christmas tree, no nothing, and you're worried about an application that you mention over and over is extra for you. So please with all due respect, I cannot keep taking away from me to give you me. It does not make sense. You do not listen to me. You don't hear me. You literally are coming at me about a situation I cannot fucking control.

"When I just said as soon as I have the money, you will have it. I don't know why you think if you send someone a unicorn, you now have the mean green to send it back, even if I didn't pull the money."

"You can control yourself," I said. "Stop deflecting and running mind games."

"It was enough to pay for four shields. I'm not running a mind game. I just showed you my account, and you are literally making this night about EGO. Heather, honestly, I'm bowing out of this conversation."

"I'm praying for you, and I wish you nothing but the best. Let's be friends, but do pay me back what you owe me. It can be little by little, but pay me what you owe me."

He tried to call me, and I told him that it wasn't a good idea if we talk because he was cussing and used profanity.

"I'm done with this conversation, Heather," he said. "Have a good Christmas."

"You have a good Christmas, too, Kyrie. But for the record, when you started pursuing me, you made it seem that you had everything together and that you were super successful. I'm thrown because everything that you presented to me wasn't real. Maybe you should be more realistic with yourself about your means before you present fallacies to the world."

At that point, I was shook! I was very sad but still content because he was acting crazy. And I had enough. I think I went to bed early that night because I was over it all. I woke up in the middle of the night at around 1 a.m. I went to Kyrie's live on the EGO app under my fufu (fake page).

He was playing music and having a full Christmas Eve party panel with Cloudy, the girl from his auction and Foreigner Bae from Barbados. How could he be having a party after we just broke up? How was he in such good spirits after we were done? Was I missing something? It was safe to say I was disturbed by this. I was hurt by this. I didn't know what to say or do.

So I went on my page and went live. I was venting to the few people in my room about what I just saw. As I was venting, Number One Woman, Kyrie's number one contributor on the app, came into my room.

Something in my spirit told me to ask her to speak off of the app. I asked her if I could call her, and she said yes.

This conversation with Number One Woman would explain everything that I needed to know.

STORY 17
Answers

Kyrie told me goodbye.

To say it was sudden is an understatement.

I remember how much he had changed at the end of our relationship. Because he was mirroring a new target, he shifted his demeanor, clothing, interests, music, vernacular, goals, etc.

When I questioned these changes, he brushed me off but secretly reveled in my misery. This was his ideal scenario, knowing that I was still committed while he was securing his next victims.

Something in my spirit needed to talk to Number One Woman. So I asked her if we could I talk off the app.

She sent me her phone number. I got off my live broadcast and called her. I started the conversation by telling her that I was dating Kyrie and that we'd been dating for the past two months. I told her that a lot of stuff was not making any sense with him because we were getting into all of these fights and arguments for no reason at all.

When we got into an argument, we'd say these bad things to each other. But then the next day, he'd call me like nothing had ever happened, or he was trying to have phone sex with me to make up with me. I just didn't understand what was going on.

So at that time, she released a heavy sigh and whispered, "Wow." After a pause, she continued, "I wish I had spoken to you before now because I would have told you a lot of information."

"What would you have told me?"

"Kyrie and I were in a relationship. We met on EGO, and he pursued me romantically. We started supporting each other on the app, and we started going together. We were boyfriend and girlfriend. I went to visit him in Chicago. I stayed with him at his house. He came to Baltimore where I live, and he met my family and my kids and everything. We were in a relationship for a couple of months."

"Wow, really? Because he told me that he had never talked to anybody on the app."

I was so shaken. I couldn't believe what I was hearing. This was so new to me. I even asked him what his relationship with Number One Woman was.

"He told me that you were just his number one contributor on the app, that you liked him and that you asked him to come to your birthday party," I said, "but he didn't look at you like that. He saw you as a friend."

She immediately interrupted me and said, "No, we were in a relationship, a whole relationship."

Number One Woman and I talked all night about everything dealing with Kyrie. All of the little nuances, all of the little things that he would do like his sporadic behavior, the lies, the deceit, him acting crazy, hanging up the phone, and getting mad with the both of us for no reason.

She even told me that he would do the same things to her, like calling her back after an argument to have phone sex with her. She also told me that they were having phone sex the whole time he and I were dating. Number One Woman provided me with several receipts that included sex text messages, pictures, and videos of him masturbating on FaceTime.

This hurt. I thought that this was my man. I thought that he was my one and only, but here it was. He was still having a full sexual relationship with Number One Woman, and I didn't even know it.

So all of this put everything in perspective. Why at certain times, he wouldn't want to have phone sex with me, or he wouldn't want to talk to me because he had a whole other situation going on. I was hurt and distraught. I couldn't really believe what she was telling me, but it all made sense. Now this was why he couldn't be present with me or why he didn't want to continue on with me because I was trying to make it where he was just with me. I was asking too much of him, and he didn't want that because he was trying to juggle Number One Woman and me.

I found out later that it wasn't just me, but we will save that for later.

I was so thankful that Number One Woman told me all of this information about her and Kyrie's relationship. It mirrored mine to a tee. The only difference between me and her was that he caught back up with her on her board on EGO. She stopped gifting him and told him she wasn't going to give him another Mean Green until he caught up with her.

She was smart enough to say, "Hey, let me stop this before it goes too far."

Unfortunately, I wasn't that smart. I didn't tell him that he needed to catch up with me. I just kept giving him gifts on the app. But everything that happened to me happened to her from everything that he said to her, even the way that he treated her, the same words that he spoke to me, he said the same things to her verbatim. I couldn't believe what I was hearing.

"Number One Woman, how do you think I can get my Mean Green back?" I asked.

"The only way that you're going to be able to get your stuff back is if you threaten or scare him."

"Okay, I guess that's what I have to do."

It wasn't my goal to spend the night of Christmas Eve in deep pain and with swirling negative thoughts, but that's exactly what I did.

Christmas morning, I woke up and didn't get any call from Kyrie. No Merry Christmas, nothing. I played with my daughter and made sure her Christmas was good. I watched her open all of her gifts and smiled as she did so, but I could not shake what I had learned. I had spent the last two months with Kyrie, and he had betrayed me and lied to me. Everything was a lie, everything. I didn't know what to do. I was hurt. I was sad. When not in front of my daughter, I was a crying emotional wreck. Every emotion that I could feel was present: rage, pain, hurt, and despair were in my psyche.

Throughout Christmas day, I still didn't receive any calls, any texts, not even a Merry Christmas from him. I went to my friend's house for Christmas dinner.

At that time on EGO, there was a big incentive where if you stay on live for five hours, then you could get a lot of Mean Green.

Everybody was going live for the required hours. I went live at my friend's house and then I saw that Kyrie was live. So with all the information that I had, I went into his live.

I asked him when he was going to be able to pay me back the theophanies I gave him for his PK.

He immediately went from zero to one hundred real quick. Totally cray-cray on me. I was very calm. I wasn't trying to embarrass him. I was just asking a simple question because I wanted to have witnesses so that people would know that he owed me.

He literally went off the handle and said that I was storming his live broadcast. He cussed me out, and then he kicked me out of his live. He then ranted to Woodie and Temi because they came in his live and in his box. He totally portrayed me like we weren't just in a relationship. Like I was a nobody and that he was being embarrassed and he had to fight for what he believed in.

I watched from the window (logged out account-EGO TV) and then screen recorded his live broadcast. I listened to everything that he was saying to Woodie and Temi and couldn't believe it.

Once he cooled off, he started to show Christmas gifts that he had. He showed that he had a Gucci purse. This baffled me because he just told me yesterday that he only had three dollars to his name. How could he afford Gucci?

So I told Number One Woman what happened.

"Why did you provoke him?" she asked. "You have to play the long game."

"I don't know. I wasn't trying to provoke him. I was just trying to, I don't know what I was trying to do, but now it was do or die. I didn't know what else to do."

"The only thing you can do is threaten him." He pretty much blocked me from every channel. He blocked me from his phone and his EGO page. I really didn't know what to do.

When he blocked me from his page, I texted him immediately.

"Babe, I'm sorry. I didn't mean to disrespect you; please forgive me. I love you. I didn't mean to hurt you. Please unblock me."

"Please do not contact me. I do not want to even be a friend to you. Your disrespect is definitely my breaking point. I am not a slave to you because you supported me. I never asked you for anything. And because you've been doing too much, you feel dumb. I'm removing you from my list. I will not be making any keepsakes for your sorority. I don't need your money. I certainly don't need someone like you in my life. This relationship is done for the last time. You need help, serious help. It is not my job to see you through."

"Please don't do this, Kyrie."

"Heather, do not contact me anymore. I'm done."

"I don't think you really mean that. You said you loved me and can't live without me."

"I love myself more."

"You need me."

"I refuse to have someone in my corner whose act is predicated on what I can give back. You have problems, and I'm done. I can't live because of you. I'm not doing me because of you. This conversation is done."

"But we said we love each other, Kyrie. You said you love me. You call me and make love to me. You said that your dick is mine and that you want to build a life with me. You told me that I need you to cum on your dick and that you need me and love me. Please. Don't do this. I've forgiven you so many times when you have done bad things to me. Please don't do this for real, for real, please give me a call."

When he blocked me from all of his networks, I immediately went to his Facebook page and saw that he didn't block me from that platform.

So under Number One Woman's advice, I threatened him.

"If you don't pay me back, what you owe me, the unicorns and the yacht that you promised, I'm going to make your life a living hell on this app until you do."

I wrote that and meant it because he was trying to play me. He was trying to play me, and he was trying to erase me like I was nothing. I didn't appreciate that. Give me back what you owe me.

Do right by me or else.

STORY 18
The Snake Rears His Ugly Head

I fell in love with a lie.

The person I fell in love with never existed. Kyrie created his persona just for me. He saw how wonderful I was and copied my characteristics. He pretended to like the things I liked so they would be more believable to me. He knew I was smart and wouldn't want him if he portrayed his true nature. He made me believe that he was madly in love with me. He made me believe I was the center of his universe, and then he stopped playing. He knew he had me caught in his trap. He knew I would kill myself trying to get back the person I fell in love with. He didn't care. Kyrie never cared. It was never about me. It was about him, trying to feel human and be as good a person as me. He would never manage to do that. It was not in his nature. He treated everyone this way. I wasn't his first victim, and I wouldn't be his last.

On Christmas Day, I was so depressed. I had my last PK of the Holiday, PK incentives on the app. I was very emotional during the PK, and my friends were very supportive in how they were gifting me.

The next day, later in the evening, after I got off of EGO, I spoke to Number One Woman, and we were talking about the situation. When we were on the phone, Kyrie called from a fufu number, and I clicked her in. He apparently was watching me on my live broadcast from a fufu as well. He immediately started calling me stupid bitches and talking to me crazy about the situation.

He also told me that his mother was in the hospital because she was bipolar schizophrenic and because she saw the message that I left on his Facebook wall. He said that she was hyperventilating and that they had to take her to the hospital. I told him to cut the bullshit and that I knew everything about Number One Woman and how he was playing me and that he had a girlfriend. I told him that Number One Woman was on the phone, and he yelled, "Charelle! Charelle!" And then hung up the phone.

She didn't answer him, but he immediately called her. I didn't want to mention her name, and I felt bad that I opened my mouth. I texted her and told her that I was sorry because my emotions took over me.

"Please give him a piece of your mind for me," I said. She called me back to let me know that he said there was nothing between us, that we only had sex one time and that I didn't even make him cum.

The most important thing that she told me that would carry on a chain of events was that he said that he was just using me for money. My world crumbled when I heard this. I couldn't believe that he would say that. I thought he loved me. I really did.

A few minutes later Kyrie called me with his aunt Loretta on the phone with him. When she tried to speak to me, he would yell uncontrollably at the top of his lungs profane words and threw insults toward me. He called me a liar, saying that I was married and acting a plum fool. It was like there was a mad man on the phone. A new psychotic entity that I didn't know. It was extremely disturbing.

His aunt called me to work the situation out, but it was evident that he didn't want me to speak to her by myself. When we spoke, I started from the beginning and told her that we were dating, and then he dropped me like a bad habit because I was asking for him to meet me halfway on the gifts that I gave him.

I told her that when I addressed the issue at hand, he would go off the handle, and eventually, he blocked me from his phone and on EGO. That's when I sent the Facebook message. I told her that was my only recourse to getting my money back. I also told her that her nephew preyed on older, plus size women and took advantage of them on EGO.

"He tells them lies, preys on their emotions, and uses them for his own financial and sexual gain," I said. "He flies out to come visit them and uses his sexual advances to get whatever he wants or do whatever he wants. He makes women basically fall for him."

I told her that we had a business relationship on the app, and he was taking advantage of my emotions, my giving nature, my kindness, and had used it to his advantage until it didn't work for him anymore. When he felt like it was too much for him and he didn't know how to communicate effectively or do things in a proper manner, he started lashing out and started being disrespectful.

This whole experience with Kyrie had been a rollercoaster ride. He lied to me the whole time. Everything that he said had been a lie. As I kept pulling back the layers, I kept finding out different things that he lied about.

People that he was talking to, people that he dealt with, and the fact that he had a girlfriend that I didn't even know about. In fact, I asked him specifically about the young lady in his Instagram pictures. I asked him if the girl with the white hat and the white dress on was his girlfriend. He told me no.

I also found out that he was dating several people on the app and doing the same thing to them. At that point, Kyrie interjected, screaming, and hollering, "She's a lying bitch! She's married! Fuck her! Hang up the phone on that bitch! It's her fault my mother is in the hospital!"

"Really, Kyrie," I said, stunned.

"Because of what you wrote on Facebook!"

"I did *not* put your mother in the hospital.

"Don't put that on me," I said. "This is all karma for what you're doing to people. So when you treat people badly, Kyrie, this is what happens. You have been nothing but disrespectful to me, nothing but mean to me. I didn't know anything about your mother. I'm so sorry that your mother's in the hospital, but here's the deal. You cannot treat people like this and not expect it to affect the people around you. So you have to take a look inside and see what you're doing to people. Because it has consequences. Your actions have consequences. I'm sorry. You cannot play with people's hearts. You cannot play with people's emotions."

His aunt confirmed that his mother was in the hospital and that's why he was acting crazy and irate. I also told her that as I started investigating, I found other women that he did the same thing to and that he told his other contributor Number One Woman that he was using me for money. That's why I was asking for the money and gifts back.

"Ms. Loretta, I just want him to pay me," I said, suddenly so very exhausted. "I just want him to pay me what he owes me. He called me yesterday and told me that I wasn't getting anything. He wasn't going to pay me anything. Ms. Loretta, I'm calling all aspects out on him, and he doesn't like it."

Kyrie was yelling in the background. "She's lying! She's married! I didn't want her!"

"Ms. Loretta, I'm going to get off the phone because I can't continue to have a conversation when he's yelling at the top of his lungs. Please call me back. Here is my number."

When she called me back, she assured me that she would pay me back the money in full in increments of five hundred dollars starting January 8, 2021. She seemed like a reasonable lady, but there was something shady about her as well. She told me that if I wanted to talk about this some more that I could call her. She also asked me not to speak to him about our conversation and to keep everything between us.

I also called Bamm, Live Thrive founder, for help. I told him what happened, and he said that he would help me get my money back. In fact, he called Kyrie and let me listen. It was horrible. Lie after lie and more lies. Listening to the conversation was very disturbing. I truly had deep feelings for this man and to hear him talk in such disdain about me was a horrible feeling.

Kyrie told Bamm that he was with his ex-girlfriend at his house for Christmas, and she bought him a Gucci bag. This was a lie because she was actually his girlfriend. I found that out later on. He actually bought her one as well because he showed his friends on his live broadcast.

When Bamm asked what the extent of our relationship was, Kyrie told him that we had a mutual dealing with each other, that it was really nothing, that we weren't in a relationship and that we only had sex one time. He told him that it stopped when he came back from Atlanta because I was married and had severe emotional issues. He told Bamm that he couldn't be with someone who was married.

Now, folks, from the very beginning, I told Kyrie that I was legally separated and hadn't seen my husband since May 2019. This was an example of him twisting the truth to make me look like a bad person and him as the victim. He told Bamm that I was a forty-four-year-old woman who had a lot of issues that I hid from him. He said that once he realized that I had all of this emotional shit going on, he tried to be my friend when he came back from Atlanta.

Another example of Kyrie playing the victim came when he told Bamm that now, because he wanted to be my friend, I was asking for all of these gifts back. Bamm told him that he didn't want people to think that he was a gigolo. That's when Kyrie told him that he made six figures before EGO, drove a Benz, had a Rolex and five businesses. He said, "I don't need any of these bitches' money."

After a pause, he asked, "Didn't she send you a unicorn, Bamm? You know how many people she has been gifting? Heather gifts people without command."

He also lied and said that I was sending gifts to him without consent before he traveled to Atlanta. This was not true. We were sending gifts to each other because we agreed to be allies to each other on the app. That's how we met through Woodie.

Kyrie told Bamm that he genuinely liked me. That he was genuinely trying to be there for me. But because I hadn't figured out my life, now I was saying that he conned me. He said I reminded him of his mother who was clinically bipolar and who he had to drive to the hospital because she saw the Facebook post that I wrote. He also said that he was not hiding anything, but I was painting a picture that he was fucking bitches for Mean Green and using women.

We will learn later that this is exactly what he was doing.

During an auction that Kyrie was involved in during the time when we were feuding, I sent him a yacht, which is a very expensive gift. I sent the yacht because I wanted to show him how much I cared about him and supported him. I also sent the yacht because he told me that he was going to send me one and unicorns and go broke supporting me. No one else came to this auction to support him or send him Mean Green. I was the only one. I remember him asking me to come or told me that he was in it, but he didn't ask for anything but was insinuating it by his tone.

He told Bamm that he asked me on live if I wanted the yacht back, and I said no. I probably said that, but I honestly thought that we were a team and that we had each other's back. I was wrong.

Kyrie then began to say that I was dumb, and his family didn't play fair. They knew my management company, they had my address, and they were really about to report me. He also said he wanted to call his cousins and say green light and go to my house.

Bamm told him not to make it like that.

"I'm not giving her four racks," Kyrie declared. "It's the day after Christmas, and this EGO shit is too much, and people need to be in the real world."

Bamm asked Kyrie for a resolution and reaffirmed that Heather was a real person.

"She's not regular. You have to treat this situation with more delicacy than sending bitches to her house to beat her up."

"I have a brand, too, and you can't threaten someone," Kyrie said. "She threatened me."

"But you know Heather. She's a nice lady."

Then Kyrie lied and said that I called him a faggot five times.

Bamm said that straight women do that all the time. "But she wasn't saying that when you were fucking her, right? You both were saying things to hurt each other, but I think you genuinely like her because you wouldn't have sex with her if you didn't."

Kyrie then told Bamm that he was compromising himself and that wasn't fair.

"You can be a friend. We've had so many issues besides this EGO shit. I can't be with someone that does an act and then throws it in your face."

In reality, we didn't have a lot of issues. He was a habitual liar and manipulator. I was asking for accountability and holding him responsible for his actions as my partner, and he didn't want that. So instead of doing the adult thing, he put on this full-scale production.

Next, he lied and said that he was in the art store one day arguing with a client, and I took it upon myself to invest two thousand dollars into his company. He wasn't at an art store; he was arguing with his aunt, and he was in his apartment when I sent the two thousand.

"If you take the two thousand and the gifts on EGO, that's how you get the four thousand. That's what she is asking for," Bamm said.

He said that he asked me if I wanted it back, and I said absolutely not.

"She probably didn't want it back at that point because it was real for her," Bamm said. "Somewhere along the line, that realness left for her and that's where she felt like she got played or had been played so then she backed out of it and wants her money back because you played her. That's a natural response."

Bamm was really trying to find a solution and help out the problem. He was giving Kyrie very viable options to come up with a resolution. Kyrie wasn't listening and did not want to work it out. Every time Bamm came up with something, he would pose another problem. Kyrie answered Bamm with that's understandable but now you are contacting people and telling false narratives? That was a little extreme.

"I don't have connections to your people to give them false narratives about you," Kyrie said. "You literally were doing things that you knew that I can't do back. I never asked her to send me a yacht. You expect me to give you all these gifts back at once? I don't owe her a hundred thousand. I didn't ask for it."

Bamm said, "If you really fell for her, you can amicably have a conversation where she can apologize and y'all can talk about how you can pay back what you owe her, and you can be back in the same space. You don't have to argue back and forth because you know each other."

"Heather is one of those types of females where you want a man to talk to you and now you want to control that man. You don't want me to respond to you. Every time I respond to you, you are calling me a faggot. Now, I'm sensitive and you can't say stuff to people and not expect a response. Every time I respond, I'm wrong. I literally told her that you are getting your coins back on my live broadcast. You are stupid because my number two contributor, Number One Woman who you hit up, don't even give a fuck about what you are talking about, Stupid! You're dumb. She also pressed Temi too for the eight shields that he didn't ask for. I didn't ask for anything from her and when I do, I'm joking."

"She was giving because she is very supportive," said Bamm.

"You forget that I flew all the way to give her a custom art installation commission, and you act like I didn't do anything for her for free. You know how much I charge by the hour for that? Please."

"Kyrie, how many times did y'all have sex?"

"When I was there? Like twice. I wasn't there the whole time."

This was a lie; he was with me the entire time. Like stop giving false narratives.

"My family lived twenty minutes away from her; she was not the only person I was in Atlanta with. Stop. Truth be told, she was not even legally separated. All I gotta do is go to her husband and say one thing, and her world would crumble."

"I know for a fact she don't fuck with her husband."

"It doesn't mean nothing; she is not legally separated and that's law," Kyrie said. "Truth is truth, you're not supposed to date someone until you are legally separated. When y'all go for a divorce, they say that you are cheating. Y'all have a child together; they will take your child."

"Calm down, and you all should try to work it out."

"After this, I don't want to be near her. She's got issues. She is a talented trainwreck. I can't. I feel like I'm in high school. That's why when I'm on EGO, I dibble and dabble. Bamm, I'm retarded. I will smack the shit out of somebody."

"Kyrie, all of this is your fault. You made choices. Y'all had a situation, and it got out of hand. Don't get mad at anyone but yourself. But just talk it out. Y'all shouldn't be so frustrated that you don't come to a human resolution. Even though she tried you on your live, I think it came from a place of her not being able to get through to you. An adult would try to have a conversation. Do your part and try to have another conversation."

Kyrie told Bamm that he could call on three-way because he wasn't not calling me. "I called her yesterday and tried several times," he said. "And then you sitting here telling my aunt that I'm taking advantage of women and prostituting myself all over the country? Bitch, are you serious?"

"Have you had sex with someone else off the app?"

"Yeah, before I met her. This was way before I came to Live Thrive."

Now this last statement from him I didn't understand. As we continued to fight and make up over and over, some of his mental issues started to come to the forefront.

"I'm going through a lot, and this is why I don't really do serious relationships with people because I'm battling a lot," Kyrie said. "So I don't try to give people that, especially people that are sure of themselves and comfortable with themselves. That's not fair."

This whole conversation that Kyrie had with Bamm was my first glance into the depths in how far he would lie to get his point across to look like the victim and the bigger person. He literally took the story and twisted it to fit his own personal narrative. He would continue to do this throughout the rest of our story together.

STORY 19
Mediation

Kyrie was a master manipulator and liar to the tenth power, like all narcissists. When I confronted him with what he did wrong, and he didn't want to take responsibility for his own actions, he would manipulate me by putting the focus back on me. Kyrie loved to bring up something I did or needed to do, using my imperfections as a way to avoid taking responsibility for his own actions.

He actually liked knowing my difficulties or flaws. This gave him ammunition and gave him something to hold over my head to use against me. He also used a technique called *triangulation* against me with Number One Woman. His goal was to deflect some of the tension, creating another conflict to take the spotlight off of the original issues. He also wanted to cause friction between me and Number One to ensure that we did not exchange information to become close or join forces against him. But it didn't work!

At this point, Number One Woman and I were having a *real* connection. We became friends and are still cool to this day. Kyrie did not like this because we could see through his bullshit together. At the same time, Easy Lay was telling me not to trauma bond with her. But she was like my long-lost auntie. She was really a sweet person with a kind heart. The things that she told me really helped me out and gave me perspective on what exactly was going on with Kyrie.

After talking to Kyrie's aunt, I felt a little relieved that I was going to get my money back. Now, I had to gear up for the next big event to happen: the Zoom mediation with Bamm. For the mediation, I made sure that I looked very good. I put on a nice outfit and beat my face to the "Gawds." My presence was poppin'!

Despite my mixed emotions, seeing Kyrie in the Zoom made my heart race. The fact that he, too, looked very good didn't help me at all.

"Everybody," Bamm said to start the mediation, "let's stay respectful throughout the whole conversation. It is really about building a solution and coming to a resolution. It is hearing both sides and having closure so that both of you can feel a hundred percent comfortable moving forward. I'll also let you say what you want to get done with this conversation today as well. What are your expectations for today's conversation?"

Looking irritated and bored, Kyrie replied, "I just want a solution. I'm not trying to disrespect anybody. Me and Heather both have a brand, and I feel like EGO is not something that's worth tainting what me and her have separately. I'm just trying to get to a solution that makes sense for the both of us."

"Okay, and you, Heather?" Bamm asked.

Taking a shaky breath, I said, "I wrote a letter to read so that I can stay calm and articulate myself in the best way possible. I don't want to get emotional, and I don't want to get mad."

Kyrie rolled his eyes and turned his gaze from the camera. Bamm gave me a small smile and a nod. "Go ahead," he said.

At this point, I was nervous as hell. I wanted to get all of my feelings out, but I was scared. I had no clue what was about to happen at the end of this mediation. I was so happy that Bamm was here to mediate, but I didn't know what angle Kyrie was going to come from and what he was capable of doing.

Closing Letter to Kyrie

I first want to say that I forgive you. I forgive you for all of the wrongdoings and the way that you have treated me. I forgive you because God says forgive, and I don't want to block the blessings that are coming to me.

I forgive you, but I will not forget what you did to me and how you made me feel. This relationship started as friends on EGO. When I sent you a unicorn on Bamm's panel, I did that because previously we corresponded about becoming alliances on the app and then whatever was given would be returned equally on both sides.

Our phone relationship started when we exchanged information to discuss the fact that Bamm didn't return the unicorn like you did and how I could go about handling the situation from there. You began to text me several times throughout the week, making small conversation that eventually turned into you showering me with comments and shooting your shot by calling me your EGO boo.

From there, we had several text exchanges about how you weren't my type and one thing led to another where you told me you were pansexual, that you never slept with or messed around with men or transexuals but that you dated them.

I also asked you very specific questions to see if you dated anyone or messed around with anyone on the app. You said no. I also asked you if you had a girlfriend, and you said no. From the information and intel that I have received now, I know that all of what you told me were lies.

From our conversations/text messaging/FaceTiming on the phone, our relationship grew and moved very fast, and it was scary and exciting at the same time. I was truly frightened that I liked a person so much whom I hadn't even met. I feel now that it moved so fast because that's how you hook and reel women in.

You make them fall in love with you fast so that they won't leave you. You tell them that you love them, that you want to be their husband, that you want to be a stepdad to their child so that they feel that you genuinely have real feelings for them. I thought that everything that you said to me was true and believed everything word for word that you told me.

After you swept me off of my feet and had my heart, you bought a plane ticket to come see me in Atlanta. This was very scary, and all of my friends told me not to do it. But I trusted you because you said that you had my back, and everything would be fine. You spent the next six days with me, and it was the best time that I had in 2020. The amount of passion and lovemaking that we shared was unparalleled, and I truly thought that I was in love, and you told me that you were in love with me. While here in my house and in my bed, you kept speaking love into me and affirmations of how special I was to you and how you wanted to be my husband and be a stepdad to Morgan. You even did some great things like put together Morgan's potty and my end tables to show that you could be flexible with some of the qualities that I needed in a man.

There were also some red flags that I saw as well, but I ignored them because I really wanted this to work out between us.

The first red flag was when we went hiking, and you didn't want to mess up your five-hundred-dollar Jordans. You were in such a rage that I literally saw heat and fire coming out of your face. That really scared me. I also saw that you didn't possess any gentleman-like chivalrous qualities, such as opening the door, pulling out the chair. When we got back home, I got really emotional at my house because of the red flags that I saw, but immediately when I told you about them, you tried to change them, and you explained why you did the things that you did because of where you came from and your upbringing.

When you left Atlanta and went back to Chicago, I immediately saw a change in you. It freaked me out. But I asked and told you if you weren't interested in me, let me know and I can move on. But you said no, everything was fine. You just had to work and that you were really busy.

The only times that you seemed to have time for me were when you wanted to vent about EGO or if you wanted to have phone sex. The morning calls and evening good night calls/texts were few and far between. Then we started getting into arguments because I would ask you about our relationship and that I needed more time from you. Whenever I would try to talk to you about anything, a rage would come out of you. You would yell at me and also hang up the phone several times. After these arguments, you would always call me after 2 a.m. and speak to me in a very sexual manner and try to have phone sex with me to get back on my good side.

Next, we decided that you would come back to Atlanta the weekend of December twelfth. On the phone with you, I started looking for flights. You told me that you were waiting for your unemployment to hit, but you would pay me back via Cash App for the ticket.

Days later, I asked you for the ticket and you exploded on me, saying that you were stressed and that you didn't make your quota on EGO. That your number one contributor was MIA and that you didn't have money to move your next art collection along. I asked if there was any way that I could help ease the stress and started trying to give you pointers on your business. You flipped out on me again, saying that I was trying to silence you and not let you be heard.

I immediately apologized and said I was just trying to help and only wanted to give you a solution to the problems that you were having. We spoke again and the real issue was that you didn't have any money to move forward with what you were doing. So I asked you for your Cash App so that I could help you out of love and give you a loan. I sent you two thousand dollars so that you could buy art supplies for your art show. I told you that it was an investment in you so that you could get your collection started. I also told you that it was a loan and that I was helping my man and I was in a committed relationship. Now I know that was not the case.

When we started down this road, we spoke about reciprocation and how we were going to help each other out, and that was what we were going to do for each other. But we also spoke about it, and you told me that you would go broke helping me. You told me that you would send me a yacht and all the unicorns to catch up with me on my board and that you were going to be my Number One contributor. This has not been the case. As I keep watching and observing, I see that you never had any real or good intentions for me. Like you told your number two (Charelle-AKA Number One Woman) contributor, you were just using me, and there was nothing between us. I know that this is true now because of how you are talking to me, reacting to me, and treating me.

I didn't deserve any of this. The lies, the deceit , the mistrust, and all the mental/verbal abuse.

I know that you did the same things to Number One Woman (Charelle) because when we spoke, she told me the exact same situations that I went through with you. The only difference is that you gave her back what she gave to you. You are also plotting to recruit the next crop of BBW older women to take advantage of as well. This has to stop.

You think that I am weak, stupid, and too nice. But I'm not. I'm going to advocate for myself and for anybody else that needs my help against you.

Kyrie, you are a narcissist, and you only care about yourself.

Kyrie, I am holding you accountable for your actions. I am calling you out on all of your negative behavior and Jezebel spirit ways. Do the right thing and do right by me.

There were plenty of times where we could have ended this peacefully and still remained friends, but you said no and that you were here for me, happy with me and didn't want to lose me.

This has been one of the worst experiences of my life. I just want to be paid what I am owed so that I can move forward with my life.

What I need from you:

An apology. Your STD results that I never saw. The two theophanies sent by the end of the month (December). The rest of the one hundred thousand given back to me by the beginning of March. The two thousand dollars returned back to me by the beginning of March. Not to do this to any other woman.

Addendum

At the end of our mediation meeting on Sunday, you gave me an apology, and you returned the theophanies/dragons. You said that you would return the gifts by the beginning of March. The only thing that you didn't agree on was the two thousand dollars. You said that you would possibly give half of that by the beginning of March.

"No offense," Kyrie said, "I'm grown, and you're grown. I'm not about to go in detail, like you just did. There's some pieces to that letter that I don't agree with. Half the things that you're saying, I would never agree to. I said that I was building with you, and I was getting to know you, but this narrative that's like being told now that I've deceived you? I never, never, never remembered mentioning replacing Morgan's father. I never even met your child. I met her on video. Yes. I do have love for her."

I had no clue who I was dealing with. Everything that came out of his mouth just baffled me. Who was this man? Who did I fall in love with? Why was this happening to me? Why can't he take ownership in his mistakes?

"I feel like, respectfully again, I'm just not going to go into detail. I just want to move to a solution. The reason why I said that I would start gifting you back is because you kept mentioning it after it was just gifts. Just like I told you before, just like when we met with the unicorn, and I sent you back, anything that I said that I was going to send was going to get sent back.

"My whole thing is that even in those messages, I said, I'm going to get you as soon as I get paid. Even still to this day, it's Sunday, no banks have dropped my check. I'm not lying about the check that's coming. I haven't gotten paid. So I can't recharge. I haven't sent any unicorns. I haven't sent anything to no one. I have no problem sending you the two theophanies or two unicorns. I'm just trying to resolve this.

"Now, the two thousand dollars for your business, along with all of this stuff, I have no problem paying you. Maybe I don't agree with the timelines, just because one, I feel like they're not realistic only because, you literally just mentioned in your letter how you did this stuff out of kindness, but now just because our situation is now not working, you're literally asking for everything back, and it's like, no disrespect, I never charged you for the art installation. I charge people by the hour.

The gall of this dude! He was coming there to help me. Never once were prices involved. I couldn't believe what I was hearing.

"I'm not saying to you now pay me back what I did for you in Atlanta, so it's like, we can go it tit for tat regarding what we did for each other. I feel like that's where we get to the opinions. All I was trying to do was trying to separate from this situation because me and you both know this was not the first argument that we had. So I feel like if all of this is over EGO gifts, I can just pay you back, and then we can just part ways. That's what I was trying to do. I wouldn't lie. Now, you're coming in all my live broadcasts asking me the same questions that I literally just answered on text messages.

"I never went on your platforms and did that to you. Fast-forward, my aunt sees my Facebook stuff, and my mom sees it, too. So all of this stuff when I felt like we literally had a solution. I said I was going to give you back the things that you asked for. The only discrepancy that I got is because now you're throwing in the two theophanies and 100K, so that's now one hundred twenty K.

The only reason that I went on his Facebook and wrote that message was because he blocked me, and I felt like I was stuck. It was the only way to really reach him.

"Heather, well, it's not, it's not one hundred twenty K, it's a hundred K minus the two theophanies. So that would now be eighty K."

"Including the theophanies," Bamm said, "it's one hundred K. Real quick. I want to make sure that I mediate appropriately. Kyrie, what of her terms do you not agree with?"

"I feel just because we've had honest conversations and we've never had a conversation with me saying that my business is in need," Kyrie said. "We met during the time that I was preparing for a pop-up art show. You thought I was frantic and doing all this other stuff. I mentioned to you that I didn't get loans and stuff like that, but I never asked for any financial anything. I didn't ask for that money.

On EGO, the only gifts that I literally asked you for were the two theophanies, so this whole narrative that I used you and pulled things out of you? You're mentioning Number One Woman, I gifted her, she gifted me. I'm not running anyone for their money.

I've been who I am before anybody has met me. So my whole home, my car, my closet, my wardrobe is built on me trailing and tricking on women? I think that's a little bit absurd. Like I can be Googled, just like you. I have no problem again, solving this, but I'm now not going to, bit by bit tear you down and now take shots at you. I'm not going to do that. Because once again, I'm trying to solve this situation. Like I said, this check is supposed to drop hopefully, tomorrow, and tomorrow is Monday."

Kyrie is just going on and on about nothing. He doesn't apologize, he deflects, he is truly full of shit! I'm so over it and tired of defending myself. His words are empty promises and filled with air. I wanted to pop the shit out of his fake ass balloon!

"There's so much that I need to respond to. I think I'm going to forget points," I said. "Number one: I'm not taking any shots at you, Kyrie. I'm just telling my truth and how I feel. This is what I perceive. This is what I see. When you say you've never deceived me or told any lies, that's not true. You told me you never dated anybody on the app. You were having a full-blown relationship, phone sex relationship with Number One Woman the entire time that we were dating. I have the videos. If you want me to show you the videos and pictures of your conversations, I can."

"I don't care about any of this. I only care about the solution," he said. "I don't care about any of these details about what her opinion is. No disrespect, but this isn't a psychological situation. We're not on a couch. I'm grown. She's grown. I'm now not talking about my personal business like that. The only reason I agreed to this Zoom call is to get a solution with these gifts. I don't want to talk about any personal visits of what I did."

"Is that because there is a lot of mistrust and deceit and everything that you said, Kyrie?"

"No, disrespect, but that's not Bamm's business."

"It's not Bamm's business, but you wouldn't let me talk to you to work this out like adults. All you did was try and over talk me, call me names, and get out of pocket."

"Let's not argue," said Bamm.

"I'm not trying to argue," I said. "When you shut down somebody, when you hang up on them, when you block them and you don't let them talk to you, these are the consequences to your actions. Every time that we had a fight, you said that you weren't going to pay me back shit. So honestly, this whole time that I've been tolerating and putting up with you in these final stages was so that I can stay in your good graces and have you trickle the Mean Green back down to me. That was the only reason why I was staying in this.

"But when you start doing things that you do, like being irrational and yelling and cussing and going off, I have no choice but to go to your social media so that you would get my message because you blocked me. With Number One Woman, I needed to talk to her because I needed to know what was going on because I was losing my mind from listening to you. You would tell me you loved me, wanted to be with me, but your actions are speaking louder than the words, and you don't spend time. You don't do anything because you're honestly not into me, and you don't want to be with me. So all of that, like all of this game and this facade that you have put on for me, I called her because I needed to know what in the hell was going on here.

"Talking to her gave me a lot of closure because now I understand why you're not calling me. He has several girls that he's dealing with. But here's the deal. Don't play on my time. Don't play on my emotions. Don't play on me because I was in this for real for you to be with you because you pursued me, and I loved you. So when you say you're talking to find the solution, when? I've tried to give you solutions several times. I've tried to talk to you."

"That's not true," Kyrie said.

"It is true. I tried to talk to you. I've tried to be amicable with you. I've tried to reach out to your friends to try to reach you. But, Kyrie, you have made this very, very difficult for me. Very difficult for—"

"Let me—"

"Just let me finish, Kyrie. Let me finish. I didn't interrupt you."

At this point, it's all about him! He always makes it about him. I am distraught and over this entire conversation. Bamm looks like he is over it as well.

"Thirty more seconds, Heather," Bamm insisted.

"I didn't want the two-thousand dollars. That was a gift to help you. But when you tell somebody, oh, she ain't shit. Ain't nothing happened with her. The relationship was nothing. I was just using her for money. Then that's when it's not a gift because that's painful. That hurts. Everything I did was out of love. But what I can't accept is you using me and you telling people that there's nothing going on with us and that you were using me for money. So that is why I'm asking for all of this stuff back now."

"You see, I've never been a type of individual even after I've dealt with someone to go to other people about you. You went and mentioned me to so many other parties. Number One Woman and I had a situation back in June. The only reason we agreed to still deal with each other was because we didn't have a connection on that level. It was something totally different. I just said I don't need anybody for money. So this whole narrative that I used you for your money, no offense. I grew up around money."

"Let me say this," Bamm interjected, "I just want both of you to put yourselves in each other's shoes for a second."

"Okay. No offense. Bamm, I didn't finish," Kyrie said. "Heather has had at least two to three minutes. I'm starting to feel this is two against one. The point of this conversation was for me to not now dissect the dynamics between us because we're going to get into opinions, and we can be here for hours. She has a right to her opinion. I have a right to my opinion. The only thing I'm talking about is what literally happened. I'm going to bring up the message that I sent that night before she came on my live.

"In that message, I stated moving forward, we need to be friends. I'm not able to deal with you, and you keep bringing me down. I'm being a thousand with you. I can't even when I have three dollars in my account. I never in my life have asked you to take anything from your child, so please with respect, don't put that on me.

"I have my parents here. I can't even do it for them because I have nothing. It's Christmas, no tree, no nothing. You're worried about an application that you have mentioned over and over is extra for you. So please, with all due respect, you know all of this was a little bit extreme, but you and I both know that we were definitely arguing before this point. All I was trying to do was simply just step away. I have proof that you have also in your phone, that after I tried to step away; you kept picking and you kept going. All I was trying to do was just not to get to where we are today. You know what I'm saying? Because contrary to what you believe, I have respect for you, which is why I still haven't come to your platform. Which is why I'm still not trying to say, come here and do what you're saying that I'm doing. So I don't have to, I'm not going to defend what I know is my truth. I'm just not going to do that.

"So moving forward, you said that you wanted all of this by March, coming tomorrow or no later than Tuesday, you will get the two theophanies. Can we just go back to this breakdown again, so I can know what we're getting? That's just all I want to get to because I'm not going to now dissect my relationship as a grown man. I'm sorry, I'm not doing that."

Kyrie had a way of talking in circles. Using what Narcissistic Abuse Survivors call "word salad." This was when the Narc makes completely no sense at all. There is no rhyme or reason for what they are saying, and it's pointless. Welcome to Kyrie's word salad!

"Put yourselves in each other's shoes, and let's just move toward a solution that you both can agree on about the finances," said Bamm, "'cause that's the main thing for Heather currently. I think that you both just mentioned that you have respect for one another. So continue with that respect."

At the time, this was the main thing for me. I had no idea what I was dealing with. I just initially wanted an apology and my money back—until I found out more information.

"Kyrie," Bamm continued, "based on what you said, I'm not trying to be two against one at all. Again, if you feel like I'm not being supportive of you in this conversation, definitely speak up again, but I'm not trying to have anyone's side, I'm just merely trying to mediate the situation. Also, I want you to feel comfortable that the information that she's displaying in front of me is not going to come back out or be sent to anybody else. You already know how I am. I'm very honest. I'm very truthful. So I don't want you to feel that you're not being supported because you're being supported just merely by me even taking the presence of getting into this conversation."

"I hear you guys," Kyrie said, "but the fact that my mom is sick, I'm just like this situation for me, no offense, has been a lot already."

A lot for you? My mind screamed. *You are the epitome of a lot!*

"I'm not saying you're doing anything wrong, but I'm trying to say don't persecute me for not grabbing your side in this space 'cause me being in this space right now is being on your side," said Bamm.

"So, I can understand why you don't want to talk about these things in front of Bamm because it ultimately makes you look bad because you have your truth," I told Kyrie. "I have what I have to say. Then there's the real truth."

"You see what I mean?" he asked.

"That's her opinion," said Bamm.

"But in her opinion, *your* opinion, Heather, do you still have to tear me down?" Kyrie asked.

"Kyrie, can you, can you take responsibility for what you've done?"

"I have no problem, but I can sit here and nitpick about you."

"Can you apologize? Can you take ownership for what you've done, for what you've done to me? Can you do that? That's the first thing, an apology. Can I get an apology for you hurting me and breaking me down to the marrow of my bones? Can you apologize for that? Because you're sitting here and you're deflecting and you're trying to get off the phone and just get this done when you're not taking ownership for what you have done."

"I'm not trying to deflect. My mother's actually on her way to my house. She's staying here, and I don't want to just keep this energy in my house and around my mom and my house. That's the only reason."

"Can you apologize for what you've done, Kyrie?"

"Heather, Heather. I apologize. I really do. I can say you weren't honest, either. You weren't honest about where you were emotionally. You and I both know that I had to subject myself to things with you as well. This whole thing that I'm narcissistic, you know, I can take, and you can tear me down left and right. I know the truth about me. I do apologize, you know, but like I said, I'm not going to sit here and be negative. Like it's not going to do anything for me. That's also why I'm not responding because if I respond now, I don't want to come across as negative. So I'm just really just trying to keep it clean cut, honestly."

"Okay and I am, too. I'm brutally honest. I have no problem explaining where I am emotionally or anything. I'm a very sensitive person. I told you that from the beginning. I first showed my emotions when you were here at my house because I thought I was crying because I saw that there were some discrepancies in our personalities, and we wouldn't get along. There were some things that didn't match. I was sad about that because I really liked you, and I wanted this to work. But then when I saw you were changing those things, I changed my mind set and my process.

"Now moving down the line, you saw me on an emotional roller coaster because of what you were doing to me by not spending time, by not being available for me, spending countless amounts of time on EGO, where I didn't feel like I had a boyfriend. With that brings self-doubt. It brought in a whole set of insecurities for me because I am reverting back to the child like Heather because I'm thinking that this man doesn't like me because he's not spending time with me. I would email, text you, and verbalize it to you, and every time I would verbalize it to you, you would check out on me and say that I was destroying your business and you couldn't work.

"You also said I was taking everything away from you. So that is why I have been emotional because I didn't know where I stood with you. And you know what? I want to apologize for that real emotional time when you were supposed to come back to Atlanta, and you didn't. When I went through the whole process and the crazy stuff that I did and said. I apologize for that. But that's how madly in love I was with you and wanting to be with you where you lose it a little bit. That was one time that I did that, and I apologize to you for that."

"We ain't never, never," Kyrie said, "and I mean this, I put this on my best friend's dead grave, my grandmother's, my mother's life, we never really said we were boyfriend and girlfriend, never."

What is your definition of boyfriend and girlfriend, I thought, seething, *because we were shole acting like it! Maybe that's the ole school in me. If we talk on the phone, spend time together, and are FUCKIN……. We go TOGETHER!*

"That is true. But I thought because of all of the things that we were saying, doing, we were in a relationship, and you were mine."

"That's why I kept saying, we were working toward that direction."

"You would always call me wifey and my wife and all of that, too."

"Wifey is not a wife? Okay."

"She's also not a butch queen," Bamm said.

"I don't even know what that is," Heather said.

"Right. But I say that we (LGBTQI community) use those," Bamm said. "We use those terminologies, wifey, stink, fave, bae, boo, you know, husband, we use those terminologies."

"I apologize if you feel like something that I was saying was misconstrued, but I'm not saying this to be rude to you, but I never was trying to lead you on. Just to be transparent, you already know what you're dealing with outside of me anyway, and I was giving you time for that."

Kyrie seems as if he is being sincere at this point, but Heather was always upfront with him. She was transparent throughout the entire relationship.

"I didn't need any. I told you, I don't need any time for that because I'm legally separated in California. I filed for divorce here in Georgia. My marriage is over, and I told you that."

"Well maybe I needed the time."

"Because I haven't seen Chaz Brierson since May of 2019. Okay."

"So first one on the list was the apology. That was the apology. Second on the list is the one hundred K."

"No, the second thing was your STD results that I never saw from your doctor."

"I can get those to you. I don't have nothing."

"Well, I need to know by seeing the paperwork. We had unprotected sex one time. So that puts me at risk for anything. I want to be safe. I've got to go back to the doctor, but before you even came here, we both got tested. I can give you my test results as well. I would appreciate yours."

"No problem, Heather," Kyrie said, clearly annoyed. "No problem because I really want this situation to be over at this point, honestly."

"Okay," Bamm said. "When can you get that to her?"

"I will have to call my PCP in the morning and figure out if they can. When it's negative, they don't give you a print out. I didn't get a printout saying that I'm negative. My doctor called me saying everything's cleared. So now I have to call him and get the results. Once I figure that out, Heather will know."

"Yes, sir. The two theophanies you said you can send by the end of the month. He said that earlier. The rest of the one hundred K, which is really would be eighty K after you send the two theophanies, by the beginning of March. Is by the beginning of March a date that's doable for you?"

"Yeah."

"Okay. The two thousand returned back to her by the beginning of March, which was—"

"I don't agree with that," Kyrie interrupted. "It's not because I don't have it, but I've never, in my twenty-nine years of dealing with somebody, given people money and asked for anything back. I bought engagement rings. I bought Audemars Piguet watches. I ain't never asked for anything back. I really think that is based off of an opinion that I said that. There's no written proof. Number One Woman didn't show you a text message that I said that."

"The proof of what? That you—"

This dude must have Heather bent!!!!! Why would Number One Woman Lie??????? Plus she showed Heather several receipts with time stamps!!!!!

"First of all, I took you for your money? No disrespect. What money? Like you're not, it's not like you're paying my rent, my car note. Why would I sit here and say, I used you for your money?

$2,000! Boy bye! You cried holy cow to get it, and I fell for it! The nerve!

"I don't know. I don't know why you told her that. I don't know why you told her that, maybe to save face with her?"

"But you don't know why I told, you don't know if I told her."

"Ok if or why?"

"Did she verbally tell you, Heather?" Bamm asked.

"Yes. She verbally told me several times."

"Which is an opinion. Like that's crazy."

"So, that's one thing you disagree with on the list," Bamm said. "Okay. Let's tackle the last point quickly and come back to this. Not to do this to any other women was also on the list. I think those are general. I think you already said it is not your goal. Again, this is on her list. So I just wanted to honor that and say that, too. Now about the two thousand dollars, what do you all want to do about that?"

"He can do a payment plan," I replied. "My thing is that just with all of this and how he is, I'm disgusted at this entire experience. I want my money back."

"So this narrative is that I was taking from you?"

"You were, Kyrie. And you were trying to play me, and it's just bad. It's so bad. You didn't have to do me like this, Kyrie."

"Heather, no disrespect. You have nothing financially that I need. That's not to take away from who you are. That's not to talk bad about you, but there's nothing that, no one... I will never. God is my source and the finisher of my faith and will always supply all of my needs. I will never look to anybody to be a paymaster, never to pay anything. You just said that you mentioned you gave me the money out of what you wanted to do. I've never asked you for anything. The only time we got to me asking for something was when I asked for the Theophanies, and I said that I was going to give them back."

"Kyrie, everything that I gave you was because of how we talked about—"

"But notice the things that you're mad about and that you're addressing are things that other parties said. She just now said that she's asking for the two thousand dollars because of what Number One Woman said."

This would be a totally different conversation if Kyrie wasn't a pathological liar! He literally told Number One Woman that he used me for money and now is saying that he didn't. Whew Chile…

"I didn't say that. I said because this whole situation is disgusting."

"When she mentioned it earlier in the conversation, she did mention that it was largely because of the fact that somebody stated that she was being used for her money," Bamm said, "but I think she also did this thing later on that she's just supposed to discuss this, so she feels as if she wants the money back because you weren't a real friend to her. Then that was a gift that she was giving somebody who's her friend. That's what I'm hearing from that. That's what I'm saying to you, Kyrie, that I just want us to all just chill out. We know where we are, we both know how y'all feel about each other. Y'all both know what space y'all are in."

"But even still, I will never be in a romantic affair with someone and then go to other parties and believe those other parties now."

"That's you," Heather said.

"No, it's not."

"Because, I'm looking at everything that you're doing and the way you're treating me and not giving me what I need as my partner or my dude. I'm saying, this is not adding up. So if I'm looking at all of this, and I'm seeing how you're treating me, how, when I give you a yacht on this app, you call me and say, but you told me you were going to give me a yacht. You said, 'Heather, I'm going to give you a yacht and every unicorn and catch up.'"

"I didn't say that. Do you have proof?"

"Come on now. Stop doing this. Stop lying."

"Ok, so we can move forward," Bamm said.

Move forward to WHAT, I thought, truly believing I was in an episode of *The Twilight Zone*.

| ¦ |

After the mediation, Bamm and I reconvened and discussed everything that happened. He honestly didn't think that Kyrie was going to give me back the money and that I should try my luck with the aunt. Recalling these events brought back a lot of feelings for me because Kyrie was a master manipulator and liar. He really didn't expect me to read my letter and put all of our business out there for display. I had to because I needed him to feel my pain.

What I didn't know was that it really didn't matter because he was a narcissist, and they don't feel anything or have any real emotions. From the mediation, Kyrie proved that he likes to have a rebuttal for everything. He doesn't *just* listen. His goal for listening is to respond. Period.

I'm Getting My Money Back

As time moved forward, Kyrie showed all sorts of new things—and new women.

With a narcissist, the *new* girl usually isn't new. He has them lined up before he discards one—like how Kyrie had his line of women before discarding me. First, it was Stormy and then Big Mamma. It wasn't their looks or age that made him choose them; they were submissive, overly trusting, overly forgiving, easy to hook and thought Kyrie was God.

There was no love or emotional attachment whatsoever; it was purely about securing supply through sex. Big Mamma stroked his ego, provided financial resources, and waited on him twenty-four/seven. He made it look like they had never been happier, but that was all part of the false image. He was killing two birds with one stone: lovebombing them and making me feel unworthy.

The same day as the mediation with Bamm and Kyrie, I also emailed Ms. Loretta a letter stating what we spoke about on the phone and how much he/she was going to pay me back. Basically, Kyrie owed me $4,840.

- $2,000 for fabric
- $140 for Southwest Airlines ticket
- $2,700-EGO Trades/Investments (approximately 100K in Mean green)

I wrote that per our conversation, Ms. Loretta, on behalf of Kyrie Jenkins Dubois, had agreed to make payments to Heather Moore in increments of five hundred dollars starting January 8, 2021, via Cash App. Nine payments of five hundred dollars and one payment of three hundred forty dollars.

The next day after the mediation, Kyrie came to my PK and dropped the theophanies. I came by his live broadcast after, and he was in a panel with Temi and Blaze. I thanked him for giving the theophanies back. He was very upset that I came by and did this. He didn't want his friends to know what he was doing—good or bad.

I also started deep diving in investigation, looking up people that he was friends with. I followed his girlfriend and her mother on Instagram, and I started looking at her stories and her page. I also watched his live broadcast, and he had a whole new set of friends and BBW's that were following him.

I also saw in his live broadcast that he was getting close with Big Mamma. I think she was his next victim. Cloudy was also around his lives a lot more and being extra flirtatious with him. So much so that she actually invited him to visit her in Virginia. I kept a close eye on Cloudy and watched how she moved in his live broadcast. As I watched, I saw that she was gifting him with large gifts, and I immediately knew that she was next. Because I followed her on the app, I caught her one day in her live broadcast and asked if I could talk to her off of the app, and she agreed. We exchanged numbers, and I called her immediately.

I opened the conversation by telling her that I had some important information to give her to help her avoid what I had just been through. I then asked her what Kyrie told her about me. She said that he told her that I was like a big sister to him and a mentor.

"What?!"

He even told her to befriend me because she wanted to join my sorority and I would be a great mentor for her. I told her that Kyrie and I had been dating for the past two months and that he also came to visit me. She told me that she thought that they were dating, too, because they had been talking on the phone every day and had been having phone sex since before his auction in December.

"Wow, just wow" was all I could say.

Cloudy and I spoke about how he maneuvered, and she basically told me everything verbatim that he did, and it matched how he was with me.

The typical way that a narcissist "lovebombs" you includes

- showering you with compliments,
- giving you praise,
- telling you how beautiful you are, and
- letting you know that "he wants you."

These were all of the same things that he told me and the Number One Woman. Cloudy was such a sweet and kind young lady who totally understood what I was doing to help her. She had dated a narcissist before, so she knew exactly what was going on and didn't want to take part in it or move forward with Kyrie. I was so happy that she understood and was going to get rid of him. Me and Cloudy became good friends because of this and talk to this day. I also started supporting Cloudy on the app and asked her not to let him know that she spoke to me; she agreed. Eventually, Kyrie saw that I became her supporter and backed away from her by blocking her on the app and by phone.

After the big Christmas Eve breakup and the Christmas Day fall out, I realized by watching his live that he had a girlfriend. Her name was Rittany, and she was a plus sized girl in her thirties. She had a face that looked like Edna from *The Incredibles* with horrible acne and a body shaped like Grimace from McDonald's.

From her bio on her Instagram page, she was a fashion stylist for mostly COGIC (Church of God In Christ) church folks. Her mother was a pastor of a Pentecostal church. Her style was very gaudy and outlandish. It actually made her look very unattractive. She also wore a lot of makeup that didn't complement her naturally. It seemed as though she hid her pain through all of the makeup that she wore.

As the New Year came in, I noticed on Kyrie's Instagram and his girlfriend's that they were more vocal with the presence of their relationship. I wasn't watching while we were dating. Maybe this was going on during our time, too, I thought. I had no reason at the time to look. I wish I was nosey then.

They spent New Year's Eve together at church for a watch night service. He made her a custom dress (an ugly one), and he made his suit as well. They both posted pictures on Instagram. If I had known that he had a girlfriend, I would have never, ever dated him or given him the time of day!

Because Kyrie or Rittany noticed that I checked their Insta stories, Kyrie called me one night, going off on me again with his aunt on the phone. He basically wanted to know if I were going to contact Rittany. I asked why he was so concerned if that was not his girlfriend.

"Rittany showed me two screenshots that show you and someone named Tyla started following her on Instagram," he said. "You on your backup follow page heathermoore.com and someone named Tyla Cat Eyes. It was a light-skinned woman. If I'm not mistaken, she also followed me on EGO. So did you guys try to follow Rittany on Instagram?"

I told him that I had three to five Instagram pages that I followed all of them on months ago.

"Okay, so why would Rittany so happen to just hit me up about this now?" Kyrie asked.

"I don't know."

"So you have not tried to follow Rittany recently? You're not trying to reach out to her?"

"No. Do you want me to reach out to her? Isn't that your girlfriend?"

His aunt then chimed in to let me know that she was on the phone but lied and said that she just picked up the phone. She was there all along.

"Blowing up my reality is not going to get my attention," Kyrie said. "That's just going to cause me to go the legal route to fight this, and I don't want to do that.

"We both have stuff to lose—"

"You can't hurt anything that I have going on," I interrupted.

His aunt chimed in and said, "Per our conversation, we are going to work everything out via our agreement, and he is going to pay you back everything. I took your word as a woman and trusted that word. If you have another problem, you should address that with me."

"I did," I told her. "He's doing the same thing to other women, and he continues to do those things that he was doing to me."

Every time I started talking to his aunt, it took time to get one sentence out because Kyrie interrupted after each word; he didn't want her to know more information.

"So are you now reaching out to Rittany because you want to tell her everything?" he asked me. "Is that what you are trying to do?"

"Does she need to know everything?" I asked.

"Rittany doesn't have anything to do with you and Kyrie," his aunt said.

"When I met Kyrie, he said he didn't have a girlfriend, and he hadn't dated anybody on the app. When you lie to me, and you say all of these untruths, that's not cool."

Kyrie's aunt took a deep breath, and I rolled my eyes. I felt a hard deflection coming on.

"I'm talking to you as a woman," she said. "You said when you met him, he didn't have a girlfriend. Let me ask you a question: Do you have a husband?"

"I am legally separated from my husband," I said. "Legally separated means I do not have a husband."

"No, it does not. It means you're working toward leaving your husband," she said.

"Like I said, I haven't seen my husband in a year and a half. I am not married."

At that point, I realized that she was just as deranged and delusional as her nephew. She continued on by saying that he said that he didn't have a girlfriend at the time and because I was taking someone else's word (which I wasn't), I was going by what I saw on Instagram. Because of this, I never trusted him in the first place, and I wasn't his friend. She continued saying that we were both adults, and we chose to deal with one another, and there are consequences to those actions.

I had to stop her.

"I would've never even talked to Kyrie if I knew that he was fooling with people on the app," I said. "He lied to me. He deceived me. I know he did. I see all the receipts."

Ms. Loretta was still trying to talk, but Kyrie interrupted her and said, "Because you feel like I lied and deceived you, what was the end goal? Do you want your money back and to blow everything up? Because even still at the end of the day, again, blowing up anything is not going to propel me to pay you. I'm here on the phone with you, not my lawyer, not the cops, not on EGO. I haven't reached out to any of your parties or anything."

"You can reach out to anybody," I said. "You can reach out because I'm a righteous woman. I have not done anything wrong to you, Kyrie."

"You are a forty-four-year-old woman with a two-year-old daughter," Loretta said. "You don't have anything to lose?"

"No, not from this."

"You don't think this is extortion because I work for a prosecutor."

Can you say, Bat Shit Crazy!"

"No, this isn't extortion," I said. "Kyrie and I had an agreement that we would pay each other back all of the gifts on the app, and he broke that! He also sends negative texts saying that he wasn't paying me back shit when I was in the hospital after my surgery! When he starts threatening not to pay me, I go back to my original plan to make his life a living hell!"

"Now, Heather, I told you to tell me if he contacts you," Loretta said. "You didn't contact me. If I had known then, we could have solved this situation, but you didn't tell me that he reached out to you."

"Ms. Loretta, I was really trying to handle this amicably like adults, but Kyrie goes on tirades. I would really prefer to just talk to you. Because you keep saying that I have people hitting you up and stalking you, but you literally say what I talk about in my live broadcast, and there are always EGO TV watchers in my room. So who do you have stalking me? You really need to tell him to fall back and watch how he talks to me because I'm not the one!"

"If you see any of his people contacting you or messing with you on your live broadcast, let me know."

This was where the conversation went left! Kyrie started on one of his tirades and completely lost his shit, yelling at the top of his lungs and apologizing for everything.

"Like I said," he began, "again, I don't have nobody watching your stuff. I'm trying to handle this situation. I want to just get it out and just get it over with. That's all I'm trying to do. That's what I've been trying to let you know from day one. That's what I was trying to do. That's why I kept saying my energy was always the same. You're going to get your stuff back, but I don't know anybody on God's earth that wants to continue to be disrespected and then give somebody something.

"I have no problem giving you what I owe. Heather, no one else is on this phone but you, me, and my aunt. When you gave me the two thousand dollars, I appreciated it. Everybody knows what really happened between me and you. I'm not trying to tear you down. I'm not trying to defeat you. I really fuck with you! Still to this day, I still fuck with you!

"I'm sorry you feel like I lied to you. I was not trying to use you. I was not trying to manipulate you. I'm sorry for not telling you about Charelle, but I didn't tell you in order to manipulate you. I did not think I was going to love you the way I did! I'm sorry, but I am not trying to hurt you. I'm not trying to kill you. But please trust me that I'm going to give you your shit back. I'm going to. But you don't have to hit anybody up. You don't have to watch anything. I got it. I'm going to give it to you, but just trust me!"

Ms. Loretta said, "Okay. So just like you spoke a little loud, maybe you weren't yelling like that, but you spoke with passion about your point."

"I told him to go last so he could be heard."

"That's the thing, both of you feel passionate about this, both of you just feel like, okay, this happened. I wanted to be done, but I want to be good with you after it's done," said Loretta. "There's no reason for y'all not to be good as adults. Y'all are both creative people; y'all both got shit going. The point is when you do negative shit to people, negative shit comes back to the whole family. Right? It's a whole new year. He said he is gonna give you back what he owes you."

We ended the conversation with Loretta and Kyrie agreeing to pay me back all of the money by March. I was a happy camper. I thought that I reached a good point with them. That there would be resolution and we could move forward and move on amicably. What I later learned is that this was a quick fix in the world of a narcissist. He would tell me what I wanted to hear and also his aunt. Then he would eventually blow it all up and fuck it up. After we all got off the phone, Kyrie called me back to talk further.

The Real Kyrie

Trauma bonding began with the good and bad inconsistent reinforcements between Kyrie and I. The traumatic bonds between us were stronger than typical human bonds and required much more work to break. I was addicted to the brain chemistry attached to the anticipation and traumatic bonding surrounding the relationship. Because the relationship was so utterly unfulfilling, I was left with a constant state of emptiness, which was temporarily assuaged with each encounter with my object of obsession: Kyrie.

After we hung up the phone with Ms. Loretta, Kyrie called me, and we spoke for about two hours. This was the first time that I really saw a vulnerable side to him. This was the real Kyrie. He was damaged, fractured, hurt, and a victim of trauma.

"I'm feeling like it's too good to be true," he said. "I understand what you're saying, and I would feel deceived as well. But I'm just trying to tell you my connection with you was real, and I was not trying to deceive you like that. Of course, the way that it is coming out is going to now seem that way. I understand that, but again, I'm still going to tell you I apologize for it. That's not what I was trying to do. I'm not even trying to pay you so you can now not even retaliate. I understand what you gave me, and I appreciate it.

"So I'm going to give it back to you. It's just a principle. I can't even look at you face to face and disrespect you because I genuinely care. I always told you this, like you are a dope, amazing person. I'm not trying to take you down. Like I'm not trying to disrupt your platforms. I'm not trying to do any of that. I understand the situation, that it hurts, and I'm sorry for it. Heather, listen. I'm sorry. I can't keep repeating it enough.

"I'm just telling you, you're going to get your stuff back from me, that we agreed upon. I hope you continue to heal after your surgery. I hope you have a speedy recovery. I wish you all the best with that. I'm not trying to wish nothing bad on you at all."

Wow! All I could say was wow! Because he literally had been acting bat shit crazy and not taking responsibility for any of his actions. Deflecting and blaming me for everything, the typical characteristics of a narcissist.

I responded with the fact that his apology spoke volumes about him and made me feel so much better. But I also asked him if he could not do this to anyone else because I was watching him and seeing him set it up for the next victims. I told him that I was not a vindictive or spiteful person, but everyone isn't like me.

I didn't want him to run into the wrong person and then he end up with a "Thin Line Between Love and Hate" situation going on. He told me that he wasn't sure what people had told me about him, but this isn't what he did.

"Did you have phone sex with Cloudy?" The question caught him off guard.

"I have once or twice recently," he said, "but I'm about to stop that because I'm turned off by her, for other reasons that don't even have to do with this."

"But you were having phone sex with her the whole time you were talking to me. That's not cool."

He immediately started playing the victim. "See, this is why I need to leave EGO."

"You shouldn't leave EGO. You just can't do this. Kyrie, you can't be fucking with these girls like this."

"Heather, let me explain something to you. Cloudy is a very sexual girl. Okay. Cloudy has had phone sex with like seven people on EGO."

"That doesn't have anything to do with me. The only thing that matters is that you were supposed to be with me, and you were messing with other girls. That's a violation. I wasn't fuckin with nobody. I was only involved with you. Kyrie, when you do stuff like this, the best thing for you to do is to just come clean with everything. Because I don't go looking for this shit. It comes to me. Don't use these girls like this."

He kinda got emotional like he was caught and tried to save face and said that wasn't what he was doing. But he knew that I knew at that point. He played the victim and started saying this was why he needed to leave EGO.

He then tried to change the subject by saying untrue things about Number One Woman. That she sent pictures of her vagina to him. I later found out that this was not true. At the time, I didn't know it, but he was a master manipulator and professional liar. He then backtracked to go back to the information about Cloudy, saying that he was drunk one night and played the questions game with her on a panel.

I saw that panel because I was watching from the window. Cloudy, in fact, asked him if he had dated anyone off of the app and he said, "Yes, two people."

He also was trying to downplay what they did. Saying that he wasn't talking to her. When in fact, they were having phone sex for several weeks. He apologized for entertaining stuff when he shouldn't have and said that he was human. But then went back to being the victim, saying how many people in his family were sick and dying of COVID-19. He said he didn't have time for all of this. But in reality, he did because he was literally talking to me, Cloudy, Number One Woman, Rittany, and many more girls at the same time.

"Kyrie, moving forward, you need to keep it professional on EGO," I said. "You probably shouldn't be talking to anyone on the app, especially if Ms. Rittany is your girlfriend. 'Cause that's not fair to her. Okay? Now you can lie and say that's not your girlfriend. I won't contact her, but she doesn't deserve you cheating on her. You had sex with me and the Number One Woman unprotected. Like, you can't do that. You don't know what I have. You don't know if I was HIV positive or anything. You could have taken something back to her. That's not cool. I don't mess with other people's men. I don't do that. If I had known you had a girlfriend, I would have never talked to you."

"I understand what you are saying, but our relationship is all over the place. Heather, listen, I'm dealing with it. Okay. I've learned my lesson, and I'm trying. I'm gonna give you your money."

"I'm glad you hear me. That's all I wanted. You are good with me. You don't have to worry about me. Your apology and us talking tonight has helped me tremendously. So I appreciate you, but don't do wrong by Rittany. That's not fair to her because you wouldn't want nobody to do that to you."

"I understand, but it's been done to me so much."

"Two wrongs don't make a right. I've been hurt, too, but I'm not out here hurting people. I treat people the way that I want to be treated. I love people the way that I want to be loved, and you saw that."

"It's just, it's hard," he said. "It's a lot, man; it's just a lot that I haven't told you about me. I don't love myself. I used to take Ritalin and stuff when I was younger, like I told you, I've been locked up. I've been in psych wards and shit. Like I've been through mad stuff. Like, you know, there's stuff with me being attracted to men. Like, I just don't love myself. I think something's wrong with me. You know? Like I just don't love myself. I've tried to kill myself twelve times; yo, like shit is real. I go through a lot. I feel like people don't even know who I am. So how can I give my real self to people?

"Heather, I just really liked you. I've never met somebody that just wanted to be a real friend and support me. The reason why me and Rittany clash is because we're together on and off, and her family doesn't like me. She's just the type that looks for gratification. She posts things all the time on social media but just because she's posting us doesn't necessarily mean we're good. She's just doing it so she can now get the attention. She and I have been in counseling for like two years now."

"So why don't you spend time with yourself, instead of being in all these relationships and focus on you and building yourself up?" I asked.

"I don't know, I guess I get lonely. After my best friend got killed, my life shifted, and I wanted to die, too. Sometimes, I pray that if I die, my life would be easier."

"So this is teacher Heather coming in. Your past does not create your future and your present. You are a king and you're destined for greatness."

"Look at what I did to you. Like I wasn't trying to do that and look at what happened. If I just would've been honest and just told you what the situation was and just dealt with it. We wouldn't be in this position. Like you said, I still did it. I hurt you. Like even with Cloudy, like I need to just cut this shit off. Like it's not even worth it. I don't know why the fuck I be doing half this shit when I do it. Because when I do it, I can't even find the words for it. Never mind it doesn't matter."

"No, it does matter, even the fact that you literally fucked me up, like to my core. I didn't know what the fuck going on. I was like, what the fuck? This was the worst experience I've ever experienced in my life. I still love and care about you. I want you to be well. I think you are so talented."

"I'm a talented train wreck."

"You can fix that. You can work on that day by day. But you have to do some self-love exercises. I have to do some self-love exercises because I should have cut this shit off a long time ago. I really should have the first time when you raised your voice at me, when I was like, goodbye, it should have been done then because I know better.

"Cause people don't talk to me like that, and I should've let you go then. I let you creep back in because of my low self-worth when I'm dealing with men. I know I have low self-worth when I'm dealing with men, and I thought it was gone. I revert back to the little fat girl, the little fat Heather who nobody loves. But I'm going to fix my shit. I'm going to counseling on the sixth and start my sessions so that I can get myself right and get on the path of righteousness for me. Because I'm about to go through this whole weight loss transformation' and I'll be damned if I lose all this weight and I'm still fucked up or have insecurities. The first step to recovery and to redemption is admitting that you have issues and that you have things that you need to work on. So kudos to you for taking the first step and for even telling me all of this. That speaks monuments and volumes about you. So I hear you. I see you and you can change.

"But here's the deal. Kyrie, don't treat people badly because you feel bad. Treat people the way that you want to be treated. If you always hold that mantra close to your heart, you won't have any problems. No matter what happened to you, if your family's fucked up, if your life experiences are fucked up, let all that go. Let all that go and move on and treat people with kindness. Treat people with respect and work on you. You need to leave everybody alone and focus on you and get your life together and get your mind right. You don't need to be in a relationship. You don't need to be talking to anybody. You don't need to be doing any of that shit. You need to work on Kyrie. Do you want to be well, or you don't want to be well? It's as simple as that. Come clean with her and say, 'Hey, I'm not, well. I'm not doing things that are the best for me. I need to work on myself. Is it okay if you give me time to allow myself to work on me?'"

At that point, every piece of advice that I would give him to get better and make wiser decisions, he would shoot down or make another problem staying in the victim role. We kept talking in circles, and he told me that he was going to lose his girlfriend and that his family situation was messed up and there was nothing that he could do to change it.

I tried to pour into him with positive affirmations to lift his spirit. I really believed in how talented he was and that I thought that at the end of the day, he was a good person and could get better. I told him that the world needed him. They needed his brilliance and his artistry.

He also started going back into what happened with Cloudy and how he wanted to quit EGO. He was caught and couldn't believe it. I told him that he had to take responsibility for his actions. Flirting with people and taking things off the app was not a good look.

The problem came with him because I later found out that he did it on purpose and moved on flirting with Big Mamma. He also blamed his behavior on how he was raised. Stating that his grandmother had several men, his aunt did the same thing and that's where he picked up these bad behaviors from. He stated that he didn't have a normal upbringing, and his life was very unstable in regard to the behaviors that he witnessed from who raised him.

As we kept talking, I reiterated that if his relationship with Rittany wasn't working or if she couldn't accept him for who he was, then he should leave her alone. He told me that she didn't know that he was pansexual or that he was in the ballroom scene. I told him that he needed to be with someone who loves and cares for all of him wholeheartedly.

"Who the fuck is that?" he asked.

"Well, you just lost it, sir. Because it was me," I said. "I meant what I said about loving all of you and accepting you for exactly who you are."

I still didn't know what I was dealing with in Kyrie. I later found out who he was from my spiritual advisor. All he said were half-truths. It sounded real good, but his actions would eventually speak louder than his words.

STORY 22
New Supply and Old Supply

Abusers look for certain characteristics in people. They like compassionate, empathetic people who will constantly understand and overlook their constant transgressions. They like 'ride or die' individuals who are fiercely loyal, no matter what. But it was a misconception that all victims have no confidence or suffer from low self-esteem.

Pathological people groom victims and slowly break down their sense of self and diminish their self-worth. It is not always the other way around. Many victims often feel the loss of their prior more confident selves. Narcissistic people know themselves; they know they are selfish and entitled. They know they won't last with other selfish entitled individuals, so they look for people who are the opposite of themselves and have the morality and values that are missing in them.

At this time, I was recovering from my gastric bypass surgery. My cousin Mecole and Myra were in town to help me with Morgan. Mecole witnessed all of the fuckery that was going on with Kyrie. She in fact was listening to all of the conversations that we had on the phone via speaker.

After the conversation with Kyrie that I recorded, I realized that he had a lot of mental health issues. I also realized that he was into men more than he let on. I really felt that he was a homosexual who was ashamed of being gay and used women for a cover up. His sexuality continued to unfold as we continued. I felt sorry for him and wanted to help him in any way that I could.

So I started sending him affirmations for him to speak into himself. When I started this and talked to him about it, he acted as if we never had a conversation about his issues, and he didn't want me to make mention of it. I really didn't realize at the time how much I really was in love with him. Things were still moving so fast, and I was just trying to keep up. I kept seeing him on EGO and would come by his live broadcast often. Every time I would come by, he would speak, but it seemed as if he was nervous. I also saw a big movement with him and Big Momma. They would line up often and would be in each other's live broadcasts flirting heavily.

This was disturbing to me because me and him just ended. I spoke to him about it, and he said that he didn't know what he was doing because she was married with three kids. But eventually, he told me that he liked her because she had a nice smile. We would still talk and text from time to time and come to each other's lives. He was working on some new sculptures that I liked, and I told him to save me one.

Then he texted me and told me that he was coming to Atlanta and that he just wanted to let me know. I asked him why. He said because he wanted to tell me before someone else told me. He was coming for an LGBTQI ball. He was styling a few people for some of the categories, and it was a big deal for the gay community. He also asked if he could stay with me. I said no! He said he was just joking. I told him to make sure that he used the ticket credit for his flight to the A that I had bought for him. He told me that he would.

A day or so later, he told me that he could still hear me. Then said sorry after I didn't reply right away. He was referring to the way that I climaxed when we had sex. This was his narcissistic way of pulling me back into his web. After he wrote that, I called him to talk about it. We both admitted that we wanted to continue with what we were doing sexually on the phone and in person.

After we established this, we had phone sex. A day later, I called him to have phone sex with him, and he was too busy. This was his typical narcissistic behavior. He was only available when he needed his needs met and never when I wanted to get off. During this time, I also would fly through Big Momma's live broadcast and speak. He would be in there and would text me immediately asking what was my angle and was I sure I was good? I wasn't good, but I was just going through the motions.

We continued to talk on the phone and text. He would tell me about his plans for Atlanta, and I started to help him look for Airbnbs. He also continued galivanting with Big Momma more and more every day. Almost like he was putting on a show. As I was helping him find places, he started to talk about Temi and said that he might not stay with him because he was inviting people to stay with them. He didn't like this and expressed his frustration to me. I also asked him if he could style me for the balls. He said yes and that we would go shopping when he came into town. I told him to deduct his fee off of the money that he owed me.

Then the shit hit the fan! He called me cursing and yelling out of control about Number One Woman. He asked if I spoke to her and if I told her things about his aunt and our arrangements. I'm a brutally honest person, and I said yes.

But later on, I realized that I hadn't spoken to her. He was furious with me, and I apologized profusely. But it didn't work; he told me that he didn't want to see me in Atlanta and hung up on me. I begged him to not do this. We were doing so well and making such great strides in our friendship again. I sent him two videos telling him that I needed him and that he was a light in my life and not to tell Temi or his aunt and to let's work this out.

I also sent him text messages apologizing and saying that I thought that me and Number One Woman were cool and that I was wrong for talking to her. I told him that we were bonding over our situationship and that now I see that she wanted to keep up the mess. I told him that I saw that she was trying to play us against each other because she still loved him. I asked him to please call me so that we could work it out. He never called me.

After all of this happened, I found out that he was lying about all of this. Number One Woman wasn't trying to keep up any mess. He was. He didn't want us talking to each other because then we would know what he was doing. Playing us all! In fact, he got into an argument with her because she wouldn't give him back a unicorn because of what he was doing to me.

So he got mad and took out all of his frustration on me, thus starting the fight that we had.

At the same time, Kyrie was also becoming more visual on EGO with Big Mamma. Big Mamma was a member of the Regular Retreat family. She had three kids and was married. She had a pretty smile but never showed anything but her face in the camera on EGO. As time passed and she got more involved with Kyrie, she gained more confidence in herself. When I first started watching her on EGO, she was timid, shy, and only stayed in one spot on her couch and on her computer.

As time progressed, she started showing her body and baby! She was a SSBBW: Supersized BBW. She actually had the body of Danny DeVito as the Penguin in the Batman movies. She was just a taller version of him.

At the beginning of January, they were always lining up in their live broadcasts together, and he flirted heavily with her, saying things like I wondered if we can get married on EGO. He continuously gave her big gifts, and she looked so happy. I even went by her live broadcasts to say hello from time to time. He didn't like that and asked me, "What is your goal?"

I didn't really have one. They were also always buying each other in auctions and changing their names to each other. This literally infuriated me because when I bought him in an auction, I didn't even get a Coke and a smile. I eventually asked Kyrie what he was doing with her, and he said he didn't know because she was married. I told him that I didn't like it. He kept flirting and pouring it on thick. I wondered if he was doing this to make me jealous.

As I continued to do more research on narcissists, I found this out: *The new girl* (i.e., Big Mamma) *usually isn't new.* The narcissist had her lined up before he discarded me. It wasn't her looks or age that made him choose her; she's submissive, overly trusting, overly forgiving, easy to hook, and thought he was a God.

There was no love or emotional attachment whatsoever; it was purely about securing narcissistic supply through sex. She stroked his ego, provided financial resources, and waited on him twenty-four/seven. It might've looked like they've never been happier, but that was all part of the false image. He was killing two birds with one stone: lovebombing her and making me feel unworthy.

Rittany, on the other hand, from her Instagram, was very flashy and a self-proclaimed church stylist. She was a BBW, too, and Kyrie loved his BBWs. Probably because he felt that they had low self-esteem and could run games on them. Which he did very well. She was also shaped bad. If there was a character that she looked like, I would say Grimace from

McDonald's. Her stomach hung over her knees, and she never wore shapewear to control her fat tissue. Her style was very extra and gave the illusion that she needed to be seen. In her pictures on Instagram, she would always wear a ton of makeup, which really took away from her looks. I started noticing her more around Christmas when I started investigating her page and his page. They spent Christmas together and then New Year's Eve. I never paid attention as much because I had no reason to be suspicious or so I thought. With Rittany, he told me that they weren't together from the start. He was mad at her because she never mentioned that she wanted to pursue an art career and that she was taking his dreams and making them her own. He also would talk negatively about her all the time on the phone and in his live broadcast when Big Mamma was present. This was his plan to make his exes look crazy, so that you wouldn't believe that they were with anyone. Everything was always the ex's fault.

After the argument about Number One Woman, Kyrie was in an auction. In the auction, he was bought by Big Mamma, and she changed her name to Kyrie's Big and he changed his EGO name to Big's Kyrie.

Seeing this hurt me to my core, and I couldn't take it. When I bought him in the auction, he never changed his name to my name. Now, he was openly expressing his love for this chick he just met. I was so hurt. I didn't want to do this anymore. So I opted out of the situation.

I called him, left a message, and said that I didn't want to do this anymore. I wished him the best. I wouldn't say anything about our situation, but I didn't want to be involved with him any longer.

I cried myself to sleep. I was hurt, I was distraught. I let go of the man that I loved.

STORY 23
Praise and Worship

A smear campaign is designed to stop you from exposing the narcissist and to get you to defend yourself against blatant lies.

They want you to defend yourself so they can further the drama. Kyrie's smear campaign carefully and strategically used lies, exaggerations, suspicions, and false accusations to destroy my credibility. He would hide behind a cloak of upstanding heroism and feigned innocence in an attempt to make as many people as possible think his efforts were not based on his vindictiveness but on upstanding concern.

Kyrie began his smear campaign against me using his flying monkeys.

At this time, I had met a whole new crew of folks on the app that had become a support system for me. The main person who would become my 'ride or die' for the next couple of months was Tyla Cat Eyes. She found my page by being in John Mississippi's room. In her profile picture, she was fair skinned and beautiful. She gifted me often and loved my energy. She started coming to my lives in December and became a very good friend to me and supporter of my live broadcast.

During the last couple of weeks, she could really tell that my spirits were down because of what was happening with Kyrie. She offered her help to me off the app and said that she was available if I needed to talk to someone. I took her up on that offer, and we talked every day for six months after the breakup with Kyrie. She was such a kind and patient person and never judged me for what was going on and the decisions that I made. She was such a blessing to me for her kindness, compassion, and heartfelt advice that she offered me throughout my struggles. She became the sister that I never had.

After I spent the night before crying myself to sleep, I woke up refreshed and ready to let go of Kyrie. I went on EGO Live to start my praise and worship because I prayed to let go of him and let God!

I was having an amazing praise and worship service, thanking God for letting me learn about myself by going through the trials and tribulations with this man. I was ready to let it go. I was listening to my favorite Gospel songs and was praising the Lord for more than an hour. I listened to "We Fall Down" by Donnie McClurkin, "The God in Me" by Mary Mary,

"I Give Myself Away" by William McDowell, "I Surrender," and many more. This was cleansing for me and therapeutic. I was really letting it go. Not only was I feeling it, but so were my followers. They were enjoying me being vulnerable and allowing myself to heal on EGO.

Then all hell broke loose! A person named Onika came in my room and asked what I had against the gays.

"What?"

Tyla Cat Eyes kicked them out. Then a person named Candy came in and said they were talking about their brother, Kyrie.

"Excuse me? What are you talking about? I don't have a problem with Kyrie. We are good."

She then asked me to come on a private panel to get to the bottom of what was happening. Tyla and others were in my room, and they told me not to go. Candy kept asking and commenting on my live broadcast. I told her that I would end my live broadcast and come over. I didn't know why I ever did that because I literally walked into a lynch mob.

I came into the live panel, and Kyrie was on the panel having a typical Kyrie tirade. He was going off on me saying that I was trying to destroy his brand. That I went on his platforms and threatened him and that I was defaming his name on EGO. He was literally yelling at the top of his lungs and painting the picture that I was a psychopath who was trying to really hurt him and his brand.

On the panel was a very masculine, loud, and disrespectful woman named King Ugly. She was the founder of a new family called the Regular Retreats. There was also a girl named Candy, who was also a member of the Regular Retreats. These two people were very close to Big Momma. They had apparently connected quickly with Kyrie as well because I never saw any of these people around him when I was with him three weeks ago. King Ugly was very defensive of Kyrie and was taking up for him immediately. She was very judgmental of me and didn't let me get a word in edgewise.

Candy was a little better, but they both were on his side. He obviously had been speaking with them for them to be agreeing with him. They seemed as if they only cared about what he had to say. I sat there on this panel embarrassed and couldn't compete with the level of fuckery that they were displaying because I wasn't a match for the low vibrational levels they were exhibiting. I basically sat there and tried to defend myself, but I ended up looking like a plum fucking fool. They went on and on bashing me and taking up for Kyrie. Tyla Cat Eyes came up to speak, but it really didn't do anything.

Next, Kyrie's friend, the one who liked him, came up and added his two cents. This was interesting because I talked to Temi about everything, and he knew my side of the story, but he also added to the foolishness as well. Saying that we were in a new year and why were we still dealing with this.

In actuality, it only had been maybe three weeks since we fell out. Seeing him respond this way infuriated me to no end. I was livid. I was also angry at the fact that all of these people were now involved in what me and Kyrie had going on. Kyrie was in fact doing exactly what he didn't want me to do: air him out on EGO.

When I sent him that message ending everything, I never planned on saying anything or trying to embarrass him in any way. How dare he do this to me? As I sat there on that panel and listened to him bash me, it just started to destroy my spirit piece by piece.

We previously worked through all of what he was claiming that I did and were going to move past it or so I thought. I figured out later this was typical narcissistic behavior to develop flying monkeys to fight your battles for you so that you look like the victim, and that's exactly what he did. Temi, Candy, and King Ugly were his flying monkeys. They were on the attack against me.

After this all happened, it took me a couple of days to realize WTF happened and how it affected me. The more I thought about it, the more I wanted revenge and wanted to wreak havoc on his life. I hated him for what he had done, and he was going to pay for it. I asked Kyrie the next day why did that to me—just because I sent him that voice message. I wasn't going to attack him or do anything to him to harm him or his brand. He responded that the only communication we will have would be tentative based on what was agreed. Outside of that, he was done with this, to which I responded, "You're right. My bad."

I was such a respectful and kind person and now looking back at this, why did I put up with this kind of disrespect? Why was I complying with him like I was wrong? Why didn't I speak up for myself? Why did I let him control this narrative?

I continued to watch his and Big Mamma's live. I didn't know why I was torturing myself because that's exactly how I felt. Seeing them make goo-goo eyes at each other and share the affection that I once had killed a part of my soul. I would still try to call him, but he would ignore my calls and texts. I became very desperate. I turned for his attention, and he wasn't giving it to me.

So I enacted the most desperate/rock bottom of acts that I could. I texted him and told him that I wanted to commit suicide.

"I hate you for ruining my life," I said. "Morgan isn't going to have a mom because I'm checking out of this life. I hope someone invites you to my funeral. Thank you for making me kill myself, Kyrie. See u in hell."

He responded, "Heather, can you please stop putting this on me? I am not doing anything to you. This is becoming way out of hand."

Now, I really didn't want to kill myself; I just wanted him to see me. I needed him to come to me. I felt abandoned, betrayed, and discarded. I felt like he didn't give a fuck about me, and I had no other option but to resort to this new low.

It didn't work. He went on EGO and told Woodie and Temi in their lives what I had just said to him. Why would he do that? Then they talked about me like a dog, too. Woodie said he didn't play around with issues like that. Temi said that I was lying and that I would be doing a motivational video in the morning. I knew then that they were not in my corner, could not be trusted, and were not my friends. This hurt me. More so about Woodie than Temi because, from the beginning, I never really liked Temi. I knew he was a snake, and there was something that wasn't right about him.

Because I saw that in their lives, I texted Woodie that I was feeling suicidal and asked him to pray for me. He didn't respond.

To this day, I haven't heard from him. He was never my friend. I also called Bamm and told him the same thing to keep the lie going. Bamm responded like a true friend and told me to let me know if I was ok and that he loved me and needed me here.

After that, I asked Easy Lay to call Kyrie to have a heart to heart with him about me. I wanted her to do this to help out, but it didn't. He just lied and said that he never loved me and that I was crazy, which made me feel even worse.

The next day, I had a Box PK where I got almost fifteen boxes! I didn't want to do the PK, but I had to because I had business arrangements made. I was crying because I was distraught about Kyrie but also crying tears of joy because so many people showed up and out for me. I was living the worst experience of my life in real life and on this app. I couldn't hold in my feelings, and it showed during my PK. I know he was watching me and laughing in my face. All I could do was try my best to make it through day to day.

STORY 24
F… You, Then F… You

Kyrie used his "Flying Monkeys" against me. Those were the people who he manipulated to take his side and believe fabricated stories that had no grounding in reality. Flying monkeys were the enablers who support the narcissist no matter what!

He chose Temi, King Ugly, Candy, and the Regular Retreat family to be some of the most obedient and compliant sidekicks to abuse me on his behalf. The stalking, threats, and harassment continued for months.

A whole week passed since the suicide incident. I knew that Kyrie was coming to Atlanta for the LGBTQI balls and Pride weekend for the gays. I definitely had plans for his arrival. I was going to fuck him and then fuck him.

Previously, he told me that he was coming to Atlanta, and we made plans to see each other. He actually was going to style me for the balls. After our argument, I hadn't spoken to him since the lynch mob that he orchestrated on EGO the week prior. I knew that he would arrive on the Friday of MLK weekend. So I waited until I knew that he would be flying before I planned my attack.

I went to Big Mamma's live when no one else was in there and asked if I could talk to her. She said yes because she wanted to know why my name kept coming up and why there was such a big problem with me.

When we spoke, I asked her what she knew about me. She said that Kyrie told her that we were dating and ended up having sex one time and that I was a problem. I told her that that was a lie, that we dated for the past two months and had sex four to five times a day for six days when he came to visit me in Atlanta.

I also told her everything that happened to me with him from the beginning. She couldn't believe what I was telling her because Kyrie painted a totally different picture. I also read and let her read my closing note that I read to Kyrie in our mediation with Bamm. She was in shock and couldn't believe what I was telling her. I also let her listen to the recordings that I made of Kyrie apologizing and acting a damn fool. I told her what type of person that he was and that she should leave him alone. I told her that he was going to use her for Mean Green, that he preyed on older, plus size women and had dated several women on the app. I told her that he also had a girlfriend and was setting up his next round of women to take advantage of.

I asked her if they started having phone sex, and she told me yes. She also told me that he told her that he wanted to spend the rest of his life with her, get married, and live off of the grid together. I told her these were the same types of things that he told me. I fell for it, and I wanted to help her avoid the pain that I was going through now. I told her if I had known the type of person he was, I would not have dated him. This was the worst possible pain a person could feel.

"Sister to sister, please leave him alone because this is not what you want. I wouldn't wish this amount of turmoil on my worst enemy."

As we talked on the phone for the next couple of days, I told her what my plans were. Operation Fuck You, then Fuck You. I told her that I was going to entice him into coming to my place, and I was going to have sex with him one more time. Then, I was going to send a letter to his girlfriend detailing our relationship and letting her know everything that he did to me.

I just asked her not to confront him until after he got back to Chicago. She told me that she wouldn't and that I had her word. I talked to her several times throughout that weekend to see where her head was at.

She couldn't believe that he lied to her and told her so many untruths. I thought that she would be ok, and she wouldn't have to go through the pain of everything because she was going to listen to me and take my advice. I was wrong, and I will tell you why later.

And the operation began!

I made sure that I was fly AF for the ball. I wore my new Ivy Park blazer that he picked out for me when we went shopping a month earlier. I wore a beige bodysuit under it and a pencil skirt. I complimented the outfit with a fly ass camel fedora and some banging snakeskin boots. By this time, I had lost about twenty pounds from my surgery, so I was definitely feeling myself. My makeup was flawless, and I wore a blue sequin mask that he made and gave to me to complete the look. I was ready to make a statement and be seen.

I met King, my former student and friend from the app to accompany me to the ball with his boyfriend. They were ready just in case there was any foolishness. We got to the ball, and the first person I saw was Kyrie with a gaudy fur coat on. He looked like a mess in my eyes. He also reminded me of a weasel. He seemed smaller in stature and not as good looking, as I remembered.

I knew that I looked amazing, and he saw me. I stood out like the beaming star I was. I was like a princess at the ball. He was with Temi. They both looked out of place, and Temi looked a mess with what he had on. But that wasn't anything new. His clothing choices were never stellar. After the ball, they high tailed it out of there, and we went to the after party. I was excited because this was the first time that I had been out since the pandemic. John Mississippi and Bamm were at the after party, and I was so glad to see them. We took pictures, popped bottles, and had a great time.

During the party at around 2 a.m., Kyrie called me twice from That's That because he was blocked on my phone number. I let John see the call.

"Heather, don't answer."

Then he texted me and said, "I don't know what to say."

I didn't answer the text. My mission was successful! He saw me and wanted me, but I wasn't going to let it go so easy. I had a blast that night and went home by myself.

The next day, I called and asked Big Mamma if she had spoken to him, and she said yes. I told her that I saw him the night before and that he texted and called me. I also reminded her of my plan. She told me that she was trying to act as normal as possible with him. I told her thank you.

The next night was another ball. King told me that he wasn't going to go with me, so I had to find someone else to accompany me because I didn't want to go by myself. I asked my friend from college, Juan, to go with me, and he said yes. That night was part two of my masterplan. Once again, I was slaying in my choice of wardrobe. I decided to put on a crop white balloon top with another pencil skirt, but it was sequin. I complemented the sequin skirt with the sequin mask that Kyrie had made and given me. My makeup was flawless, and my natural twist out was poppin'! My shimmering accessories added an additional flare to the ensemble. I was werkin' it!

Juan and I got to the ball around nine-ish, and it was packed. There was no way in hell that we were in the middle of a pandemic with the amount of people there packed in that place. When I arrived, I saw a lot of people from the App like Bamm, John Mississippi, and many others. The app was full of folks from the LGBTQI and ballroom scene, so they were in full attendance.

Maybe after about thirty minutes, I spotted Kyrie, sitting by himself looking as if he wasn't having a good time at all. He had on that silly fur coat again, looking totally out of place. Juan and I posted up near Kyrie so that he could see us. He did. I saw him several times looking our way and looking directly at me. I didn't see

Temi at the ball or with him. I didn't speak to him at the ball and walked past him several times to ignore him but to make sure that he saw how beautiful I looked.

When we left the ball, I called him to see where his head was. He hung up on me several times. I repeated the words that he spoke to me: "I don't know what to say." He said he didn't know what I was talking about. I said that's what you said to me yesterday. We went back and forth with small conversation until I finally asked him if he wanted to "do one more for the road?" He asked where was I at? I told him that I was at home. He asked for my address, and I asked if we could meet at a hotel near my house?

He asked, "Is this a setup?"

"No."

I called him and told him that I would meet him there. This was at 3 a.m. I waited about ten minutes and told him to meet me at the Waffle House off of I-20, and he did. Then he followed me to my house. We talked for about five minutes, him looking at me crazy and me doing the same to him. There was an unspoken tension in the air.

Once we got over that, we got hot and heavy. Kissing, touching, caressing, but it was different this time. It wasn't as good as I remembered. He was mean to me in bed. Making demands, telling me not to make noises. I asked him later why and he said because he was mad at me.

His penis didn't seem as big as it was before, and I was really over it. After we finished, I started asking him questions on why he did what he did to me. He told several people that he never said he loved me and that there was nothing between us. I asked how he could say that when he had told me more than a hundred times that he loved me and wanted to spend the rest of his life with me. He immediately got mad and eventually stormed out of my house in the middle of the morning because he didn't want to take accountability for his actions.

I called Big Mamma that day to tell her that he came over and we had sex. She was shocked and couldn't wait until he came home to confront him about everything. Two days later, she did just that. She confronted him about everything, and he did what he did best: lie.

He said that he never came to my house and that he was with Temi the entire weekend. He then called Temi on three-way to confirm it. This was a lie. He and Temi fell out during the trip because Temi wouldn't give him a key to their Airbnb, so Kyrie was locked out of the place for a while. That's when he came to me.

After he left my house, I also sent an email to his girlfriend Rittany.

Hello.

The circumstances that have caused me to write this letter to you are disheartening and hurtful. You do not know me, but if I was in your position, I would want someone to reach out to me and let me know the situation at hand.

My name is Heather Moore, and for the past two months, I have been in a tumultuous relationship with your boyfriend Kyrie Jenkins Dubois. When we started this relationship, I did not know that he had a girlfriend. In fact, I had suspicions because of your Instagram page and the pictures and comments with him that you could possibly be his girlfriend. So I asked, specifically, is this young lady your girlfriend and he blatantly said no. I, in fact, drilled him on not having me look like a fool and if you were his girlfriend, let me know. He told me that you were not and that he hadn't been with you in a year.

I met Kyrie on EGO, where he pursued a romantic relationship with me. I am attaching a letter that explains our entire relationship and where it went left so that you will know exactly what happened. I am also attaching voice recordings of our conversations so that you know that I am not fraudulent or telling any lies.

In addition, to everything that you are reading here and listening to in the recordings, Kyrie continues to seek out, prey, and use older vulnerable plus size women on the app for sexual and financial gain. If you want more information, download the app, follow his page, and watch for yourself. Kyrie also told me that he had never talked to anyone else on the app. That was a lie as well. Before, he had a similar relationship with one of his contributors, whose EGO ID name on the app is the Number One Woman. Her real name is Charelle. I believe they dated for around two months before me. She visited him in Chicago at his home, and he also traveled to Baltimore to visit her as well. He continues to have phone sexual encounters with her currently. Now, he is pursuing another young lady on the app and has plans to visit her in Maryland soon. Her name on the app is Big Momma.

When I started investigating Kyrie and digging up information, I started to look more closely at your social media pages and really saw for my own eyes that he had a girlfriend. Through mediation with his aunt and others, we came up with an agreement for him to pay back the $4,700 that he owed me from cash and from gifts on the app. The first recording was a result of me digging for more information and the aftermath of him confronting me about it. The second recording is him apologizing for everything and finally admitting that he has a girlfriend.

I thought through our conversations that Kyrie wasn't going to continue with this deceptive behavior anymore and not do this to any other women. But I was wrong. I also tried to be a friend to him because of all of the mental health issues that he has but that failed as well. There is money involved that he owes me, but I'm just going to chalk that up as a loss, and my main goal is for him not to hurt anyone else.

I'm coming to you woman to woman out of respect. If this was happening to me, I would want to know. Please feel free to respond to this email if you have any more questions.
Sincerely,
Heather Moore

After I sent this letter, I didn't hear anything from his girlfriend. She didn't contact me or respond back to the letter. I told Big Mamma that I sent it. The same day I think Rittany opened an EGO Live account because she checked out my page. I sent her a message there letting her know that if she was trying to be incognito, she might want to be careful checking accounts because you can see everything on the app. The next day, Kyrie called me from a Google Voice number, but I didn't answer. I remember it because he called me from the same number last month.

After all of this, when I spoke to Big Mamma again, she told me that she was going to continue with Kyrie. He told her that he didn't have a girlfriend and she was gonna continue to get "her bag." I emphasized that she shouldn't do this. I asked was her self-esteem so low that she wanted to risk it all for him? I realized at that point that she was worse off than I was and couldn't see the forest from the trees. He had already penetrated her mind and soul. She was under his spell, and it didn't matter what I said or showed her. She was gonna believe him and that's exactly what she did. She in fact had severe low self-esteem and thought that he was the best that she could get.

They continued going live and lining up with each other, acting as if they were a happy couple. My plan didn't work. His escapades went on unscathed and unbothered. I also saw through Instagram on Rittany's stories that she was still with him as well. She would show in her Instagram stories that she was often with him at his house. As I read more about narcissists, I learned you should never reach out to the girlfriend. They will never believe what you say about their man. She was so much under his spell that she would never even think twice about believing me over him. This also goes for the new supply. He had them both brainwashed. This sucked for me because I was really trying to inform them of the real. For it to fall on deaf ears was painful.

STORY 25
I Feel Like Shit

The lesson learned from trying to do the righteous thing and expose Kyrie was that you cannot tell another woman about her man, especially if she has low self-esteem. I was literally trying to use "woman code" to help both Rittany and Big Mamma. They wanted so much to have a man that they ignored everything that I told them. Because of this, my plan failed... horribly.

In fact, it made me feel like shit. To add insult to injury, I still wanted to be with him. I still wanted to talk to him. I thought blowing up his spot would make me feel better, but it didn't. He kept going on live with Big Mamma, lining with her and laying it on thick, and his relationship with Rittany was still going strong. He had his girls, and I had nothing. I spoke to my good friend in LA, Natalie, about what was going on. Natalie was an angel from God for me during this time, just like Tyla. She started advising me on what to do to move forward. The first thing she told me to do was to start writing in my journal about how I felt. So that's what I did.

Journal Entry #1: January 28, 2021

Today, I had my second reading. It was great. The information that I received about Kyrie helped me tremendously. I am finally releasing all of the negative energy. This has been the hardest experience of my life. The energy, the euphoria that I felt is something that I want to feel with my husband. Kyrie was the catalyst for me to get healthy, to experience love, to know validation, and to be worshipped.

He was drawn to heavyset women because he could be healed by them. If he validated them, he would get healing. He used sex for validation. I just blew him up a week ago. But I still miss Kyrie. I feel a void in my heart when I'm not talking to him. I love Kyrie or the experience of him. He opened up a part of me sexually that I haven't felt in a long time. I can feel love again. He's not the one though. I felt so alive waking up, talking to him. His text messages brought me so much joy. I thought I found someone who was genuine with me. He knows how to romance, but he doesn't know how to be in a relationship. The compliments, the way he talked to me. The way he looked at me, I felt like he was piercing into my soul.

|│|

At the same time I was journaling, I also was on EGO and went to Louie's live. Kyrie was there, and I spoke and gifted everyone on the panel. I didn't speak to Kyrie or gift him. Soon after, Temi came onto the panel; I knew Kyrie had called him to do that. Temi and I got into a heated argument. I blocked him and Woodie the week prior because of what they said about my mental health. He also owed me nine shields because I would gift him to shut him up when I was with Kyrie. I told him that I didn't fuck with him after what he said about me. He was blocked from my pages, and we no longer had to deal with each other because he was fake and fraudulent. He said a few horrible things about me and thought that he was going to come up on the panel and say whatever, but I was letting him have it in the comments.

I told him that he was beneath me, and that EGO was the only thing that he had because he was a nobody. He called me a fat bitch and said that I was ugly. I told him to move out of his mother's house because he was a broke ass loser. Basically, Kyrie was using him to fight his battles, which was pathetic because Kyrie was lying to him about everything as well. Temi didn't know that he was at my house in Atlanta while he was coming to his defense. Temi was Kyrie's number one "Flying Monkey." Kyrie used

Temi to validate his story and take up for him. He used him to do his dirty work. When all of this was going on during the panel, Louie was embarrassed, but he wouldn't let me up to have my word. I apologized for making a scene on his panel, but I later spoke to him about how unfair it was that he didn't let me speak my peace.

As a chain reaction and payback for what Temi did to me on that panel, I emailed Kyrie's other flying monkeys, The Regular Retreats. I emailed the founder King Ugly, co-founder Candy, and member The Grinch. King Ugly was a member of the LGBTQI community. She was a very hard-faced woman that seemed as if she had been through a lot in her life. She was given the short end of the stick and would return that short end to everyone she came in contact with. She was very mean spirited, negative, and downright ugly person in mind, body, and spirit. She seemed to be a very tortured soul.

This app gave her an outlet to unleash all of her hurt and insecurities or project them on other people. She was a bully. Looking back, I hate her for the things that she said and can only pray for her healing.

Throughout the next couple of months, she would comment on me and knew nothing about me. She was going solely on the lies that Kyrie was feeding her. Later on, I would find out that she was transitioning to become a man. This explained the inner turmoil that she was going through and how unhappy she was that she would pick on me. She hated herself. The Grinch was a trans man who seemed to be big on the app and within the Regular Retreats family. I didn't really know a lot about him. He seemed to be one of the power players, so I included him in the email.

Then there was Candy. She was friends with Big Mamma in real life and was the co-founder of the Regular Retreats. She was a plus sized girl who never showed anything more than her face on EGO. She was definitely ashamed of her body, like her friend Big Mamma. In fact, both of them had extremely low self-esteem and self-worth. EGO gave them a sense of false confidence because they had a family who backed them. But in reality, they felt very small and low and hated who they were. They lived a very sad reality but hid it through the app. Months later on her Instagram, Candy came out and said that she was having bariatric surgery. She also posted on her social media of how depressed she was and how she was a train wreck. All of my suspicions about her self-esteem were correct: she hated herself. She seemed as if at the heart of it that she had good sense, but clearly she was a follower as well. None of them took the time to really hear or get the truth. They were Kyrie's new flying monkeys. They were going so hard for Kyrie and had no idea who he actually really was.

I sent them the original email that I sent to Kyrie's girlfriend.

Hello Candy, The Grinch and King Ugly,

I am emailing you because I need for you to hear the truth about Kyrie Jenkins Dubois.

Two weeks ago, I was attacked verbally in my EGO Live Broadcast and led to a panel orchestrated by Kyrie for your family to come to his defense and railroad me. At this panel, I was made out to be a liar and someone who was not telling the truth. I did not take this lightly. It was very disturbing watching all of this unfold, as if I was the crazy person in this situation. As a result of that panel, my spirit led me to contact your family member Big Momma and inform her of all of the pertinent information. I informed her that she is being set up to be used the same way I was and several others on the app and that she should be careful. I also wanted to make sure that your family knew as well.

I believe in providing receipts so that you don't have to just take my word for it.

Below I have provided and attached:

- *The email that I sent his girlfriend Rittany about what he was doing.*

- *The letter that I read to him in a mediation session with his Family Leader detailing our entire relationship and what I needed for him to do moving forward.*

- *Recordings of two conversations where he admits all of his wrongdoings and the fact that he has a girlfriend.*
- *Pictures of his visit to my house in Atlanta, GA.*

This is a prime example of being careful who you align yourself with on this app. Clearly, you all had no idea who you were dealing with. At the end of the day, we are on EGO to make money. I'm pretty sure that you wouldn't want to align yourselves with someone who is a professional con artist, manipulator, and liar. It's not good business. I always stand for what's right, and I would want to know the truth about the people in my circle.

If you have any questions, please feel free to respond back to the email or unblock me on EGO and contact me there.

Respectfully Submitted,

Heather Moore

After I sent this email, none of them contacted me. In fact, they would still line up with him and gift him on the app. The Grinch went on live with Kyrie and said that he thought that the whole thing was BS. This spoke volumes about what people would believe from a psychopath that they knew nothing about.

During this month, Kyrie would call me from several numbers, and we would talk. I actually talked to him on January 31, 2021, and I asked him to forgive me. He was very combative on the phone and would not take ownership and responsibility for what he did. He would also go live and be very distraught about all of what was happening to him as a result of what I did. So much so that he would have tirades about quitting the app and how worried he was about the EGO TV watchers in his room. He was also really putting on a production on EGO when he would line live with Big Mamma. Asking her if they could get married on EGO and flirting heavily.

Not to mention all of the auctions that they would buy each other in. If it was true and he was serious, it was beautiful. But I knew that she was his next victim and his next narcissistic supply to keep him going. He would keep this charade going for the next seven months with her.

STORY 26
The Obsession

I didn't realize it at the time, but I was smack dab in the middle of Narcissistic Abuse. I didn't feel worthy of his time and attention. I felt like there was something innately wrong with me and like I was crazy. I felt completely lost and unsure of anything with a chronic continuous sadness that never seemed to subside.

Kyrie made me feel full of shame and inadequacy, overwhelmed and out of control. It felt like my heart had been ripped from me where I was completely disrespected, disregarded, and unimportant. At that moment, I was hopeless, helpless, and confused.

I was a broken person.

On the other hand, because I was so consumed with what was going on with Kyrie, I forgot that I was a month out of my surgery, and the weight was coming off! I was truly feeling myself! I took pictures of myself naked in the mirror and was loving what I saw! This temporarily made me feel better, knowing the progress that I was making.

But I was still losing my mind about Kyrie. I became obsessed. I found comfort writing about it in my journal.

Pre-Journal Entry: January 31, 2021

I texted him and said that I wanted to speak to him with no drama or disrespect.

"About what? Like what is your goal?" he asked.

"I wanna tell you I'm sorry, and I wanna be done. Please call. I need you to hear me one last time."

Natalie coached me on what to say so that he would call me, and it worked. He called me at 2:05 a.m., and we spoke for ten minutes. He was very mean to me when we started the conversation. He definitely had a wall up. When I started reading the letter to him that Natalie helped me craft, he didn't let me get far without attacking and being on the defensive. This first conversation was hard, and I wasn't able to get everything out.

We ended the convo by me asking for some masks, and he hung up the phone. I called several times, and he didn't answer. Then either he picked up, or he called me back at 2:24 a.m. This time, he let me speak my piece, and it was very emotional. I was able to truly tell him how I felt about him and how much he hurt me and how he changed my life.

I told him how he opened me up sexually when I felt I would never feel the same way or feel for a man ever again. I told him why I sent the emails to Rittany and the Regular Retreats because of what he did to me on EGO. He hurt me to the core with that. We spoke about him coming to Atlanta and if he did, would he come see me. He said it would crush Big Mamma. I told him I wouldn't tell her anything. He said he shouldn't have called me back and that this was wrong. Then we got off the phone. He called me two minutes later and said his dick was hard. I told him I was so happy! That I thought we would never have phone sex again. I was so horny and happy that I could do it one more time.

We had phone sex, and then he said he didn't cum. He just said that to try and hurt me. I gave him the recording of me climaxing so he would have it for inspiration. I tried calling/texting him for the next couple of days, but he didn't respond. This was the first time of many more to come of him ghosting me.

Journal Entry #2: February 3, 2021

Right now, I feel like shit. I'm in love with a psychopath that doesn't give two shits about me. I'm sexually open and want to have sex with anyone I come in contact with. I hate him for making me feel this way. I hate that I ever met him. I hate that I didn't run at the first signs of foolishness. When we had that argument and I said I was done, why did I let him talk me back into this? I saw the crazy, but I stayed. I knew something wasn't right, but I stayed. How can I get rid of this pain, this feeling? Because even though I am hurting, I am completely obsessed with him. He doesn't deserve my time of day. How is it possible to do this to someone and how is it possible to stick around for this bullshit? I hate myself for not letting go and releasing him, but I honestly don't know how to let go. I'm gonna pray because I haven't asked God to help me because a part of me is hoping that he will like me again. WTF!

Journal Entry #3: February 5, 2021

I had another reading today, and I feel so much better. Yesterday, I was so distraught. Today, I am taking steps to heal and make myself whole again. I even took naked pics in the mirror. I was feeling myself. I LOVE HEATHER MOORE. I did see Kyrie on the app, and he looked REAL good with his hair cut. He is so fine. I also listened to the recordings and heard him say that he did care for me. I think this comes and goes for him. Depending on the day and the person. But it doesn't matter, onward and upward.

I went to Big Mamma's page and spoke to her. She was cordial. It was very interesting because she didn't speak to me the last time I came by her page. My spiritual advisor said that she is a hundred times worse than I am regarding Kyrie, so leave it alone. She has to learn on her own.

Journal Entry #4: February 7, 2021

I window licked a lot today, which is watching a live broadcast from an unregistered, untraceable EGO account. Jay (a host friend of mine on EGO) took my name because I bought him at an auction. He came by Kyrie's live, and everyone in there told him it wasn't me. But he kicked him out of the live broadcast. Jay was pissed. I wonder what does that mean? Did he kick him because he saw my name? Because he didn't want me buying anyone else? He took new pics, and they look very good. I have to stop doing this to myself. I have to work on getting myself together.

Journal Entry #5, 6, 7: February 8-9, 2021

Yesterday, I watched his live as he was in a PK with Big Momma. It made me cringe. The production that he was putting on for the world. Then me and Tyla got off, and I went live. We lined with Trap D, and he told me his Stars would troll for me to get Kyrie together. I was so happy. They showed me how they would change their names to mine. They did this in a matter of seconds. I talked to Uncle Tony who was a member of my family Denied Access. He was also a convict on Death Row. I told him what happened with Kyrie. He told me that he would help me get his page banned. He also told me how much of a douche bag Reimo the founder of Denied Access was and how he played Easy Lay. I couldn't believe it. Basically, he did the same thing to her that Kyrie did to me. When I talked to Easy Lay, I told her I was so sorry that happened to her. I said to her that we should do a panel to expose them both. She told me that she wasn't gonna let no man see her sweat and that she had a brand to protect. I told her I had a brand as well and got off the phone with her.

|¦|

Previously, every time that I would explain something to Easy Lay, she would be very judgmental and non-compassionate. This side of her informed me that she was a total bitch. When she responded to me about confronting them, this was another example of that. Unfortunately, when I spoke to Uncle Tony, he told me that he spoke to her and that she wasn't my friend. That she said I was crazy, stupid, and dumb. She basically told him all of my business about Kyrie. This infuriated me! She violated the girl code. I thought she was my friend. I couldn't confront her though because

Unk didn't want me to. Also during the evening, me, Teri and Tyla were window licking in Kyrie's live. One minute, he was on camera, and then the next, it went dark. It stayed like that for an hour. We heard a female voice in the background. I knew that it was his girlfriend Rittany. They were talking about fabric and materials.

There was also Jamaican music playing in the background. I think he put his phone in his pocket because she didn't want him on EGO. After about an hour, I saw a comment on his live from Lady Red 2, "Brother you are being mannish."

I looked at the live and heard that he was performing oral sex on her because she was moaning. Then I saw Big Mamma fly through the live.

She said, "Hey, you're in the dark." I then called Big Mamma.

"See, I told you he has a girlfriend, and I'm not crazy," I told her.

She said she texted him and asked him what that sound was? He said he was watching porn. Then she had a PK with him, and she didn't say anything. She didn't confront him or anything. I don't think I could have sat there and looked him in the face after he did that. It spoke volumes about how she felt about herself.

Later that evening, Bamm came by my room, and I told him and sent him the recording. He told me that the leaders of his family confronted Kyrie about it. Kyrie flipped out on them and dropped his badge. I was so happy that all of this bad luck was following him.

STORY 27
February

What you'll read in stories twenty-seven to forty is the in-depth look into the constant gaslighting, ghosting cycle that Kyrie put me through. These chapters are difficult to read because it shows how low a person can be under the grips of a narcissist. These stories are raw and vivid with sexual tales that are lustful, open, and out there.

|¦|

At this point, I had a team of two people who were watching Kyrie's lives, recording and getting information back to me: Teri and Tyla. We coordinated when to watch and record all of the videos. The reason we were doing this was because we were trying to establish a pattern that Kyrie was using women on EGO, in particular, older, plus size women. They often told me to stop watching and window licking his live broadcast because all it did was hurt me. They were correct, but I couldn't stop.

Tyla would always tell me, "Why visit hell when you are an angel?" or "Everybody is not your assignment. That's why you're drained. #selfcare."

Tyla was the first person to tell me that she thought Kyrie was a narcissist, and she was right! If it wasn't for her and my spiritual advisor, I wouldn't have known what was going on.

She also brought the term "Lovebombing" to my attention. After this, I started looking for a therapist because I was in very bad shape. Tyla told me to repeat "I love Heather more."

I said this often, but it was very hard for me to believe and follow it because I kept getting sucked into Kyrie's web.

There were quite a few things that happened on EGO in February. When I went to Big Mamma's PK and dropped on her, she dropped back. When I dropped on her, Kyrie was furious. Big Mamma also told me that she wanted to still be connected to him to get her bag. She also continued to drop Mean Green on him in his live broadcast. I fell out with Easy Lay, and the last day I talked to her was 2-12-21. I couldn't trust her. She told all of my business to Uncle Tony and said that I was crazy and stupid, all the while paying Reimo's first and last month's rent plus deposit. TRoss was one of Kyrie's plus size contributors, who went off on Kyrie, and he went on a tirade about me. Tyla trolled him, writing, "All the women are tired you using them for mean green! U are a scammer, the truth is coming out!" He was furious.

One of my former students wanted to help me with Kyrie. So he called him and acted like he was an attorney. We recorded the conversation, and he was brilliant. He really sounded like a lawyer. He told Kyrie that he was calling to collect the debt that he owed. He also told him that we were trying to work this out so that we wouldn't have to seize his assets. His aunt called back, and they tried to call from different numbers because they did a reverse look up on his cell phone.

My former student also called him saying that he had a delivery for him. My student was too smart for them. You could really tell that they were seriously shaken over the conversation. After this conversation, Kyrie called me from a private line three times. I answered the last time.

"Hello," I said.

"Hello."

"How may I help?"

He hung up.

I also enlisted one of my sorority sisters who was a real attorney to call Kyrie. She did, but he wasn't as shaken with her.

On Valentine's Day, there were a lot of pics and postings on Instagram from Rittany. She and Kyrie did a photo shoot where they wore matching lime green velvet outfits. They really looked good. I must admit that I wish it was me with the representative of Kyrie that I fell in love with.

I asked Big Mamma if she wanted some more receipts. I also window licked her live. I didn't have to send her the receipts about Kyrie because she saw them for herself. I watched her face as she saw, and it looked like her world was taken right from under her. I felt bad for her. She texted him and said, "I really think you should work it out with her. Y'all look great together. Enjoy your night with her."

In the footage on Instagram, Rittany cooked for him and showed her cards and gifts from him and the matching pics in lime green. As I saw him in the pics with Rittany and on EGO with Big Mamma, I wanted to call him. I constantly thought about him all day and every day. This was extremely hard.

How could someone do so much bad to you, yet you still want to be around them and talk to them? I was so jealous of Rittany and Big Mamma. They had my man. They were talking to him, and I wasn't. I hated seeing them with him. It really made me want to have another "shiny dude." One that looked better than him.

A few days later, Kyrie called me from a private number.

"Why are you looking at my EGO profile?" he asked.

"Are you seriously calling me at one in the morning for this?"

He hung up. I called him back, and he did the same thing. I told him to stop calling me and hanging the phone up on me.

"If you want to talk to me, then do that."

He then asked if he could put his dick in me.

"No. Absolutely not."

He hung up after that. Later in the day, I had a photo shoot to celebrate losing thirty pounds, the first milestone in my weight loss journey. Number One Woman called me afterwards and told me that Kyrie called her and asked why she was in my live broadcast and if we were best bitches now? This confirmed that he was window licking my live broadcast and watching me as well.

That evening, I had my first entertainment panel with Nicco Annan from *P-Valley*, a TV show on Starz network. It was amazing! There were more than eight hundred people in the room watching the panel and eighteen EGO TV watchers. I knew his people were watching. I was so proud of myself for bringing real Hollywood content to the app. I was trying to move forward on the app in spite of everything that happened.

Because of how Kyrie opened me up sexually and because of all of the weight loss, I was extremely horny all of the time. I even joined several dating websites to look for men. I masturbated a lot and often, especially when I saw Kyrie live.

I called him one day to tell him that I changed my mind and that he could put it in. He didn't answer. I sent him a message asking him if he could get me a parting gift... a metal dildo from Nordstroms. He didn't respond.

Kyrie started programming to show that he was a good person. He was trying to do damage control because of how he was exposed. So on Monday's live, he started having a motivational panel. As I window licked and watched him wearing all white like he was a saint, it infuriated me. I hated looking at him acting like he was "Saint Peter" or somebody. So I called Don-Trap D to unleash the Stars on him. The 'Stars' were Trap D's fans, family, and supporters. There were about a thousand of them.

They went to his live broadcast and trolled the shit out of him. They called him a Mean green Thot Scammer and said give Heather her Mean green back! It was brilliant. I was so happy! The sheer level of disgust in his face was priceless! He had his friends, including Ramel, in the live, and they were shocked and couldn't figure out where all of these trolls were coming from.

I saw seven layers of disgust come over Kyrie's face. He tried to play it off at first, but he couldn't last. He was so embarrassed. It served him right though. For all of the disgusting things that he did to me. He texted all of his flying monkeys for help. Temi, The Regular Retreats, Big Mamma, Candy, and King Ugly. They couldn't stop it though. The Stars got him good.

After that, he said that he wanted to be messy for a moment and showed my text about the parting gift on his live broadcast. He had no moral compass or code. This showed me that he would do anything to make himself look good or not stupid. This pissed me off. I wanted to contact all of his supporters and tell him about his shenanigans.

February Journal Entries

February 13, 2021

Kyrie started calling me from private numbers.

February 17, 2021

This was the next time that he asked for phone sex.

February 25, 2021

I went to Malik's live, and he was PK'n Kyrie. Malik was a guy on the app that I met through Kyrie. They were in the same Ballroom house. He was a gay male, college educated and very nice. His spirit was always genuine and pure. I also spoke to him off the app about what happened with Kyrie. He was very supportive and knew that Kyrie had issues and different sides of him that most people didn't know about. He counseled me and helped me with advice on how to handle Kyrie. I was truly grateful to him for helping me. When I went to the PK, I gave Malik Mean green. Kyrie got upset, very upset. He made a big deal about it and had a mini tantrum. Malik told him that he didn't want to be in the middle of it. I called Malik the next day to talk about it.

February 26, 2021

Today, every time I go live, I have two EGO TV viewers. I know Satan (Kyrie) is watching me. I wanted to tell him, *just pay me back my money, so I can leave you and all of this alone.* I really want him to know that. But I don't think that will work. Yesterday, I had a very good therapy session. The therapist told me that she was a psychic, too. I really like her a lot. She told me how to break the cord from Kyrie. I don't really know if I'm ready to do that yet. I'm contemplating sending the trolls out to get Temi at his PK. He should feel the wrath.

February 27, 2021

Today, I came to Big Mamma's live, and she spoke, and we made small talk. As soon as I left, I came back on as an EGO TV watcher.

She immediately started talking about me and said, "I'm surprised she didn't drop any Mean Green on me."

At this point, I realized that she was two-faced. I was never going back to her live broadcast, and I wouldn't try to help her anymore.

February was fulfilling for me because I got some retribution. I was able to get back at Kyrie a little bit. I also had some success on the app so that was rewarding as well. Knowing what I know now, I do wish I had of done a few things differently. But all is fair in love and war. Right?

STORY 28
March

The month of March was very eventful and emotional, so much so that I wrote a timeline of what happened verbatim. There were many different moving parts that were coming from all of the characters on EGO. They all played a part in many of the dynamics, changes, and the climax of the entire story.

March 1

I submitted a case report/request for Judge Mathis and The People's Court. I knew that if I went there, the show would pay for all of the fees and also his part of the case if I won, so it would be a win-win situation. I was trying any outlet to win with him.

March 3

Kyrie was live on EGO in the car with his girlfriend Rittany. When Big Mamma came into his live broadcast, he didn't show her the same love that he usually showed. He was riding with Rittany to the fabric store. When he got out of the car to go in, he started talking about Rittany to Big Mamma in the comments. He was totally disrespectful to her. He spoke about everything, like her always having to get her way and that she thought the sun revolved and set around her ass.

March 6

Kyrie was lined up with Terri Meid. Terri was also a fashion designer and an amazingly nice person. I had previously told Terri about the situation, and he was very supportive. He also supported me in my live broadcasts and would give me Mean Green. As soon as I flew in the live, Kyrie saw my name and immediately started to panic, and his demeanor changed. It was very interesting to watch. I started to give Terri Mean Green. A few at a time.

Then all of a sudden, Kyrie called his flying monkey, Candy from the Regular Retreats Family, to come into the room. He was commenting to her, "See, this is what I was telling you about. We were just lining freely."

I was confused. Terri supported me, so I supported him. Kyrie did not like that. But to me it was a free country, and I could do whatever I wanted to. So I sent Terri Mean Green, and then Kyrie instructed his monkeys to send him Mean Green to win the PK that they started. I recharged my account because I loved a good challenge. In the end, I won; Kyrie lost the PK, and Terri won. After the PK was over, Kyrie was furious and complained about it to Candy. The small victories mattered to me.

March 10

King Ugly of the Regular Retreats said on her live that I got handled by Kyrie. "You thought you could throw everything you had at it," she said, "but it didn't work."

"Hello, Heather," Candy commented because they knew that I was watching from the window.

March 16

I was watching Kyrie through the window, and then I went to John Mississippi's live broadcast because he was lined up with him. He looked really good because he had a haircut. I called him and told him I missed him. He hung up on me.

I called back the next day to try and talk to him again. I asked him to not hang up on me and that I wanted to extend a final olive branch to make things right. He said some terrible things to me once again.

"I fucked you, and you couldn't handle it."

"I don't give two shits about what you have going on in your life."

"We will never be good, and we will never be good because of you."

"Take me to court, Bitch! I don't give a fuck."

These were the horrible things that Kyrie said to me.

March 17

After I sent Big Mamma the email that Kyrie was CC'd in, King Ugly went onto her EGO TV live broadcast and said, "You can't get paid off of your residuals, so you have to use my sister as a storyline because whoever and whatever show don't want ya.

"I ain't blocked the hoe. I want her to come in here so I can read her. You are gonna leave my sister (Big Mamma) alone."

Her Regular Retreats Family members, Candy and HideousT, chimed in.

HideousT, who is possibly the ugliest woman I have ever seen, commented, "Come to me. Knuck if you buck, Bitch, Heather, little pissy ass. You are here to make a bag, not chase penis, bitch. You've been threatening to go to court, just go to court. He needs to get a restraining order because she is bat shit crazy."

"I heard the men down in Georgia like your size," Candy added. "They don't wanna deal with you because she is bat shit crazy."

"Fuck, Heather; she can't stop you," said HideousT. "Maybe one day, she will wake up and see that she can't stop you."

But actually, I did stop his bag. Even though they may not admit it, they didn't rock with Kyrie the way he wanted them to. Eventually, he got off EGO, which was an extra source of income for him. If none of this had happened, he would have really taken advantage of them and their Mean Green.

Big Mamma had a way of throwing stones and hiding. She liked her wack ass goons of dysfunction to help her because she couldn't fight her own battles. The situation with me and her had nothing to do with them. She would act as if I was the crazy one, when in fact she asked me for all the intel on Kyrie. But she didn't tell her loser ass family that.

Later that evening, Kyrie went on EGO Live and talked about our entire Olive Branch conversation with Ramel and Temi in his box.

He said that I emailed Big Mamma and blind cc'd him about a conversation that they had.

"And she did that because I'm not entertaining her," he had said. "This whole thing that me and Big Mamma are a thing? We are cool. We are friends. Now, because I won't take an olive branch, you send emails. I'm annoyed because I have been ignoring it, but now she keeps on professing to get life. My fucking God, yo, it's really fucking annoying."

Now the truth of the matter was that I emailed him because he hung up on me and called me a bitch when I was trying to work the situation out. I was also making him aware that me and Big Mamma had been communicating and that she actually wanted all of the information that I was giving to her. Once I realized that she was a backstabbing, two faced, penguin looking heifer, I had to let the truth be known.

In fact, Tyla Cat Eyes would be on the phone with me and her. I would always preface anything that I would say to her by asking her if she wanted the information first. I never gave her any information about Kyrie without her agreeing and requesting it. She was very good at saying one thing to me and presenting another side to everyone else.

"You cannot harass someone because I don't owe you anything," Kyrie continued ranting. "I'm not your child's father. Just because I owe you Mean Green. Because you want to be relevant. If she is this big entity, why am I an entity to her?"

"I'm tired of this," Temi said.

I get it that everybody is tired of this, Woodie agreed from the comments.

"This has literally affected my pockets," Kyrie said. "She has contacted people that I do business with. So I get that everyone is on this. Simply ignore it, but this is why I get frustrated with her."

"Bamm is on a panel with her," he continued. "John fucks with her. And all of this is cool? What the fuck is the significance? She's living off of SBA money. It's not her money because she's not on TV like that, let's be clear. She picked up the SBA check when she sent me the unicorn. Taking government funding and putting it on the app. Period. Now, bitch, you wanna make it like I'm fraudulent, everything in this house is attached to me. Kyrie is my name; you can Google me. So first, I don't want to deal with you. Then I'm a scammer. I don't give a fuck who's watching. I know she's one of them. I can't even say suck my dick from the back because she will enjoy it. That's the crazy part. This shit is annoying. You can't keep antagonizing somebody; she is literally provoking me to wrath. Everyday."

"I don't even know what to say," Ramel said.

"There isn't anything that you can say," Temi said.

"I hate seeing him this frustrated," said Ramel.

"I tell you one thing, nobody better not come to my house to try nothing," said Kyrie. "Because I will beat the fuck out of somebody. That's on period. You can take that as a threat, I don't care. I'm calling you, but I had you blocked from T-Mobile a month ago. How the fuck can I call you?"

Someone in the comments asked what happened, and Temi replied, "Apparently, she called him last night."

Woodie was trying to make light of the situation in the comments. He would say things like "How is the weather? What did you guys do today?" He was trying to change the subject by infusing humor. Ramel made a comment about what happened, and Kyrie did not like that. Kyrie wanted his friends to believe his lies and follow everything that he said. Temi chimed in, agreeing with Ramel and said, "Me, too."

Kyrie interjected and said, "Ramel, if this was happening to you, how would you feel? Stop saying I need to leave this alone. The bitch is harassing me and stopping my bag."

"What do you want me to say? I'm leaving it then," said Ramel.

"I have been isolated by several individuals that I thought I fucked with about this situation," Kyrie said. "People are trying to act like I have a problem or had a problem and that's my fucking issue. I used to call

Temi's phone everyday with an emergency, and he would answer. Now he doesn't even answer my calls. I don't have no fucking problem! I'm not fucking crazy. You don't see me deranged over some fucking pussy on an app. That's my fucking problem."

"As your friend, what is the expectation?" Ramel asked.

"I don't want to be treated like something is wrong with me," Kyrie said. "Like I have a disease, and that's how I feel like I'm being treated, no shade."

"Who do you feel treated you like that?" Ramel asked.

"Louie, Temi, to an extent," he said. "All of that I just mentioned, and no one commented."

"I don't comment because my words are not gonna make a difference, and it's gonna make you feel like I'm against you," said Temi. "As far as ignoring you, I don't. My phone is on do not disturb me because of my late hours. As far as Louie, I told you before that everyone doesn't feel comfortable with this situation. You don't know what people would do or for what. They are still your friends.

"Prime example, when the bitch said that she was going to kill herself and all this other bullshit and was looking to Woodie for a thing, Woodie doesn't deal with death, so he avoided it. It's not that they don't like you."

Clearly, Kyrie was bothered by the sheer presence of me, and he was more distraught than he was letting on. So much so that he would have hour-long rants about it on his live broadcast.

March 18

The Second Entertainment panel was with the celebrity twins from Euphoria, Trap D, Bamm, Fatha Dollaz, and Tay Jones, my agent. This was a very successful panel. There were more than twenty-five hundred people in the room! It was a success!

March 20

He asked Beauty Defined to come up in the box to make sure he wasn't being catfished. She couldn't do that because then he would know that it was Heather. Beauty sent him an expensive gift to bait and distract him. He took the bait, and he began to talk to her from then on.

March 21

Rittany was posting her outings with Kyrie on her Instagram. She was wearing a silver sequin dress that he made. She had a horrible shape, so she looked a fucking mess in it. This was the same day that I got his address, so now I could move forward with my court case against him.

March 23

EGO Fight: I was lining up with a guy from Chicago, and we started talking about me coming to Chicago. I told him no thanks because of a guy I dated on the South Side.

On the live, I said Kyrie's entire name: Kyrie Jenkins Dubois. Apparently, Kyrie was watching from the window because he then came into the live on his Fufu-Mufasa page. At that time, I acknowledged that he was there for the guy I was talking to.

The next thing I knew, I was banned for ten minutes. He got me banned by hitting the report page several times. He then went on his page and went live for an hour talking about me. Ramel and Temi were in the live with him. My friends Rhapsody in Pink and Tyla came in to take up for me. He said so my many horrible things about me—calling me a whale, saying he didn't touch fat whales, that I used SBA loans to buy Mean greens, among these other spiteful things:

- Spoke negatively about my daughter: Did you feed Morgan today? I hope you fed her. Since you wanna say my government, I'll say your child's name.
- Called me a bitch
- Said he wanted to put his hands on me.
- Called me a dick ass muthafucka

- Said I looked sick
- Said I worshipped the ground he walks on
- Told me to use my SBA loans to unban myself
- Said that I was poor
- Called me an extra
- Said that all the roles that I had were as an extra
- Called me an 'F List' celebrity
- Said he didn't give a fuck
- Said he gave this bitch chances
- Said that I didn't have a court case
- Said that I would get sued because I was defaming his character
- Called me predictable
- Called me obsessed

"Keep threatening me, my niggah; You don't think I can sue you for your Toyota Prius and your apartment that you rent," he continued.

He went on to say that if he took a shit, would I want the toilet tissue out of his ass? He asked did I want his drawers. He said where I lived and if I wanted him to mail his drawers to me.

"Fuck with me if you want to. Remember, I've been to your residence. You've never been to mine. And you keep trying me."

He also called me a paymaster, said that I called him a faggot. I love being around the gays but said I was quick to call someone a faggot. He said I threw a unicorn before he said hello, called me dumb and a stupid ass. He showed my phone number on EGO TV, saying that he blocked me. One of his friends said that I should get touched in the comments, and he agreed with them.

"Let me email Lifetime and Tyler Perry and tell them about your characteristic traits," he said, laughing. Someone called him on the phone and said something to him. He responded with, "Record me saying what? I don't give a fuck. Y'all want to stop me? This is not gonna happen. I don't owe this bitch nothing. When I was in Atlanta, Heather got an SBA check, cashed it, bought Mean green with it, and sent me a unicorn.

"My overall numbers on EGO are higher than hers, my quotas are higher than hers. But I'm fraudulent. Called me a stupid bitch again. I thought you were gonna fuck the masseuse. Oh damn, he didn't want you. Tell her to take care of her child while she is chasing after a man who doesn't want her. Oh yeah, those pants that you wore when you were at your college homecoming looked like you had a dick in your pants, and you need to pull them up."

I started a panel with Rhapsody in Pink, Number One Woman, Nila, and Laglare. I never spoke negatively about Kyrie, and I just told the truth about what he did to me. I let my friends read him and get him together.

During the live show, he called me twenty-three times, trying to get me to end the live. Temi also called me around sixteen times. Temi and him both tried to come up to my panel, but I didn't let them. They had their chance on his live. They were not gonna be given a chance to embarrass me again on my platform. On my live, I let the audience listen to the recordings of him saying that he owed me the money, that he loved me, and that he had a girlfriend. All things that he was lying about to everyone else. There were at least fifteen EGO TV watchers watching. The real truth was finally coming out. I had held all of this back and didn't want it to go there, but he started it. In true narcissistic form, he was trying to create his own reality and narrative to deflate the truth. So I had to speak.

March 24-25

Kyrie started trying to connect with Beauty Defined, calling her "Hey Love," asking when they were going to talk off of EGO.

March 26

Big Mamma's husband died. I saw her live, and she was crying. Her family members came to her live broadcast to give their condolences. He committed suicide. I found this out because Kyrie told my alter EGO Beauty Defined that he shot himself, and he was on the phone with Big Mamma when it happened.

March 28

Big Mamma flew through my live and came on her Ms. Mufasa page. Me and Uncle Tony called her out.

March 29

On my Post on EGO, somebody wrote I looked miserable.

March 31

Easy Lay was now friends with Kyrie. When we were cool, she said that she hated him. I found out that they were friends by window lickin' his live broadcast.

March Journal Entries

March 4, 2021

Today was rough. I broke down. I want my money.

March 6, 2021

I spoke to two attorneys today. They were going to help me get my money back. One attorney, Ms. Johnson, I met in college. I broke down when I spoke to her. She shared with me how she dealt with a narcissist from college. She also gave me viable options on how to win, which made me happy.

March 7, 2021

My friend Kaycee told me to call my bank and say that the two thousand dollars that he gave me was fraud. I did, and Wells Fargo gave me my money back. This was a victory. I also saw Terri Meid lined with him. I went in to gift him, and Kyrie was furious He called the Regular Retreat Bitches for back up. It was hilarious watching him so mad.

March 8, 2021

Today, I was very depressed. I didn't want to get out of bed. I think I'm grieving because the loss is real now that I got my money back.

March 9, 2021

I feel rage today. I wanna contact Big Mamma's husband and tell him what she is doing with Kyrie.

March 11, 2021

I'm praying to God to help release this feeling from me. I was window licking his live. This was a rough day for me. My friend Tracy came over and prayed for and with me. I was really in my feelings. I literally watched him and her (Big Mamma) all night. I cried profusely tonight. I'm literally sick to my stomach. I hate this feeling.

March 12, 2021

I was window licking and heard him talking to Chief C about me. Chief C was a big host on the app. She was a plus size, beautiful girl who I had met a few months before. I didn't really know her though. She was explaining and telling a story about a guy that said she scammed him. So Kyrie started to tell her about me. A lot of or all of the things he said were very hurtful to me. He said to her, "How could she love me, and she don't even know my favorite color?" He also said that he didn't owe me anything.

March 13, 2021

I was window licking again, and Big Mamma said that he had two EGO TV watchers. He replied, "I'm gonna start saying, 'Good Morning, Heather.'" He was so arrogant. Then Temi got on there and started talking about me as well.

March 14, 2021

Drove home from my college homecoming talking to friends. They made me feel a whole lot better. I spoke to Reante, another host on the app, and he told me to meditate and release all of it. So I went on live and released (Kyrie) Satan. I meditated afterwards and felt really great.

March 15, 2021

Today, I had a therapy session. It went well. I window licked at night and saw Kyrie in John's live. I gifted John, and Temi commented, "Wow, here she goes."

Seeing Kyrie with a new haircut sparked me. I was very much so attracted to what I saw. So much so that I wanted to call him, so I did. I asked him did he know who this was, and he said yes. I told him that I liked his haircut. He hung up on me.

March 17, 2021

At 8 a.m., I had a call from a blocked/private number. So I called him to see if he called. He said no. I called Tyla and told her that I wanted to call, and she told me what to say. It went all the way left. I recorded the conversation. After I hung up, I sent a letter/email to him and Big Mamma. Then on EGO, the Regular Retreat Bitches were in a panel talking about it. He was also talking about it to his friends, Temi and Ramel. He was very upset. It was hilarious. I recorded it, too.

March 18, 2021.

Today, I had my entertainment panel. There were more than twenty-five hundred people in the room. It was great. We had over fifteen EGO TV watchers in the room.

March 27, 2021

He texted Beauty Defined. As we were texting, I felt the same way I felt from the beginning of our relationship: super excited. But I was playing with fire. I can't keep this going. Yes, it was great material for the book, but what if I get caught?

March 29, 2021

I was at my ex-boyfriend Chris' house in Mississippi. We had a blast. Unfortunately, all I could think about was Kyrie. We had sex, but I didn't feel the euphoria that I felt with Satan (Kyrie). It was like I was searching for that high, and it wasn't gonna happen.

March was a very hard month for me. The big EGO fight took me over the edge. The amount of depression that I was having was enough to put someone in a mental facility. I was tired. I was overwhelmed. I felt hopeless. I wanted better days to come.

Where was the rainbow at the end of this storm?

April

April Fool's Day 2021, Everyday Big Mamma was on EGO Live. If my husband just passed in such a tragic way, I would not be on EGO Live. At the time, she and her kids were living in a hotel, and she wasn't paying any attention to them. Her youngest son was literally full out crying and telling her that he missed his dad, and she was on EGO ignoring him. Unbelievable.

I got a reading the next day. My spiritual advisor talked to her husband, and he said that he opted out. It was true that he killed himself. A few days later, they had the funeral, and it was live streamed on Facebook. The sister of the husband said that he was bi-polar, manic depressive.

He couldn't be with the love of his life, so he killed himself. I believe she told her husband that she was going to leave him for Kyrie. That was the direction that she was going in because she actually believed that they were going to spend the rest of their lives together.

That's what he told her. She also told her kids that their father killed himself. Her in-laws were not happy about that. My spiritual advisor also told me that Kyrie was happy about this happening and got gratification that he was the cause of someone killing themselves. This was a code red for her. She told me that I must leave him alone because I was in danger.

April 7, 2021

Kyrie was in Maryland to see Big Mamma. I knew this because he was in a hotel room and said that it was seventy degrees. It was still cold in Chicago. So Big Mamma and Kyrie were in Maryland, and her husband just died. This was the first time that they had sex.

How in the entire fuck was this happening?

Who was watching her kids? He should be the last thing on her mind, especially if he was the reason the husband was dead. I wanted to contact his girlfriend and tell her that Kyrie was with Big Mamma. Tyla and I talked a lot about this. I asked her often to pray for me to forget about this. I hated the hold that he had over me. All I wanted to do was look at his pictures and look for signs to catch him up. Tyla told me that I had to choose to not do it and get my power back.

Unfortunately, I felt powerless. She also told me that it was pointless to tell Rittany anything because she chose to be with him. It was her and Big Mamma's choice what the hell they wanted to play in. Just like it was my choice to stay in hell watching Satan or not.

I asked myself often, why was I doing this to myself?

Tyla told me to resist the urges and choose Heather.

She told me that she knew that was hard, but I had to put my energy and time in all things that were self-care and that would beneficial to me. If it didn't line up, then don't do it.

I hated that I was obsessed. I went through my EGO TV messages and realized that he was doing the same thing to Beauty Defined that he did to me: lovebombing.

For me, it started in September. But we actually became friends on the app on October 4, 2020. He was actually talking to Beauty Defined via text and sending videos and messages to her. When I started talking to him as Beauty Defined, I was only trying to see if he would take the bait. I really didn't believe that he would really try to get with her, but he did. He said all of the same things that he said to me to her, like "Hey Beautiful, I want you, baby." He was trying to hook her by lovebombing her.

My name is Heather Moore, and I am an addict. I had realized that I was addicted to Kyrie Jenkins Dubois. I had come to the realization that I loved him.

I wanted to be with him in some way, shape, or form. If I could be sexually active with him, I would. If I could somehow be his girlfriend, I would. I knew that this was a sad existence, but it was also the root of why I probably did all of the things that I did leading up to that point. I really figured out that this was where I was.

I had come to the realization that I was an addict because I was doing addictive behavior. He'd been calling me a stalker, and I legit was. I was a stalker. I had watched his live broadcasts for the past couple of months every day, recorded, and took notes on any and everything. I used the footage to get information on how to figure out what he was doing, and it had to stop. It had to stop right then.

This wasn't one of my proudest moments. In February, I started a catfish page called Beauty Defined. With the Beauty Defined page, I found a picture of a beautiful, plus sized girl, very voluptuous, very sexy, very modelesque. I made a profile on EGO as an experiment to really solidify if all of what I thought about Kyrie was true. Was he really picking plus size dolls out to have sex with consistently on the app? I wanted to entice Kyrie, to see if all of my suspicions were true—to see if this was his modus operandi, if this was what he did as a game. I believed it to be true from my own intuition because of what I saw, but I just really had to see if everything that I was thinking was true.

On February 25, I joined EGO Live as Beauty Defined. I would go in his room, like his page by throwing hearts, sharing the live, and commenting. At first, he would ignore my comments. He would ignore them because my numbers were low on the app.

I kept talking to him, saying things when I could. I would actually comment on how attractive he was. Most of the time, he would ignore me because he thought I was a bot.

That changed when I started giving him small little gifts. I would just sit in his room, and I would talk to him from time to time. Most often, I would just chill out in there and not really say anything.

One day, he asked, "Are you catfishing me? Because I've never seen you live. I don't know what you look like."

That's when I sent him a shield, which was worth twenty dollars on the app.

"Oh, she's not catfishing. She is real," he said.

So from there, it sparked into more and more, where he would just ask me questions about my life and where I was from. Every day in his live broadcast, I would find ways to flirt with him and find more information about him. He told me that he had a girlfriend. I told him that I had just broken up with my boyfriend, and I asked him how to get over it.

"Get a new boyfriend," he suggested.

One thing led to another, and he hit me up in my inbox, saying, "Hey love or Hey booboo" or those types of words, or terms of endearment to hook Beauty Defined in the same way that he hooked me in. Then he asked when we were going to talk off the app.

One day in March, he messaged, "Hey, love."

"Good Morning," I said. "You are up early. How are you? What time are you going live today?"

"Hey, love. I'll be live at five."

I sent him a hand heart gift and said, "See you then."

On March 25, he said, "Hey, beautiful."
"Hey, Mr. Popularity."

On March 26, he said, "So when are we gonna talk off EGO?"

"By the looks of your life, I'm sure you have plenty of folks you talk to off EGO," I said. "And plus, I'm trying to work it out with my boyfriend."

He said, "Oh, well, I actually don't talk to anyone off EGO. But I respect that. It was a question."

"Okay, good to know. Wait don't you have a girlfriend?" I asked.

"Yeah. I was thinking we could be friends."

"See, by the way you look and how fly you are, if I talk to you off this app, I'm not going to be able to just be a friend...LOL," I messaged.

"LOL, why do you say that?"

"You know what you're giving, stop playing. Like you don't know."

"LOL, what I do?"

"You are funny. Boy, bye," I said. "You know, you fine AF. Stop playing on my time. Acting like you don't know."

On March 27, he wrote: "Give me your number. You're the one playing."

Then a couple of minutes later, I give him my *Beauty Defined*'s phone number and wrote, "Text me."

I let him know that we had just got back together, but he wasn't satisfying me. When I texted him, I would tell him that I was in the second bedroom away from him. Every time we spoke, he made sexual advances to Beauty. I was very strategic with Beauty's conversations with him.

Beauty Defined was very confident and sure of herself. She would throw shade at him in subtle ways when he would send her pics of his penis. She would say things like it was "cute but wasn't big enough."

She enjoyed talking shit to him, and he loved it as well. They would flirt heavily and eventually he asked her to send a video. I was scared shitless because he could never know that Beauty Defined was me. I sent him a ten-second video of me playing with myself. He sent her several videos. He asked her to come to Chicago or that he would travel to Ohio, so that he could see her. I, Heather, had several thoughts to set him up and meet him there, but I didn't think it would end well at all.

He told Beauty that they needed to arrange a visit because she had been playing in his face for months. "You know I want you," he told her, "and I know you want me, too."

He was very vocal about many different things. He didn't know it, but he was giving me/Heather so much intel about Big Mamma. He told me that they had sex when her husband died. He told me that she wanted more.

Then he told me, "Heather is still calling me."

I played dumb and said, "Who is that?"

"My stalker."

"Oh wow, I heard you talk about her on your live broadcast," I said, "but I don't know what happened. Why did she call you?"

"She left a voicemail of her screaming my name." That was not true. "I fucked her in November, and she won't leave me alone," he continued.

I told him that was hot and maybe if he slept with her again, she would leave him alone.

He then told Beauty Defined, "Nah, I have a restraining order against her."

"Does she know you have a restraining order against her?" I asked.

"Yeah, guess she doesn't care."

I didn't know that there was a restraining order against her. This would later change in June.

After this, Beauty Defined was supposed to call him. So I asked one of my former students to pretend she was Beauty. The only thing was that she was busy a lot, so it was hard to call him. She actually called him in April, and they spoke once.

He texted me the next morning and said that I (Beauty Defined) didn't call him. I made up an excuse for why I couldn't call. He tried calling her several times, but my student would be busy and didn't answer. Beauty Defined and Kyrie would text on and off for three months until I (Heather) couldn't do it any longer. It was like I was reliving the whole situation again and getting a high off of it.

I had jumped into other dating apps to try to get Kyrie out of my system. I think I had some good prospects. One of them was James. He was a local businessman from Atlanta. He was very attractive and seemed like he had a good personality.

I was literally losing my mind sexually and needed to release, so we hooked up, and it was absolutely terrible. From that experience, I realized that I had to ask specific questions and see certain pictures with certain measurements before I moved forward with another escapade.

This was probably the worst sexual experience that I had ever had. So much so that I went immediately to the adult bookstore and bought some adult gifts for myself!

April 26, 2021

Kyrie's aunt tried to get the five hundred dollars that he gave me back. I was able to block it through my bank. Two days later, Kyrie called me from his Google Voice number. I didn't answer because I was on my way to an audition and didn't want that to get me off my focus. I also didn't call back that day. During this time, I began seeing a new therapist named Ron. He was on Ego, too, and was in Kyrie's family Live Thrive. He knew all about the app and was a tremendous help to me getting over this situation. I met him a while back on a panel on the app. I thought that he would be a good fit because he was a gay male, and he knew all about the app and about Kyrie.

Journal Entries

April 4, 2021

I found out from my spiritual advisor that I had transferred my addiction to food to an addiction to Kyrie. She told me that it's code red now because he gets a thrill out of Big Mamma's husband killing himself. All I wanted to do today was sleep. I'm severely depressed. Tomorrow is a new day. Thank you, Jesus. I'm gonna have to stop looking at his pages. I must stop.

April 7, 2021

I'm sick to my stomach. I feel like she has my man. But he's not mine. WTF is wrong with me? Why can't I let this shit go? He's in Maryland with her now. I'm so jealous and envious. But why? He's a fucking psychopath. All I want to do is cry and sleep.

April 21, 2021

I'm watching his live broadcast, and I'm sick. This is my last day doing this. He said that he is gonna take me to court for harassment. I'm crying. This man has way too much of a hold on me.

STORY 30
May

Kyrie began to call me, and toxic amnesia penetrated everything about him. What is toxic amnesia? Here's an example: Kyrie always pretended not to remember hurtful behaviors, verbal abuse, and betrayals he was engaged in.

It was a part of his gaslighting campaign and designed to make me feel like I was overreacting or mentally unstable, which created doubt in my mind, thereby enhancing my symptoms of cognitive dissonance.

I hadn't spoken to Kyrie since the Olive Branch conversation at the beginning of March. He called me at the end of April, but I didn't answer. I texted him and asked why he called me on his Google Voice number. He texted me back, and we started the month out with several phone conversations. He called me four times, and when I finally returned one of the phone calls, his first statement was, "Hello, Is this Heather?"

I rolled my eyes. "I said yes it is. I'm returning your call because you called me four times."

"No, I was returning your call. I didn't have my phone on Wednesday. It was shattered, and a repair person had it and called you. I haven't called you in months. Why would I try to call you now?"

"That's what I was trying to figure out."

"I have no reason to contact you."

"Correct. That's all I wanted to know, and that's why I texted you."

"If that's the case I wouldn't have texted and said who is this? I didn't even know who this was. What the fuck, bro!"

Then he hung up the phone.

I called him back several times and also left a message. I texted him and said, "You're such a terrible liar. You called me because you miss it. Denial is a terrible thing. Let me know when you wanna be a grown man and do grown man shit. It's ok to be honest with yourself even if it's not the right thing to do. I've accepted my truth even though it's not the best thing for me."

I called him back, and he answered quickly, asking, "What are you talking about, yo?"

"You know what I'm talking about. You need to be honest with yourself."

"I have no idea what the fuck you are talking about?"

"When you do, you can call me back, unless you want me to spell it out for you because I can be honest. You can't, but I can. I know my truth."

"Which is what? His voice was whiny. "What do you want now? I don't understand, like what?"

"I want the same things that I always wanted, Kyrie. Nothing has changed on my end. What's really disturbing is you have literally been so very mean and disgusting to me, and I am still talking to you."

"I didn't ask you to talk to me."

"Yep, you're right, you didn't."

"I don't understand, what is your goal? I never asked you for anything. I just told you I didn't have my phone."

"I don't understand what your goal is. How can someone get your phone and call me from a Google Voice number? That's a bold-faced lie. Come on now, Kyrie. You gotta come better than that."

"I'm sorry you think I called you, but I didn't. Enjoy your day."

He hung up. I called right back. He answered.

"This is never gonna end," he said. "I don't get it. Do you want to be a consistent factor? You really think we can be together after all that has happened? What the fuck do you want from me, bro?"

"I say can I be candidly honest with you? Are you gonna go on EGO and say what I've said to you?"

"I'm not on EGO anymore. I know you have been on my page."

"I don't know, but I do know that you talk about me all the time there."

"What is your point because this is probably being recorded."

"I don't want to say my point because I am afraid that you are going to try to use that against me. I think that you are going to use this to say that I am crazy or psycho."

"Who else is on the line?"

"No one because it's a Google Voice call, and you can't have three way calling on there. I know that you have needs. Those needs are not met by the people that you are around or the people that you are with. I have needs that I haven't been able to fully fill. The only thing is the way that you work, everything has to be on your agenda and when you want it. It's never when someone else wants something, it's when you want it only. That is a problem for me, but we can negotiate that."

"This has to be an episode of *The Twilight Zone*."

"Are you really in an episode of *The Twilight Zone?* Because you are still on the phone with me. You are still entertaining me. You don't have to."

He hung up. I called back. He didn't answer. I texted him.

"I'm done falling for your mind games, tricks and getting sucked into your psychotic vortex. Don't ever contact me for the rest of your life. I'm blocking you on all forms of communication. I'm done, done. See you in court."

Narcissists need your energy to fuel themselves. By contacting me after a month, he was refueling himself. Any contact with a narcissist will be a way for them to regain control again and acquire narcissistic supply. Many narcissists come back just to see if you will take them back. It's an ego boost for them. Some try to convince you to take them back so they can be the ones who ultimately end the relationship. Others will only stay until they find new supply and then leave again. Because of the way they function in the world, there is no way there won't be drama mixed in with pain. They may lovebomb you back into the relationship only to go back to old patterns when they think they have you--all the while creating mass confusion and causing you a tremendous amount of trauma and pain.

I was really trying my best to be done. I was tired of the rollercoaster ride, the games, and the manipulation. But there was something in me that was hopeful. That believed that there was some good in Kyrie. That the person that I fell in love with would eventually come back and love me the way that I needed to be loved. This is the reason I participated in the on-again/off-again nature of our new found relationship for five more months. I knew that he had a girlfriend, but at this point, I didn't care. I really believed in my heart of hearts that he was mine. I needed to be with him.

I felt good every time I talked to him when he wasn't acting crazy. He had a side of him that was intoxicating, and I wanted to continue to drink from the fountain of Kyrie. I also realized that with him being a narcissist, something was changing with his supplies. The young ladies that he was dealing with were not providing what he needed to survive anymore, and that's why he was contacting me.

I also believed from his behavior that he really did have feelings for me and didn't know what to do with them. He was just as sick as I was. He wanted to be with me just like I wanted to be with him. He just had a fucked up way of showing it. You don't act like this with someone if you don't like or care for them even if it's this toxic. My friend Natalie told me that the power was always in my hands. I just didn't realize that. But now I could see. Even though his calling me was to fill his narcissistic supply, he still was dealing with a lot of demons that he couldn't get rid of. I was intoxicating to him, too. He loved every inch of my body. He loved my drive, my spice, my intellect, my artistry just as much as I loved his.

Not too long after our last time, I logged into EGO, and while patrolling the *streets*, I came into one of the Regular Retreats Family members pages by accident. I went back in as an EGO TV watcher, and they were having a full-blown talk session—about me. They called me a bitch, said that I didn't have any more jobs, that I was psycho and that I lived in Atlanta and that the men down south liked my type so why was I so desperate for Kyrie. They also said that they didn't care about anything that I said when I contacted them. That it had nothing to do with them. I have never in my entire life seen such a disgusting display of personalities. I don't know why they think I would be trying to single them out and mess with them. I could give two fucks about any of them. They were truly beneath me and would always be that. Bottom feeding, low life individuals who took the word of a manipulative liar, con artist, and narcissist. The fact that I contacted any of them was to warn them of who he was for their own protection. I'm not an ill-spirited or evil person and never sent anything to them for negative results. It all came from a place of positivity and to inform. Fuck all of them for the things that they said about me. It's a damn shame that people are so low that they would tear down someone that they don't even know.

But it's cool.

Watch me work.

Right here, right now.

Here is the real EGO storyline ... this book.

After two weeks of silence from Kyrie, he began calling me and hanging up. I would call him back several times with no response, and eventually, I left the same voicemail and text message: "Why do you keep doing this? What do you want from me? Just tell me what you want. I really wish I could talk to you for real, without you hanging up on me. If you are calling me for a basic need to be met, just say it. I understand. Let me know when you are ready to have an adult conversation."

He immediately responded with text and a call, asking me what adult conversation I wanted to have. I asked him what exactly he wanted from me, and he hung up the phone again. He called me back, and I said to him, "Please stop calling me and hanging up. It's an ungodly hour, and now I'm up."

"Are you recording this?" he asked.

"No," I replied emphatically, but I was. I had to. I had to document everything that came from him because if I didn't, no one would believe any of this.

"How do I know you're not recording?"

"Because I don't lie to you, Kyrie, I never lie to you."

This was true until now.

This was the Come to Jesus moment. This was the make-or-break moment in our saga. This was where all of the truth came out and even more truth about who Kyrie really was. We stayed on the phone for several hours and ended the conversation having phone sex. This time, I felt like we were making love. I loved every inch, piece, soul of this narcissistic asshole. He was dangerous, he was Satan, he was very bad for me, but I was in total bliss talking to him and having only a piece of him. Every part of my existence knew that he felt the same way about me. I had to enjoy these sporadic encounters because they were few and far between. Sprinkled in between them was chaos, confusion, gaslighting, and love bombing. I waited endlessly for the good times, but they didn't outweigh the bad. Deep down, I knew I deserved better, but I couldn't stop. I was a crackhead, and my crack was Kyrie.

"What do you want from me?" Kyrie asked.

"I'm afraid to say. Because you are gonna take it, run with it, talk about me on EGO, and tell everybody."

"I'm not on EGO anymore. I haven't been on EGO in almost two months."

"Every time I share something with you, you distort it and try to paint me out as a crazy person, and I'm not crazy.

"I mean, I tried to simply leave you alone. All I wanted to do was walk away, and you never let me walk away."

"I don't even know what to say to that."

"I wasn't trying to do all of that. When I hit you up in December, I definitely was trying to separate and not get so much involved. It's like you initiated all of this. You came on my page after I told you that you were gonna get all of the stuff back. Regardless of your opinion of how you feel like I didn't tell you this and I lied about that, and you keep on running with this whole notion that I have a girlfriend. So you feel that the whole world should know that I cheated. You still chose actions."

"Yeah, you're right. Everything that I did, in the scheme of things, was not good, not good at all. But even before I did all the things that I did, you broke up whatever we had because I asked you to meet me halfway on gifts that we had on the app."

"No, no, that's not why I broke it off and why I didn't want to deal with you. It was because of your emotions. I didn't want to be connected to you because of that. I had no reason to not pay anybody. First off, we all know that at the end of day, one, I'm not broke. Two, I don't need anything from anybody. This whole notion that I'm a schemer and that I'm scamming people. I ain't scammed nothing. Let's not forget you got a five-hundred-dollar Cash App, and I'm pretty sure you got the reverse fee of the Cash App that you did on my account. That's twenty-five hundred dollars. You act like you didn't get anything in the process of like months. So I don't get what you want. I don't know how to move in this scenario."

"Ok. You are asking me what I want, and I'm asking you the same thing. What do you want from me? You want me to leave you alone? Or do you want to deal with me? You have said that you don't want anything to do with me."

"Heather, are still trying to fuck me?"

"You just asked me am I still trying to fuck you. Every time I say something, you invalidate me. I just want to be honest and truthful and not be persecuted for it."

"I just asked a question."

"Kyrie, dealing with you opened up so many things in my life that I have not been able to close sexually."

"Like you having sex with a lot of people? I don't get it. What do you mean? You are speaking in codes."

"All I think about is sex. It's like a Pandora's box that won't close, and I've never had these feelings, and I've never felt like this before."

"So what happened to the masseuse, or your ex, or the person that you were supposed to sleep with after me. Was that fabrication? Like I'm confused."

"The masseuse I never initiated. So I didn't go through with that. I had sex with my ex. I had sex with two of my exes. I've been on several dating apps. I've been on several dates, I have a date today at 1:30."

"So basically you want to have sex a lot now all the time because of me? That's what you've been doing?"

"Yeah, I haven't been having sex a lot. If it happens, it happens. But there's a burning desire in me to have sex all the time. I've bought things to help me out with that. Three things."

"I don't know why I think this is being recorded."

"I mean I could say the same thing for you, Kyrie, that you're trying to set me up and make me look like a fool again. How do you feel? I know you don't care for me because of all of the stuff that I've done, but yet and still, you still call me. Do you still want to have sex with me?"

"I don't wanna answer that."

"Ok. Why don't you want to answer it? Kyrie, here's the deal. I know why you do the things you do."

"Which is what? What are you trying to say?"

"I'm trying to say, hurt people hurt people, and I do the same thing. I've done the same thing."

"My dick should not be hard right now."

"See, I know you are attracted to me. I know you are very attracted to me. One thing that I do know is that what we did sexually was on another level as far as attraction. You're attracted to me, and I'm attracted to you. So you know what, fuck it, I do want to keep having sex with you. I wish you would come here now and fuck the shit out of me. I wish I could come to Chicago and see you and fuck the shit out of you. I wonder if you would let me do that. I don't really give a fuck about all the other people you dealing with and whatever else you got going on. I just want what I want. That's the adult conversation that I wanted to have."

"We shouldn't be doing this." He sighed.

"If you are not gonna do it with me, Kyrie, you are gonna do it with someone else because you love to have sex. Right?"

He sighed again.

"You love to have sex. That's what you need to be honest with yourself about. You love to fuck. You want to fuck several people. All the time," I said.

"Can you give me a threesome?"

"Yeah, I would. Because one thing you woke up in me is my freaky deaky side."

"I think you want to see me get fucked by a man."

"If you want me to see you get fucked by a man, then I'll see you get fucked by a man. That's what you fail to realize. I accepted you for who you are."

"My dick should not be this hard right now."

"You love my pussy."

"Stop, Heather."

"Well, you do, and I love your dick. I love having phone sex with you."

"I still listen to what you sent me."

"I know that's why I sent it to you so you could have that as your gift. Oh my God! Thank you for calling me back and getting this out of the way, Kyrie. Damn niggah. Why do you keep it away from me?"

He sighed. Again.

"Why do you keep that dick away from me, huh?"

He sounded like he was crying.

"You didn't want me to have it?" I asked.

"Be quiet."

"No, I can't be quiet. You know how long I've been waiting for this."

"We can't be doing this," he said, crying.

"Look, you want me to catch a flight?"

"No."

"You sure?"

"Fuck." He sniffed.

"Because I can. I can come to Chicago this weekend. You want me to come?"

"No. Oh my God, why are you talking to me like this?"

"Because I mean it. Let me know. I'll buy a ticket today."

"No, we shouldn't be doing this."

"You're right, but I'm not about to deny what the fuck I want anymore, so now you know what's going on, and you know what time it is."

"You want it in your ass, too?"

"Huh?"

"You want it in your ass, too?" he asked again.

"I do. Uh, I really do."

"Fuck." There were, at least, ten U's in the word, and the very hard K told me he was very aroused. "You're not gonna stop me this time. You always stop me. Yes, after you cum, you always wanna stop."

"No, I won't stop. I'm so sexually free right now. I just want you to fuck the shit out of me."

"My dick is hard as shit."

"Can I come to Chicago?"

"Heather, no."

"You wanna come to Atlanta?"

"This is a lot right now."

"It's a lot, but you wanna fuck, and I wanna fuck."

"Why do I feel like you wanna hear me nut?"

"I'd love to hear you nut."

"Why do you wanna hear me nut?"

"Because I love the way it sounds, and I love the way it makes me feel." I moaned sexually. "You gon' nut for me? You stroking that beautiful dick of yours?"

"God fuck." He released a moan.

"You gon' keep calling me to do this? I would appreciate it if you did."

He sighed.

"This is why you called me last week because you wanted to do this again?"

He moaned.

"Thank you for calling me. And doing this," I said.

He moaned heavily.

"I know you said before how I could love you, but I do love you, Kyrie. And I will always love you."

It sounded like he was crying, and there was a quiver to his voice.

"I know you do."

"You know I do," I muttered. "Hmph ... wow."

"I always knew you did."

"Wow."

"Keep going."

"Yeah, you know I love your ass."

"Keep going," he said.

"I've always loved you. I loved every ounce of you and accepted you for who you were. I didn't give a fuck that you like dudes, girls, or trans whatever. Whomever you wanna have sex with, that doesn't bother me. It never did. I know you are hurt inside, and that's why you do what you do, but I ain't never wanted nothing bad to happen to you. I wanted to be here for you and still do. I know you see that, and you know that. Just like let's start over. I know you have a whole girlfriend, and you don't want to be with me. I don't think I can be with you. But at least until I can get over this whole sex with you deal, if we could just keep going."

"What if we don't?" he asked.

"It's a very hard road for me. Getting over you. It's fucking May, and I feel more intense about you than I did in December."

"I told you no one would ever fuck you like me. I told you that."

"Yeah, you did."

"I told you that, and I gave you what you asked for. Every motion, every curve I gave it to you."

"I love when you are on top of me, and you look at me. It's like you're looking into my soul."

"You touching it?"

"No, I'm not touching it right now. I'm just enjoying you."

"Are you setting me up?"

"No, I'm not setting you up. Want me to come to Chicago? Can I come this weekend?"

"No."

"Ok. Can I ever come to Chicago? To see you?"

"I don't know. I'm mad at you because you are fucking other people."

"You're fucking your people." I laughed. "How many people have you had sex with since we had sex?"

"You know who I was with."

"I don't know who you was with. If I was to take a guess, I would say Rittany."

"Yeah."

"I knew you were dating Big Mamma. Did you ever get to visit her?"

"Big Mamma is my EGO Wife," he said angrily. "Big Mamma has a whole husband and three children. My God!"

He was lying to me.

"Ok, scratch that off."

"If anyone was to ever ask me, yes, she has a whole husband and three kids. She has a whole system."

Her husband died, and he didn't know that I knew this.

"Will Rittany let you have a threesome?"

"With her? I'm pretty sure she doesn't want to see you. She is pretty much anti-you."

"Ok."

"We are supposed to be going to an adult all-inclusive island this summer."

"Ok. Y'all should go to Hedonism."

"Maybe that's where she is taking me. That's where you go?"

"No, that's like an adult resort where they be fucking."

"That's where you want to go with me probably."

"With you? You trying to take trips with me?" I asked.

"I don't know. My dick should not be this hard."

"And my pussy shouldn't be this wet."

This conversation opened me up wider with Kyrie. It started an even faster roller coaster ride in the wrong direction. For several times after this, he repeated this pattern of behavior. After this conversation, Kyrie didn't call me or text me for several weeks. I was really in my feelings. I thought that we could at least be back on good terms as far as pleasuring each other. I was wrong again.

On Facebook, I belonged to a couple of narcissist support groups. I checked these daily for inspiration and help in dealing with my narcissist. In one of the posts I saw, there was a comment about help with a narcissist from a spell doctor. This spell doctor could put a love spell on a person that you loved to get them back. I thought that this was very interesting, so I sent the spell doctor a message.

Now this is where I hit rock bottom, folks. Going to a fucking spell doctor? I totally lost my rabid ass mind! This was not a high point for me!

I asked him if he was available for a consultation. He said yes and asked if I had Google Hangout. I told him no, but I would download it. So once I did, I called him. It was a video call.

The spell doctor was dressed in red and was in a very intimately lit area. He said that he was in his temple in the UK. He also said that he was from South Africa. I asked him how he knew how to cast spells and he said that it was passed down from generation to generation. I thought that was cool. I told him about my situation with Kyrie and that I was interested in a temporary love spell. He said that he could do that. I also asked if it was possible to perform a spell on someone to remove their narcissistic traits. I wanted him to put a spell on Kyrie to be a better person. He told me yes as well. I asked him if he could do that spell first and then the love spell. But I also asked if the love spell was reversible because I didn't want it to last forever. He told me yes. I asked him how much the cost for his service and he was said three hundred fifty dollars. I said ok, and I would send that to him right away. He also asked for my picture and Kyrie's picture to start working on the spell in his temple. I sent him the picture. He told me in three days I should see a difference. I was like wow three days, and he will be a better person? Hallelujah!

So the spell doctor got busy on the spell to make Kyrie a better person. After he was finished with the spell, he would start on the love spell. He showed me the pictures that he printed out and his temple of all the people he was performing spells for. It was very impressive. I was excited because one, I wanted Kyrie to become a better person if that was possible, and two, if I could feel what I initially felt again with him, I would be in heaven.

A couple of days later, the spell doctor called and told me that he needed to talk to me about something very important. I took the call. He told me that there was a problem. There was already a love spell on Kyrie from another girl.

"What?" I nearly yelled. "Well, can you remove it?"

"Yes, but there is a bigger problem. Someone placed a death spell on you."

My heart rate picked up speed. "How? Who put the spell on him? Me?"

"All I can say is your life is in danger. If you don't let me take care of this, your life and the life of your daughter will be in danger."

Folks, this scared the living shit out of me!

That is until the bullshit arrived.

This "spell" *doctor* told me that it would cost four thousand dollars for him to get the materials and to break the spells. I was *not* about to pay that. I didn't have that kind of money, and if I did, I wouldn't give it to him.

But his words still frightened me, so I called my psychic advisor to ask for help, but unfortunately, she didn't work on weekends. I then Googled Voodoo priestesses and root workers in Atlanta and called two people for readings. The first person "Magic" was located in Little Five Points, and he told me that I had nothing to worry about and that he would make me a cleansing candle to get rid of the spirits. The second person I made an appointment for the reading told me that it was seventy-five dollars for the first appointment. When I arrived, she said that she could help me out, but it would cost five hundred fifty dollars for the clearing. I felt like I was in between a rock and a hard place, but I went to the bank and got the money. I returned, and she did the reading and supposedly cleared me as well. I felt duped and stupid because these folks just got me for all of my coins.

FML!

The following Monday, I had an appointment with my spiritual advisor. During this time, the spell doctor is blowing up my phone to see what was going on because I was in danger of the spell.

My spiritual advisor told me the spell doctor was a con artist, and he was trying to get me out of my money. She also told me to tell him to leave me alone or I was going to call the police. In the midst of all of this, he sent pictures of my daughter that he found on Facebook saying that she was in trouble—all of this to scam me out of more money.

After all of this happened, I knew that I had to be done with Kyrie. This took me to the bottom of the barrel. The lowest possible level that anyone could go to. I may not had known what was right or not, but I knew that shit like this was happening because of my connection to Kyrie.

Under the suggestion of Magic, I wrote Kyrie a letter, letting him go and thanking him for all of the lessons that I learned from and with him.

Good Evening, Kyrie.

I want to thank you for all of the many lessons that I have learned from you. These past seven months have made me grow tremendously, and I owe that to you! I want to let you know that I forgive you for all that you have done to hurt me, embarrass me, defame my character and soul. I also want to apologize for all that I have done to hurt you as well.

After our conversation last week, I really thought that we could move forward equally and reciprocate with each other our true thoughts, wants, and desires. I saw that I was mistaken, and that was ok. I have come to realize that no matter how much I want something or someone, it's not for me. I know now that I love you so much, but I also love you enough to let you go. I will always love you, have love for you, and wish you nothing but the best.

I also know that I deserve better than the scraps that you give me. I wanted so much to feel the euphoria of you that I was willing to accept anything from you. But I now know that I can't continue to do this. Respectfully, please do not contact me anymore. I will not answer. I wanted to come to an agreement before the court date, but I will just wait until we are summoned to handle that. I think that you are extremely talented, and I hope that the world will see your brilliance soon. I admire your work ethic, your passion, and, still to this day, think that you are the best thing since sliced bread.

Kyrie, I release you into the world free from me and my heart.

Love and light,
Heather Moore

This was my finale to Kyrie.

So I thought.

Two weeks later, I called Kyrie when I was in Tulsa, Oklahoma, working for the 100th Centennial for the Tulsa Massacre. For some strange reason, I couldn't get him off of my mind again. I spoke to my colleague about him and even called him from her phone to hear his voice. Eventually, I broke down and called. He didn't answer when I called. I talked to my student to see if she could call as Beauty Defined because I was that desperate to speak to him. We couldn't coordinate schedules so that didn't work unfortunately.

Then when I was getting ready to leave Tulsa, he called me back. I asked him if we could just talk, and I could slowly wean myself away from him. He told me no. That if you were addicted to crack, you wouldn't go by a crack house. And this was the same thing. I couldn't disagree with him. He also told me that he had moved on and that he was over this situation. He made it painfully clear that he didn't want to be with me and that this thing that I thought was still there was over. This really stung me deep, but I had to listen to him and believe what he was saying. I had to let him go because he didn't want to move forward or even appease my feelings at this point. There was nothing that I could do but move on and get over him, day by day, moment by moment.

I tried to do this, but I wasn't successful. I believed that he was done from the words that he said... but he wasn't telling the truth, again.

STORY 31
June

It was hard, but I was really trying to stay busy and go on with my life. Several of my friends came to visit me. My love Rihanna from LA, my brother Lou from LA, and my best friend Carlos from Alabama. They were very helpful in pouring into me and recharging my battery.

Morgan and I would also go swimming every day. She loved this. I loved it, too, because I had a whole new body and was showing it off in my two-piece bathing suits. This was wonderful because I had never worn a two-piece before in my life until now. I was also close to losing sixty pounds! Whoo-hoo! All of my hard work was paying off. At the end of the month, I also took Morgan to see her Uncle Marty. We had a blast going to see *Baby Shark Live*!

My last attempt to gain some control or to win Kyrie back was me reaching out to him to follow up on something that he said to me on the phone in May.

I called him and left a message stating that I had a solution to both of our problems. At this point, my sex drive was extremely high. He wanted me to see him have sex with a man, so I thought we could go to a sex club and fulfill both of our fantasies. I was really trying for the last time to get close to him once again.

This didn't work.

He called me a couple of days later while I was in a counseling Zoom session with my therapist Ron. This was probably the worst that I had heard him talk to me. He was very angry because I told him that we could kill two birds with one stone. I was just repeating what he said from our conversation in May.

"I did *not* say that, Heather," he said adamantly.

Because I knew he would gaslight me, I recorded the conversation, so I knew exactly what he said. No one in their right mind would believe this, so I had to have proof. Here were some of the things that he said on the phone to me:

- *Stop fucking contacting me.*
- *Leave me the fuck alone.*
- *You never even made me cum in Atlanta.*
- *You're an emotional wreck.*
- *You got issues.*
- *I don't care if I hurt you. I don't care if you said I love you. I don't want you in my life.*

- *I'm not obligated to entertain you.*
- *Stop being obsessed. Fuck a cow, fuck a bird, leave me alone.*
- *Half this shit I tell you is so that you can leave me alone.*

"Let's be clear," he had told me, "I've never had sex with a man so there isn't a man that you can see me having sex with. Leave me the fuck alone. You are blocked on every measure. You dumb bitch."

I was just trying to help fulfill his fantasy. I wanted him to be happy. Ron said that what I said was a trigger for him. Boy, was it! He was raging on the phone with me. This was the worst that I had seen him.

This was also an example of him gaslighting and then devaluing me. This wasn't the first time that he did this because it developed subtly and gradually, and it made it difficult for me to realize that I was being manipulated and abused. He was also trying to devalue me. This wasn't the first time. He did it before when he went on a tirade on EGO Live in March and other times as well. Kyrie, as a narcissist, loved the power that he had over my emotions. He loved that he could easily upset me, get me angry, and get me to react. He could even make me sad. He got a high off of this, and it made him feel like he was powerful. He also didn't want me to think too highly of myself because then I might leave him. He was terrified of abandonment, so he would do everything that made me want to abandon him, thinking he could make me stay. "Make me stay" not "Make me *want* to stay." It was all about control.

After this conversation, I knew that I couldn't go back. He crossed the line this time. I felt so hurt and mad at him for talking to me like this. I hated him for this. There was no turning back.

A few days later, after I thought that things couldn't get any worse, I was served by the Cobb County Sheriff with an Order of Protection filed by him! This was the lowest of the low! How dare he? Harassment? How Sway? Receiving this hurt me to the core. I was distraught. I was done. Fuck him. Bear in mind, he filed this Order in March, and I had been talking to him since April 28! If I was harassing him, why was he calling me?

After I received the restraining order, I tried to move on and keep busy. I went on a shopping spree at Gucci and Saks to get my mind off of things. It was only temporary because after I was done, it really hit me HARD. I didn't speak to him for a few weeks after he went off on me and the restraining order hit.

Then one day, there was call after call after call.

He called me between six and ten times. I didn't answer until the last call at around five o'clock in the morning. When I spoke to him, I asked him why he was calling me when he said that he didn't want to be in my life, that he didn't give a fuck about me, and that I was a bitch.

"I don't know" was his response.

"Wow. Really? Then, to add insult to injury, you also filed an Order Of Protection about me. So, again, why are you calling me?"

"I don't know. I keep wondering what those gifts are that you had for me."

"Kyrie, you have a restraining order against me. The police came and brought it to me like a week and a half ago, so why are you calling me?"

"I don't know."

"You don't know? After being *so* disrespectful to me, treating me mean. I'm not treating *you* mean. I'm treating you with respect. After all of the stuff that you have done to me, why are you calling me?"

"I'm not exactly sure. I be wanting to call. I remember that you record the conversations, so I don't know."

"But you said that you hate me, you don't want me in your life. You told me to stay the fuck away from you. That's what you said to me."

"You said stuff like that to me plenty of times."

"No, I haven't said anything like that to you."

"You've never said anything derogatory about me or toward me? You told people that I was a faggot."

"I didn't tell anybody that you were a faggot."

"You sent a whole email saying that I'm gay and that I'm basically scared to come out. Can you find a niggah that I've fucked? No. You still can't. You've been on EGO longer than me, and you can't. Can't no niggah even come to you and show you a picture of my penis."

"Here's the deal. If you want to have sex with a man. that's what you want to do."

"I don't even remember telling you that."

"If that's what you want to do, that's fine. I don't care. Like I told you from the beginning, I accepted you for who you were."

"But I don't want to have sex with a man."

"Okay, well, you don't have to have sex with a man. But if you did, that's okay."

"Why are we even still on that?"

"You just brought it up."

"I brought it up as a point."

"Well, that's not a good point. When I sent those emails, I was just telling the truth about you. How you treated me and was warning them about your behavior to find a solution."

"You said I was broke. I'm not broke."

"I didn't say that you were broke."

"You said that I have to con people out of their money by traveling."

"Can you pay me back the money that you still owe me?"

"First off, the two thousand dollars you already got back. I already sent you five hundred dollars. The rest you can chalk that up to the game. I'm not sending you shit."

"Okay. So, the two grand, I did get back and I'm taking that off of the tally. You or your aunt came and took two hundred fifty back from my Cash App."

"I don't know what you are talking about."

"I'm telling you that she committed fraud against my Cash App."

"Take that up with Margaret Loretta Jenkins Dubois. The fuck does that have to do with me? That has nothing to do with me. I don't even see her every day. I don't know what to tell you."

"Okay. Alright."

"You've called *The People's Court* on me. You've come into my lives and said crazy shit. I've been disrespected by you. I have."

"This is Kyrie's world. This isn't even Heather's world."

"It's not Kyrie's world."

"It is. You are the victim."

"There are always three sides to the story. That's life. You have your interpretation, and I have mine."

"We can respectfully agree to disagree. You put a fucking restraining order against me. Why are you calling me?"

"Why did you call *The People's Court* on me?"

"I called *The People's Court* because we will both get paid, and we can both move on."

"I don't need no three-hundred-dollar stipend from no court show."

"Not only will they pay a stipend, but they will also pay all of the damages that you owe me."

"I'm not going on TV, embarrassing myself talking about this shit. It's definitely embarrassing on EGO. There is no way."

"Well, you are the one who brought it on EGO, sir. I didn't."

"You started it. Yes, you did."

"No, I did not."

"In December, I called you and told you that you would get your two theophanies before you came on my live, and that's how all of this started. Again, you have your side, and I have my side. I was gonna give you your shit. You wanna know why I didn't? Because you have or act like you have a whole authoritative role, and you wanted to come at me crazy, publicly."

"I didn't come at you crazy. I just asked you a question, and then you checked out on me on the live, then you blocked me."

"Either way, how you came at me, I felt disrespected."

"I never was trying to disrespect you."

"I'm still not giving you your money back," Kyrie said. "I don't owe you anything."

"Well, we are still going to court twice."

"We ain't going to court."

"Yes, we are. One for your restraining order, we have a hearing on November the third, and then for my civil case. We're gonna go to court."

"It has to be a decision. Time. All of this because of an EGO situation. Before they even gave me the restraining order, the precinct laughed at me. The first lawyer laughed at me because this shit is hilarious. The fact that you want to even continue. Weren't you just on the back of a Nutrisystem box? What the fuck do you care about the five hundred dollars?"

"Wait, wait, wait... so you are looking at my EGO profile and looking at me and watching me, but you call me a stalker."

"I looked at your page today because I got a phone call saying that you were harassing somebody."

"A phone call saying I was harassing somebody? First of all, the only reason I answered this call was to let you know that you have a restraining order against me and ask you why you are calling me because it doesn't make any sense. If you hate me so much, why are you calling me? Who said I was harassing them?"

"It doesn't even sound like you have anything to do with it. It doesn't matter."

"The fact that you have called me a stalker and said that I'm harassing you … I'm not harassing you, Kyrie. I've never harassed you."

"Is this call being recorded?"

"No."

"For training purposes or something?"

"No."

After a moment of silence, he said, "You looked good in those blue biker shorts."

This told me that he had been watching my EGO profile and following all of my posts on there. Kyrie had a knack for diffusing the situation. He apologized to me for what he said on the previous call. He also said that he would get rid of the protective order. He seemed like a new person because he wanted something from me—phone sex!

I didn't give it to him. I held him to task about how he treated me and reminded him of all of the bad things that he said. He tried over and over to lead the conversation to the sexual realm, but I reminded him that I was not going to do this. I also told him that he needed to make it right with me: do nice things for me like take me out to dinner or buy me flowers. He said that he would do that. I didn't believe him, but it was nice to hear. We stayed on the phone for about two hours. I thought that we were on the same page with moving forward with being cordial and kind to one another. I was wrong again. This was one of many times that he would gaslight me, lovebomb me, and then ghost me. This was his pattern whenever he needed his fix for phone sex.

"So you are looking at me? Ok. Thank you. Wow. Who's left your life that you are calling me now?"

"I've been wanting to call you."

"Oh ok."

"You sure this call isn't being recorded?"

"I'm positive. Why would you want to call me, and you cussed me out so bad, Kyrie?"

"You made me upset, Heather."

"I made you upset because I was just trying to appease you."

"Heather, at the end of day, I cared for you, you cared for me. All of this shit did not have to happen."

"But you said you didn't care for me. You called me a fucking whale, dude. I never called you out your name. You said I used the F word, but I did not."

"You called me out of my name because I'm not a faggot."

"I don't even use that word."

"I'm not a homosexual," he said. "I'm not a part of the community. You have to participate in gay activities in order to be gay. What man is fucking me?"

"You know what, Kyrie? I'm sorry that whatever happened to you in your life caused you so much pain and hurt."

"Listen, it's not your job to give me that pep talk. I'm not talking from pain; I'm talking from truth. You believe in your mind because you saw me at a ball that I'm gay. I'm an artist and designer, those are my clients, those are my friends. Aren't you a straight CIS gendered woman? Now that you go to a ball, you're a lesbian. Why is it a double standard? Can you answer that question?"

"I'm not about to argue back and forth with whatever your truth is. You have to deal with that and accept yourself for who you are."

"There is no truth."

"There is a truth in who you are…my name is Heather Moore. That's the truth of who I am."

"My name is Kyrie Jenkins Dubois, everyone knows who I am. I live my truth every day. You're the only person that I've encountered in life that is on this Kyrie live your truth shit. You're the only one that doesn't see me for what I'm giving you. This is me."

"I see you for who you really are, Kyrie. And I'm probably the only girl that does. I'll let you marinate on that."

"I keep looking at your ass in those stretch pants. You missed my birthday."

"You ain't my man. Happy belated birthday."

"It was a joke."

"Bad joke."

"Can I get some cake?"

"No."

"Why not?"

"Because you are not about to use me to have phone sex on this phone tonight. You are not 'bout to get me all worked up, to have phone sex, which I love doing by the way. Then when I call you to reciprocate, you are nowhere to be found, and you call me bitches and shit. That's what we are not gonna do."

"Can we drop these charges and stop this shit please?" Kyrie asked.

"Can we drop what charges? You drop your charges first. You got a whole restraining order against me. You drop that and show me the proof, and then we can talk about it. Because I already told you I didn't want to go to court and that we could barter, and you could make me a painting or sculpture so you wouldn't have to pay me back the money."

"What do I owe you? I gave you back the two theophanies."

"You never caught back up with me on my board on EGO."

"Fuck EGO. I'm not even on there. I haven't been there in two and a half months."

"It's the principle of it."

"Heather, we are not children. I'm not gonna go back to EGO and gift you. I'm not even using the app."

"Well, make me some paintings or sculptures. Do right by me. Send me some flowers. Take me out to dinner."

"You want me to take you out to dinner?"

"I want you to do right by me. Make it right. Make me know it. Make me know if you ever genuinely liked me or had any feelings for me. You can show me now."

"I was so jealous the day you called me with that new dick, and I don't know why."

"Well, you have nothing to be jealous about because that dick was terrible."

"No one is gonna fuck you better than me."

"But you keep saying that I never made you cum. Why do you keep saying that? I didn't make you cum?"

"You did."

"So why would you say that to me? Like you are saying shit to hurt my feelings. I never say stuff to hurt your feelings."

"The only thing I don't like is that once you cum, you are done. Sex is not enjoyable. You just want to have sex for three to five minutes. I will never cum in life in three to five minutes."

"But I never tell you to stop after I cum. You can keep going," I said.

"You did. The first time. You actually said I'm done and slightly rolled over."

That's because I've gotten so used to not cumming from a guy, so I do my own thing." I laughed.

"But that ain't me."

"It wasn't like that the other times. I let you do whatever you wanted to do."

"You still want me to do those things to you?"

"Nope. I'm not 'bout to go here with you. Nope. Not doing it."

"I didn't get any on my birthday."

"Naw, I think you got some on your birthday, Kyrie. I think Rittany gave you all your heart's desires."

"Seems like you are watching me, too."

"You Gucci down to your socks, but you can't pay me my money. That is so funny."

"I don't owe you money."

"Whatever, Mr. Gucci man! So, I wanna—"

"Take my shirt off?"

"No, I didn't want to take your shirt off. I'm mad that you have on my shorts that I want. Cuz guess who can fit Gucci? Heather Moore!"

"Guess who used to work for them and just call them and get the shit shipped to them? Kyrie Jenkins Dubois. But you thought I was fraudulent."

"Well make me know it. Get me some Gucci shorts."

"I'm not getting you no twelve-hundred-dollar shorts."

"You don't really want me."

"You don't even want me."

"If that's what you think."

"Why are we even on this phone?"

"You called me, sir."

"Should I hang up the phone?"

"Do you want to hang up the phone?"

"Do you want me to hang up the phone?"

"Stop putting it on me! You make a decision. You grown. You thirty now! Dirty thirty."

"You want this thirty-year-old dick."

"There you go with your shenanigans again. Look I'm not having phone sex with you no more until you show me that you care about me."

"Oh, you want real sex."

"You gotta make it right with me, sir. If you wanna be my friend. You gotta start over. Are you gonna get rid of the restraining order?"

"Are you gonna stop making it seem like I wanna fuck a man? That shit is really getting fucking annoying."

"Kyrie, when we were on the phone, and we were having phone sex, you said to me, 'Heather I think you wanna see me have sex with a man.' Okay, so I was only going off of what you said. If that's not what you meant or that's not what you want to do, that's fine. I won't bring it up any more.

"I called you because I am literally over here dying because now my sex drive is out of this world. I play with my pussy four to five times a day. I have three new vibrators; I have a rose. I have all kinds of shit, and I want to fuck. I've been on these dating apps and have met these dudes on these apps, and they ain't shit. When I called you and left that message, I was only trying to bridge a gap with me and you to work out and be better to try and kill two birds with one stone. So I wasn't trying to offend you."

"When was the last time you had sex?" he asked.

"With Nick."

"Who's Nick?"

"The guy you said you were jealous of. But he couldn't keep his penis hard. I think he was intimidated by me."

"All that ass you got."

"You didn't answer my question. Are you gonna take this restraining order away? Because I'm a public figure and that can fuck up my record. You want to fuck up my record?"

"No, but you tried to fuck up my name. And you act like I didn't have a name like you did."

"Kyrie, we have differences of opinion. Like I said, I haven't tried to do anything to you. I didn't try to bring it on EGO or none of that."

"But you did. Heather, you sent Rittany an email; you sent my aunt an email. All of that stuff counts."

"I sent them that shit because you got mad at the Number One Woman when she wouldn't give you back the unicorns."

"I get the why, but it still happened."

"Ok. Like I said, I can forgive you for it, but you can't get over it. That's yo' ass."

"That's because, you ain't sittin' on me. Come sit on me."

"The last time we talked, Kyrie, I asked you if you wanted me to catch a flight to Chicago, and you said no."

"You were serious?"

"What chu think?"

"I can't stop thinking about you taking this dick."

"Ok, well, I don't think you are serious about it because if you were, you would make some shit happen."

"Then why is my dick hard and I'm stroking it?"

"Because that's what you do. I think that you are probably very sexually aroused and excited by me. I think that's it and that's where it stops. I think after you get your nut, you are on to the next until you want to do this again."

"No."

"Yeah, that's what it is. That's what you did the last time. I thought we were good and could talk on the phone. But you played me to the left again and then the police came to my house twice to serve me with your restraining order. Do you get a discount at Gucci?"

"Yes."

"Did Rittany buy you all that stuff from Gucci?"

"No. I make more money than Rittany."

"What does she do for a living?"

"I don't even think I should answer that question. I don't want anything to backfire on me."

"So if you love your girlfriend so much, why are you calling me?"

"Do you want me to hang up the phone?"

"I just asked you a question."

"I don't want to answer it."

"Oh ok."

"So are you ever gonna send me those gifts. Especially since it was my birthday?"

"Nope."

"Why?"

"I don't want you to use those gifts against me."

"What are they?"

"Me playing with my vagina with a dildo."

"Did you cum?"

"Um huh."

"Fuck."

"The most I could do is send you another voice recording, but I'm not sending you no video."

"Why?"

"Because I don't trust you."

"What can I do so that you can trust me?"

"You can make me know it."

"Fuck, why does your voice make me so horny?" he asked.

"I don't know."

"Fuck, Heather."

"Why don't you buy me a ticket to come to Chicago?"

"Ah shit. Ah fuck."

"Is that what you want to do? Because you are saying that you still want to fuck me. Or you just want to keep having phone sex with me?"

"No, I want it."

"Ok, well get me a ticket."

"I've been in the gym, too. I want to pick your ass up and toss you against the wall."

"Ok."

"Fuck. You didn't see that I got bigger in the pictures. I gained like fifteen pounds."

"Really? No, I couldn't really tell. You're gonna send a picture of yourself and not a dick pic?"

"I don't know how and where to send it."

"You have my email."

"I can bench press like two hundred twenty now. I have three trainers. I'm trying to look like I just came out of jail. I hate being thin. I've been the same size since the tenth grade. I wanna gain weight. People always say I'm handsome, but I don't really like myself totally, if that makes sense."

"I know. I know you don't. I hate that about you because you're beautiful."

"I'm ok."

"You can't tell me how to give you compliments and just accept the compliment."

"Can you ride my face?"

"You gotta make it right with me. My favorite flowers are sunflowers. You know where I live."

"I don't have your address."

"Yes, you do. You had me served. You have my address. And I have your address."

These conversations via phone and video call would continue on for July, August, and then ended in September. The last calls happened in November. Maybe every two weeks, he would call and lovebomb me to have phone sex and then ghost me. He was only available on his schedule when he wanted to engage in sexual activities.

Journal Entries

June 2, 2021

> Yesterday, I spoke to him, and I recorded it. I think that the best way to get over him is by weaning myself off slowly. But he doesn't want to do that. He still speaks as if he had nothing to do with anything that happened between us. He says that basically it's all my fault. Now that I talked to him, I can move on. There is no future or hope between us. He's not right for me. I know it, and I will stay away.

June 5, 2021

Yesterday, I received a disturbing call from Kyrie during my counseling session with Ron. The night before, I left a message on his phone telling him that I found the answer to our problems. To cure my sexual urges, we could go to a sex/swingers club, and I could see him fulfill his fantasy of having sex with a man.

Well, he called me and proceeded to cuss me out. He told me to never call him again and that this has to stop. He also said that he doesn't love me and basically hates me and doesn't want me in his life. Ron heard the entire conversation and was appalled at the way that he was talking to me. I was once again hurt, angry, mad, and distraught, and I took up for myself. I just want this saga to end. I hate the way I feel, and I want to be out of this pain.

June 6, 2021

Today was rough. I was depressed the entire day. Morgan woke up at 5 a.m. and would not take a nap. It's extremely difficult going through all of this with a toddler. Every chance I got today, I tried to go to sleep. I am mentally and emotionally drained. I'm hurting on the inside. I have come to grips that it is over with Kyrie. It's been over, but I can't hope, wish, or think that anything positive is ever gonna come from him. I talked to Natalie, and I was crying my eyes out. I fell madly in love with someone and couldn't let it go until now. Wow! Six months later. My road to recovery starts now. I have my candle lit. I just took my shower, and I have a 24K Gold Facial Mask on. I'm going to slowly build myself up day by day. My therapist Ron told me to do three things every day. One: meditate. Two: say I Am's. Three: journal. I will overcome this pain. I will be a better Heather after this. I will grow.

June 7, 2021

Today, I woke up ok, but I have to meditate first to get my vibrations together. I took Morgan to school, but I was mean to her this morning. I don't want to be that person. I listened to the first chapter of Oprah's book. I have to change some things in how I am raising Morgan. No more cussing, yelling, and spanking unless it's absolutely necessary. I am about to light my candle, meditate, and pray. Today, I will work on my book, organize my class with my friend Kaycee, and handle all of my business for me.

June 8, 2021

I am doing the work. I am and will be healed. Natalie got me right last night. I'm not in a competition with anyone but myself. I'm the prize. I'm the only one who doesn't know it. I'm sitting here thinking I lost, but I've already won. Remember Heather, he calls you, not the other way around. He's now working out because of me and how good I look. He's encouraging the other women to eat right because of me. I have the power. Stay the course and continue to focus on me. Meditation, prayer, I Ams, praise, worship, and workout. Build Heather's empire. Day by day, step by step, moment by moment. Heal from within and step into your greatness.

June 14, 2021

It was all fake. It wasn't real. That's what I have to keep telling myself. I keep looking at his and Rittany's social media and looking at Big Mamma's through the window. I keep asking myself what they have on me? Nothing. Low self-esteem to stay with him and believe his bullshit. He put a restraining order against me. It really hit me on Friday after I left the mall. He doesn't give two shits about me doing something like that.

How can he have an order of protection against me, but he's still calling me! I hate him.

I'm doing the very best that I can. I think my friends are tired of me talking about Kyrie. I totally understand, but if I don't talk to them about him, he stays in my mind. Him putting the restraining order against me really blew me. It really resonates that he gives zero fucks about me. Everything was a lie. I spoke to the Number One Woman today, and she told me that he asked her to come visit. I wish he never acted so seriously with me. We could have just been fucking. Crazy. I'm gonna be ok though. His birthday is Wednesday June 16. I wrote Chapter 18 of the book today. It was hard to write.

June 16, 2021

Today is his birthday. Rittany posted a video tribute to him. There was one video that I remembered because it had a tag that she was at O'Hare Airport. As I looked at what he wore in the video, I realized that she drove him to the airport to come and visit me. He is the epitome of an ain't shit ass niggah! So they were together when we were together. Another lie comes out to the forefront. Yesterday during my counseling session, I had to face some hard truths. Why am I not mad at him? Why am I still feeling pain and not anger? It's because I still love him and want to be with him deep down. Even after all of the bullshit. This is a horrible place to be.

June 17, 2021

Today is very rough! I slept all day because I am depressed. I feel a hole in my body. I stopped doing my affirmations and such because Morgan keeps waking up and staying up all night. I've been masturbating to Kyrie's videos because they turn me on. I'm still very much so sexually stimulated by his voice and the presence of him. I have to get busy and do things that make me happy to get through this. I am ENOUGH. Thank you for my weight loss. I'm grateful for my house. Thank you for my friend, Malika. Thank you for waking me up today. I am grateful for Morgan. I am grateful for my real friends. I love the woman I am becoming. I LOVE HEATHER. I am grateful for Heather. My friend Malika had a terrible relationship with a narcissist, and she is helping me get through this.

June 18, 2021

Today, I did amazing! I went to the mall with my friend Anthony from LA and had a great time! I did me today! I took pics and felt really good. I wore my new Armani Exchange clothes and looked amazing. I am proud of myself for today.

June 20, 2021

Today was GREAT! Kyrie called twice: once from his Google Voice Number at 11:40 a.m. and then again from an Illinois number. I didn't answer! I am so proud of myself! I just started cleaning and getting busy and playing with Morgan on EGO. I went live and was dancing and having a great time. I mopped, cooked, organized, and went to Big Lots. I'm so proud of myself. I can't answer his call because I don't want to go to jail. So I won't. If I do, I will state that you have a restraining order against me, why are you calling? Today was a good day.

I think he is calling me again because Big Mamma is mad at him for all of the posts that his girlfriend and him are making about their birthdays. I was window licking her live and heard her talking about it with Candy.

June 25, 2021

Today was great! Carlos, my best friend, came into town. Also yesterday, we came back from

Huntsville, Alabama, from *Baby Shark Live*. Morgan had a blast. The day after my last entry, Kyrie called four times. I answered the last time and talked to him. He's psycho. I asked him why he was calling me because he has a restraining order against me. He said he didn't know. I think he was calling me to have phone sex. I told him no and that he had to make me know it: send me sunflowers, make reservations to visit, to have dinner.

I gained my power back from this conversation. He was in the palm of my hand. I recorded the conversation. I also held him to task for the rest of the conversation. I was asking all of the hard questions. It's funny because all he would do was deflect when asked something. He's really cray-cray, but unfortunately, I still love him. It was also Rittnany's birthday week. So after Monday night, I haven't heard from him because he is with her. It's very interesting. I think he loves her, but he doesn't like her. Tonight, Carlos and I went out, and we had a blast. I haven't felt this good in a very long time. We danced and turned it out. I also looked very sexy in my leopard skirt!

June 28, 2021

Today was very productive. It's been a week since I spoke to Kyrie. He's probably trying to do right by his girlfriend. I'm not gonna fall for this shit again, getting excited to get let down. It sucks.

Kyrie was a true narcissist. Heather was doing very well this month in spite of his narc characteristics. She was getting stronger and stronger. His cycle of lovebombing followed by devaluation was intense. His gaslighting making her disbelieve reality or making her feel like she was losing her grasp on reality was exhausting. Kyrie constantly making her the enemy or the bad guy for having feelings and reactions was over the top. Also his constant lying to avoid responsibility, never being at fault for any issues in the relationship and turning all of the blame on her continued to wear on her psyche and soul. But the icing on the cake was his huge sense of entitlement. He thought that everything was owed to him.

STORY 32
July

July—my birthday month! I turned forty-five years old on the fifteenth. I wanted this month to be very special because I needed to relieve some stress and have fun! I wanted my b-day to be amazing and top Kyrie's and his girlfriends. I know that was petty, but that's how I felt. So I planned to have an amazing custom-made jumpsuit designed. It was beautiful, but the designer was trash because it arrived late.

I planned an absolutely amazing party celebration at a rooftop club in Cincinnati. I also had my second milestone photo shoot with sixty pounds lost! I looked beautiful! I was so proud of myself!

When I went home to Cincinnati, I connected with my former student Kourtney and my cousin Mecole. This was the first time that I heard and saw the validation in my weight loss. I looked TF good! Every chance that I had to go out, I did. I was so excited to be outside and be with my family.

My birthday was amazing! We had a blast. Then a few days later, we did some yacht shit. I chartered a yacht and invited ten of my closest friends to cruise on the Cincinnati River with me. I looked great and felt great. In spite of everything that was going on with Kyrie, I was trying my best to do me and feel good doing it.

A week after my birthday, I traveled to Mexico with my cousin. I truly lived my best life!

I had such an amazing time when we went to Mexico. I felt like I was twenty-two. My cousin Mecole was such a blessing to me with helping me through this entire situation. She was patient, kind, and compassionate. I love her down!

Mecole's friends Belinda and Neicy also came to Mexico with us. We were dressed to the nines and enjoyed the views, the pools, and especially the drinks. It was a great way to stop thinking about Kyrie. I felt like a new person when I returned home.

During this month, Kyrie and I spoke many times with the usual lovebombing he did and the gaslighting to get me to have phone sex with him. It worked every time. I especially wanted him to be there for me on my birthday. He actually called and texted me the night before when I was at my party. He asked me if I had some birthday dick. He loved asking me about the guys that I was seeing and how they compared to him. I told him that I had sex with my high school sweetheart. No matter how much he would hurt me, Kyrie always had a way of reeling me back in. Every time he did this, I fell for it. I tried to call him after my party to see him, but he ghosted me and said that he was with his girlfriend.

July 14, 2021, Phone Call with Kyrie

"Why are you jealous of me doing something with another dude?" I asked.

"Because I think it should be me."

"Do you want it to be you?"

"I do, but I'm pretty sure that's impossible."

"Why is it impossible?"

"You're in Atlanta, and I'm in Chicago."

"So you are basically saying you don't want it to happen."

"It's not that."

"But…What?"

"I don't know, Heather. I don't know."

"You want me to come to Chicago?"

"Maybe, I've been thinking about it. I just don't want the drama. I don't have time for it."

"Drama meaning you don't want me to."

"I'm just trying to trust you and your emotions and the way you react, but it's stuff I can't come back from. It's like I don't know, and I'm just being honest and realistic. Although you might think differently. I have a five-year relationship, and it's amazing. She will leave me, she will. Then what am I gonna have? Already you have done shit. I'm just being realistic with myself."

"Ok. So I'm not gonna contact your girlfriend."

"Even with that, it's so much."

"So much what? What are you talking about?"

"The watchin' of Big Mamma's live broadcast. I'm not trying to go through all of that. I felt like I was in fucking high school. EGO was extra money for me. That would be dope right now if I had that. I'm not comfortable going on EGO, truth be told, because of you. Every time I go live, I'm uncomfortable. I see two EGO TV watchers. Niggahs have literally left my whole platform because of my emotional shit. Like I'm gonna do all of this to bust a nut. Like is it worth it?"

"Is it just busting a nut or is it more than that? I just want you to be honest. I want to know the truth. I'm willing to tell you my truth if you are willing to listen to it. Do you want to hear it?"

"What do you mean?"

"You have really fucked me up," I said. "Like I'm literally... if you don't tell me that we are going to hook up. Me coming to the Chi or you coming to ATL. I'm gonna have to cut this off. I'm not gonna be able to talk to you anymore. I'm gonna have to go cold turkey, no masturbating, no looking at you. I'm gonna have to remove you from my life because I can't function sexually. My shit is broken. And it's only gonna work for you, and I have to get rid of that. If we are not gonna see each other or we aren't gonna fuck again, I'm tapping out. I can't keep doing this. You got your life with your stuff. Don't worry about me. You do you, and you will be great. You can move on and go on about living a beautiful life with your girlfriend, but I can't keep thinking we are gonna do something, and we are not."

"But what happens when everything happens all over again? I love you, I really need you. Then you are gonna hit Rittany up again. Contact her mom, the church. I don't have time for all of that."

"Kyrie, honestly, I can't be with you. I can't take you seriously as someone I would date. For real."

"So you want me to be a cool friend forever?"

"I mean. If you had kept it one hundred with me from the beginning, we could have been the best of friends and just been cool as shit."

"OK, you keep saying keep it real with you. I was on a break. I didn't have anything to tell you if I wasn't in a relationship. This is why I don't want to even move forward because regardless of what I'm saying, you still have what's in your mind."

"You never told me that you were on a break, Kyrie. You never said that."

"I don't have to because I was single. I didn't see Rittany until a month after I saw you. What is it for me to say?"

"It doesn't even matter. I'm not trying to argue with you."

"There is always a constant back and forth with you about this timeline. At the end of the day, I never forced you to open your legs and put my penis inside of you. It takes two."

"But at the same time, all of the stuff that you told me—"

"I know what I told you, but let's be realistic. Like you literally wanted me to stop my life and move to Atlanta."

"No, I didn't."

"I swear to God you said that you were gonna put a sewing machine in your house."

"Ok. Hypothetically, I did say that, but I was just joking, and we were getting to know each other."

"Yes, we were, but you went from zero to five hundred. You did and you said my sex was amazing. You know how many people have amazing sex?"

"Kyrie, I've never had sex with nobody the way that I had it with you. That's never happened."

"Maybe it's because you really haven't experienced life."

"No, babe," I said.

"I didn't do anything new and nothing special."

"Yes, you did. So what you wanna do?"

"I don't know. I'm trying to think. I'm not saying that I'm not gonna release the restraining order. I'm actually trying to figure that out and couldn't, so I need to call my lawyer and figure out how to do that. I don't have no problem doing that, and I'm not trying to fuck you up in the process. I'm just trying to not fuck up my peace of mind, which is very important to me."

"I really feel like I can't be one-hundred percent honest with you because you will get mad, and I don't want you to. And I don't want to fuck up your energy." I was really hoping that we were good. He seemed to be trying to move in the right direction or so I thought.

At the end of the month, he would ask me to send videos. I never did. But I used this as an opportunity to get some leverage with him. It didn't work though. I told him to be available and then maybe I could send something to him. When I was back home in Atlanta, I thought that he was going to come and visit me. Well, actually, he played me.

He never had any intention of coming to visit me, and we had an argument about it. I told him to stop playing games with me. I really wanted him to visit so that we could have sex one more time. That's all I thought I wanted. I wasn't successful. He didn't come. He told me that he was broke and couldn't afford it. I offered to pay, and he still ghosted me. I was disappointed. While I was in Mexico, he also took a trip to Miami with Big Mamma and the Regular Retreats family. They were very hush-hush about the trip and didn't post any pics or go live on EGO when they were there. I'm glad I was in Mexico so that I could keep my mind off of it.

One person who helped me was She-Bad.

I met her in June on EGO from one of my friend supporters, Excellent C. She-Bad was a lesbian and would come by my live broadcast and comment and gift me. She seemed very nice.

Excellent C also said that She-Bad and I had a lot in common because she had just broken up from a narcissistic relationship as well. We exchanged numbers and talked on the phone about our dealings with our narcissists. She was very kind and patient and was a great person to vent to. She was also beautiful! If I would talk to a girl, she would be one that I would date. We started to talk on the phone from time to time, but she didn't know that I was attracted to girls. She would always come by my live broadcast and also liked my pics on my social media platforms. She would flirt with me as well.

One day when she did that, I flirted back and messaged, "You better watch it now, girl, because I will definitely take you down! LOL!"

When I got back from Mexico, I was in a fearless mood and shot my shot. I told her that I had a crush on her. She couldn't believe it. I told her that I thought she was so beautiful. She said that she was blushing and asked had I ever been with a girl? I told her that I had only had a threesome, but I was attracted to girls.

Things started to move very quickly with her. But I was honest with her from the very beginning. I told her that I would like to have a sexual experience from her, a seasoned lesbian. I told her that I very much liked penis but wanted to experience the real deal. She said that she understood. Unfortunately, we spoke about Kyrie a lot, and she helped me process a lot of things. She was a Godsend to me. The two and a half months that I spoke to her were amazing. We poured into each other, and she especially poured into me. I will always love her for that. It got real when she really started having real feelings for me and couldn't handle the relationship. I truly cared for her but couldn't be serious with her like she wanted to be with me. We eventually had to part ways because of this.

July Journal Entries

July 3, 2021

My friend Edwin came into town to help me with Morgan. I was very grateful for him. I've been thinking about Kyrie a lot. I'm gonna soon stop looking at his pages. I can let him go. I can move on now.

July 5-6, 2021

At 3:10 a.m. and then 3:47 a.m., he called me. I was asleep. He texted me at 4:42 p.m.

"Hello."

I texted back at 8:41 p.m.: "Hey You."

He texted me the next morning at 2:39 a.m.: "What are you up 2?"

"I can't sleep," I said. We continued texting back and forth. He's very vague, and I have to try hard for him to call me. But eventually, he called me, and we had video phone sex. It was great. I recorded the conversation. My end goal was to see him again, but I don't think he wants that. Later that day, I had a massage and tried to call him to tell him about it. He didn't answer and didn't call back.

July 7, 2021

Good day today. I had a photo shoot for my second milestone of losing sixty pounds. I looked and felt great! I didn't think about him a lot today. I feel like I'm getting better and better.

July 8, 2021

We talked and had video sex. I recorded the encounter.

July 13, 2021

He texted me at 10:00 p.m.

July 29, 2021

He called me, and we talked for two hours. I recorded the conversation.

I felt like I was doing better. July was a good month. I traveled, had an amazing birthday, and had a special friend who was keeping my mind off of Kyrie. For once, I felt like I was doing well mentally and emotionally. I felt like I could breathe.

STORY 33
August, The Fall Out

July was an amazing month for me! I really got my natural life. At the beginning of the month, Kyrie texted me saying that I looked nice on my trip, and he was sure that I enjoyed myself. I kept it brief in my reply and told him that it was amazing. I didn't write anything else because I was tired of playing the games with him. I was at home in Cincinnati and trying to just really move on the best way that I could. I didn't respond as quickly as before, so when I did that, he would text me more.

Then he sent me a full-body nude picture of himself, telling me that his body was changing, and he didn't know if I would still like him. Then he called me on video. I didn't answer.

"You must be upset," he texted.

We spoke on the phone that night. He was really fishing for compliments from me about his weight gain. I didn't give them to him. I started sending him pics of my new hair color and body to see if he would give me compliments, and he didn't.

I then sent him a video telling him how good he looked because ignoring Kyrie wasn't working. I was trying a new approach for a different outcome. He didn't respond. After a few days, I sent him a pic of me in Cancun in my bathing suit, holding my butt and asked him what was he gonna do with this? I told him that I honestly couldn't stop thinking about him. I also told him to bring his Speedos to show off that beautiful body when he came to Atlanta because I wanted to break the pool in.

"Shit," he replied, "why do you keep doing this to me?"

"What did I do?"

He then video called me, and we had video phone sex. This time, it was different. He told me that he loved me and that he wanted to be with me and that he couldn't live without me. This was the one time I didn't record the conversation and wished I had. I hadn't heard him say these kinds of things to me in a very long time. I wanted to believe it and did sorta kinda, but I knew that there was always a chance that he was lying like he always did.

After we had phone sex, I continued to text and call him, but he didn't respond. I was trying to see what his plans were for when he came to Atlanta so that I could be there before my Miami trip. He made it extremely difficult for me because he didn't give me definite answers, or he didn't respond at all.

I finally got fed up with it and stopped calling and texting. He then video called me at 1 a.m., but I didn't answer. I was tired of the ghosting and bullshit. This was the night before he left to go to Cancun with his girlfriend.

Nine days later, I texted and called him, but he didn't respond. I sent him pics of myself to try to entice him to call me, but it didn't work.

Not too long after this, he called me in the early morning to ask me if … I'll let you hear for yourself.

"Did you call me yesterday or maybe the day before from a private number and hung up the phone?" he asked.

"Why would I do that? I call you direct."

"I don't know. I'm just asking a question. You're also countersuing me?"

"I'm countersuing you?"

"You're suing me for something now?"

"Kyrie, I told you that I had a court case against you a long time ago. I filed that in April. I told you that. You don't remember that?"

"What is this for?"

"It's for everything that we've always talked about, all of the money that you owe me that I've been trying to get back for months. All of the unresolved issues."

"It's not unresolved if you got a reversed Cash App on your account and you got your money back."

"Do you remember when your aunt reversed a Cash App on my account?" I asked.

"My aunt ain't me. Why don't you sue her?"

"Because that was money that came from you. She was paying on your behalf."

"This is another reason I'm not coming to Atlanta. What the fuck do you want from me, bro?"

"First of all, Kyrie, we can have an adult conversation without disrespecting each other."

"This is an adult conversation. If you take me to court, you are not gonna see me."

"Just like you have a restraining order against me that is still in place that you haven't reversed. What's up with that? I've told you before many times that I did not want to take you to court. I've tried many times to have a conversation with you to resolve this."

"You're not getting no money from me. I don't owe you anything," he said.

"Ok. I've asked you several times to reverse the restraining order against me. Have you done that?"

"I haven't gone to nobody's court, and the last time I talked to my lawyer, it was about a more important court case that I'm dealing with. *That's* what I talked to my lawyer about, not you."

"You put in paperwork against me, Kyrie, when I'm not even harassing you."

"You was."

"No I wasn't."

"You hit my aunt up and told her I was a faggot. You sent Rittany an email, that's harassment."

"That's not harassment."

"That's why the Illinois state courts processed the restraining order."

"You put a restraining order against me, Kyrie, but you are still calling me. You are still talking to me."

"Did I tell you that I booked a trip to Atlanta?"

"I don't even know what you are talking about. I haven't talked to you, Kyrie. You haven't called me."

"When's the last time you've seen me? This is the reason I'm moving the way I'm moving. You don't make no sense."

"I told you the truth. You thought I didn't file a court case against you, and I told you several times that I would. You just didn't believe me."

"I'm not going to go. I have a restraining order against you. My lawyer is gonna go, but I don't have to go. I don't have to appear, and that's the law. You can keep the case, but it's probably gonna get thrown out. At the end of the day, you go tit for tat."

At that point, I got very upset and heated. This was the first time that I fought back and went toe to toe with him and took up for myself. I was very proud of this moment.

"I'm not going tit for tat with you, Kyrie!" I yelled. "I told you that I fucking filed that shit in April, my niggah! Just like you filed your shit in March! OK, and it's just getting to you now! I told you that!"

"You sound vexed. You gotta raise your voice?"

"Yeah, because I've never raised my voice at you, and I'm sick of this shit! I'm sick of you playing with my emotions. I'm sick of you playing with my heart. I'm sick of you lying. I'm sick of you gaslighting. I'm sick of you being a gotdamn narcissist! It's all about yo' black ass! Always."

"No, it's not."

"Yes it is! It's always about you! I ain't did nothing but try to love you, try to take care of you, try to be in your life, and try to do it respectfully. And you keep spitting in my face."

"You love the theory of me. You love my penis. Jump in line. I don't owe you shit."

"You don't owe me shit. Like you said, you got a restraining order against me, so you don't have to call me no more, Kyrie. I'll see you in November."

"You're not gonna see me."

"Ok, I'll see your attorney in November for the first court case that you have against me, and then I will see them for my case against you. We can settle all of this in court like we were supposed to do from the beginning. I've tried my best."

"You just want to be a factor so bad."

"I don't want to be a factor."

"It's not working for your regular life, so you just want it to work by all means possible. This is what's flying over your head. The life that you are looking to get out of me, sweetie, you're never gonna get."

"I don't want a life with you," I said.

"Really? You do want a life with me. You do."

"I don't. I don't want a life with you."

"You check my shit. Remember, I don't check for you."

"Baby, I haven't been checking for you either. I was just trying to fuck you one more time. That's all I was trying to do. And now I don't want to do that because you fucking disgust me. Okay."

"You have been disgusting to me."

This was where I got my power back. My tone changed, and I took charge. He was shaken, too. He didn't know what to say or how to handle my confidence.

"I can't tell, sweetie," I boldly said. "The way that you call me and the way that you want to video fuck me all the time. I can't tell that I disgust you by the way that you are all up sniffing under my ass. You love my pussy, and you love me! So you can cut the bullshit."

"You must be feeling yourself since you had the bypass."

"Baby, I have *been* feeling myself. Because I've been that bitch! One hundred percent, and you know that's why you wanted me and that's why you can't leave me alone, Kyrie."

"You're not even an inch of a bitch that I'm used to dealing with."

"Because you're used to dealing with clowns. Here's the deal, sweetie. Don't let me contact Miss Rittany again since you wanna play."

"And say what, motherfucker?"

"You wanna find out? Don't let me contact that church, Kyrie, and let them know all of your tea. If that's what you want to do! Since you want to hurt feelings and you wanna go there. I have not unleashed the kraken of what I can unleash. I don't want to do that, but if you keep talking crazy and out the side of your neck to me, I'm gonna unleash it. So don't fuck with me, Kyrie. Don't fuck with me! You don't want to go to war with a soldier!"

"Heather, please. Thank you for the audition. I don't care to interact with…you really don't get it."

"You really don't get it. Because you're crazy. Because you're a sociopath and a psychopath. You don't get it."

"Wow and you're the only one who believes that."

"Because you have them all fooled, Kyrie."

"Did that feel good? You feel better about yourself?"

"I've always felt great about myself. You came into my life and tried to fuck up my life. That's what you've done."

"I only called you to see if you called me from a private number."

"No, I call you straight up." I had no shame in calling him out!

"So, is the conversation done?"

I hung up on him.

I felt so good after this. I felt like I got my power back; I was in control. I stood up for myself. I wasn't going to allow him to control me any longer. He literally wasn't ready for what I was saying and giving to him. He was such a habitual liar, and I called him out on all of his bullshit! I thought for certain that our toxic ass relationship was done.

I thought that this was going to be the end of the book for sure and was ready for it to end. At the same time, I felt like I was grieving a death. I felt lost after this fight. I didn't want it to end, but it was. I was sick about it.

<u>August Journal Entries</u>

August 15, 2021

I sent him pics of me from Cancun in my bathing suit. We video call to have phone sex. He tells me that he loves me and many other wonderful things that I have never heard him say before. Then he ghosts me, and I haven't spoken to him again.

August 30, 2021

He calls me, and we have a big argument. It's over.

August 31, 2021

For the past two months, we have been in communication. Yesterday was the final straw. I stood up for myself and told him the truth. I finally fought back and didn't go along with his bullshit. I had had enough. No more gaslighting, no more fake promises, no more lies. I was done. I didn't want to participate in his trickery and games any longer. I am moving onward and upward. Today, after my triumphant victory in the conversation, I feel like I am mourning the death of a loved one. I feel like something is missing and empty. I'm tired. I'm tired of struggling and not having the support that I need to survive. I cried to my new friend She-Bad, and she is so supportive and sweet. I'm so happy that I have her in my life. Kyrie took so much from and out of me, and she is replenishing my soul.

STORY 34
September

I traveled to Miami for the college football classic, and as soon as I arrived, I was already over it because my best friend caught COVID, and he was my road dawg, I didn't like the hotel that I stayed at, and it rained every day in Miami. I contemplated getting a plane ticket and going back to Atlanta.

Thinking Kyrie was in Atlanta, I texted him. "I'm thinking about flying back to Atlanta. My best friend caught COVID and isn't coming to Miami. And this hotel sucks." He didn't respond to that text or the several calls I made. Every minute that passed increased my anxiety and loneliness.

I desperately needed to talk to him.

He texted me back two days later: "I'm not even in Atlanta. I told you that. SMFH."

He eventually called me back.

"Don't hang up on me," I demanded.

"Heather, what is the goal? What are you trying to do? What are you trying to accomplish today?"

"I want to be able to have a conversation with you, where we can be respectful of each other."

"But why? I don't want it."

"Ok, so you are telling me that you don't want it now? If you don't want to talk to me, can I see your face? Because I need to get this out."

"You getting it out."

"I need to see your face to get this out."

"No, you don't, Heather."

"Yes, I do."

"You don't need all the stuff that you think you need. I'm answering the phone, and I really shouldn't be doing that. Like what is the point? This is toxic as fuck. Like for what? God. What do you want from me? Like I'm trying to be good, and you keep taking me backwards, bro. What do you want from me? I don't want to talk to someone in which there is a chance … Look, I don't trust you. I'm sorry. There is no conversation that we can have where I can do so.

"Your actions, I don't care what excuse you have, what emotion you wanna express. You act like a fucking little ass girl whose feelings got hurt. No one wants to deal with that. You keep on thinking that your life is more beneficial than mine. I have shit to lose, just like any real person."

"I have shit to lose, too, Kyrie, and you have a whole restraining order against me. That could, for us talking on the phone, send me to jail and have me losing my daughter. Do you want that to happen to me?"

"Now because that can happen to you, I now have to acquiesce my mind and be on the phone with you because you are gonna lose your child?"

"No, I'm not saying that."

"So, what are you asking me?"

I was on eggshells talking because I didn't want to upset him and cause him to hang up on me.

"I wanna speak my truth," I said. "I don't want you to hang up. And I want you to hear me out and don't respond to respond. But listen to what I'm saying to you."

"Heather, I'm gonna give you like two-three minutes, and you can explain what you have to say."

"Kyrie, you have equal responsibility in this. This was supposed to have been over. You've called me. You've told me things that have entrapped me back into this. I've tried to leave you alone several times. I was ok with us moving on, but every time you call me, and you engage in activities with me, that opens my feelings back up.

"So, you are saying you don't trust me and don't want this, but on the opposite end of that, you keep calling me and having phone sex with me and telling me that you love me. Telling me all of these different things. I don't know why you tell me those things if you don't feel that way.

"I don't know what to believe or trust in you. I was willing to just go along with the program just to feel the things that I wanted to feel again. But like you said, this is toxic. But it doesn't have to be toxic. I know that I am open with my feelings, but you are not open with your true feelings."

"Heather, I really want you to understand this. Mentally, I want to be by myself. I want to leave everybody alone. I'm not happy about my life and me talking to you is not gonna make me any happier. I can't. Because honestly, any further, Kyrie is gonna pull a trigger and blow his head off, and you are gonna see me in the newspaper. I can't keep doing this. Every time I say I can't, it's like I literally am about to explode. You're like I just want to get it out.

"Do you fucking hear what I'm saying? Since December, I've been scared to live a life because I have you in the back of my mind. That's psychotic. I don't want to post on social media because I feel like people are watching me. I don't want to do anything. I don't want to be who I am because of me channeling people like this. This is the dumbest shit I've ever done. I'm good. I'm fucking good, man. I'm good. I haven't called you in like two weeks. Just let me rock. Let me rock. Damn, yo."

"Well, I don't want you to be ill or psychotic."

"I'm already ill and mental disorders actually run in my family. I'm literally gonna be fucking sick. Sicker than I am. I'm losing weight. I'm throwing up every day. I'm shitting blood. I don't know what else you want from me. This is the main reason I am not going to Atlanta because the minute I get to the airport, all I'm gonna think about is you, and I'm not gonna think about what I came out there for. I'm supposed to be out there right now winning four thousand mother fucking dollars. But I'm here."

"Why are you thinking about me, and you say you don't like me?"

"Are you crazy? Did you not just hear anything I just said?"

"I did, but I don't understand what you are saying."

"That's the problem," he said.

"Make me understand."

"I can't further explain anything. Neither do I care to be on the phone. This is taking the life out of me. You want me in your life, but you've already drained me before I get in."

"I don't want you to feel this way."

"I've been feeling this way for months. I got pills. A gun. You don't know. You think it's about you."

"You've never told me." I began to cry. " I don't want you to be sick. I don't want you to hurt. I love you enough to let you go, alright? So you won't hear from me. I don't want any bad shit to happen to you. I want you to be healthy."

"Bad shit is already happening to me."

"Ain't no bad shit gon' happen from me. So I wanna wish you all the positivity and good vibes that you can have the best life."

"I don't even feel that I am enough to create something. You're fine. Aren't you on a Nutrisystem Box or something or some shit like that?"

"You're enough."

"Just leave me alone."

He hung up.

"Wow, wow, wow. I don't even know what to say about that," I whispered.

After that call, I texted him: "I pray for healing for you. I never wanted to hurt you. I will always love you and be rooting for you to win. I love you enough to let you go. If you need me, I am here for you."

I then texted him two days later, "I hope u r ok. Praying for you."

I was extremely worried about him from our conversation. It was very disturbing, but I knew that I could leave him alone if he was in such a desperate state. I didn't want him to hurt or feel any pain. If I could help ease the way he felt, I would do that. So that's what I did. I was ready to leave him alone because he was going to hurt himself over me.

Six days later, he texted me, "I hate that I can't stop thinking of you."

Whaaaaaaaaaat!?

After all that he said to me, now this? He told me that he wanted to kill himself. He told me that he was sick and couldn't function because of me. He told me once again to leave him be. But now he was saying that he hate that he couldn't stop thinking of me? This dude was certifiably nuts!

He then called me the next day.

September 11, 2021

"I know I'm not supposed to answer the phone, and I know I'm not supposed to talk to you, but I would hate it if I didn't answer and something happened to you," I said. "I love you so much, and I don't want to not pick up and something happened to you, and you needed me. Are you ok?"

"I know I said all that stuff to you the other day, but I need to really fix and try to drop this restraining order. I don't want you in jail. I don't want your kid being taken away from you. I'm not trying to do anything malicious to you. Half of this was my aunt's doing."

"So you saying that your aunt made you do all of that stuff?"

"Yes, and it's just a lot. It doesn't even matter. I'm just gonna try and fix it. I'm sorry I sent you that message."

"What message?"

"That I can't stop thinking of you."

"Ok."

"It probably made you uncomfortable, and I wasn't trying to do that."

I had to listen to the recording that he sent me. "Weeks ago?"

"Yeah of you touching yourself. I know I shouldn't be playing with my dick thinking about you. I should not be doing it."

"Nah, you shouldn't."

"Why?"

"Because you don't like me, you don't want me."

"You know why I'm upset, right?" he asked.

"No, I don't."

"Because you are fucking other Niggahs. I'm getting jealous of how sexual you are with them and the fact that you be cummin', and it's not with me."

"You don't want me to do it with you."

"Then why do I wake up and touch myself and think about doing it with you?"

"Do you really want to do it with me?"

"Are you recording me?"

"No. I'm just confused because you give me so many mixed signals," I said.

"I was gonna come to Atlanta, just to see you. But I hurt myself. My hand is like fucked right now. I can't even open a pair of scissors. I'm happy I didn't go because three of my friends got shot."

"At the Marquette?"

"Um hmm. Even Temi got hit."

"Wow. Can you travel?"

"Yeah, I can. It's getting better. I'm just in physical therapy."

"I'm going to Cleveland next week to film a reality show. You wanna meet me there?"

"I have a ball next week. In Chicago on Saturday."

"Do you want to meet me Wednesday through Saturday, the fifteenth through the eighteenth?" I asked.

"Yes, possibly. I can try. I want to fuck you until you forget about the masseuse."

"I wanna be your woman."

"You do?"

"I do. I wanna be your girlfriend."

"Fuck, Heather. Ummm."

"I love you so much, and I miss you so much."

"Um. Fuck. I feel like we would be so nasty together."

"Nasty sexually?"

"Yes."

"That's a good thing, right?"

"Would you have a threesome with me?" he asked.

"I sure would."

"Did you fuck that girl?"

"Not yet."

"Does she like dick?"

"No, she doesn't. She knows all about you, and she told me that she wanted to watch us have sex. She really loves me."

"Fuck. I've been touching myself since you got on this phone."

"You know I have a daughter, so you are gonna have to call at certain times when I'm not mommying."

"Sorry."

"I have a house guest now, too. So I can't move and shake like I used to."

"Sorry for being selfish. Sorry, I shouldn't have called you."

"I'm not saying you shouldn't call me. You need to call at certain times when she is asleep."

"I'm sorry."

"How are you gonna explain your feelings to your aunt about me?"

"She's not my mom. I don't need permission to live."

"But you always go to her when you are in trouble and need help."

"I don't go to her. She's just around and is a go-to person, but I don't always go to her. You've just seen a bad example because we had a bad experience. That's it."

"You know when I said what I said about contacting Rittany and the church, I only said that to make you mad. I'm not gonna do that. You don't have to worry about that."

"Why do I keep thinking about you riding me?"

"I probably can do that well now because I can move."

"But I wanna be the one that makes you squirt."

"Well, meet me in Cleveland."

"Did somebody do it yet?"

"No."

"Are you lying?"

"No. I don't lie to you, Kyrie. I don't have any reason to lie to you. I don't have time for that."

"Did you fuck somebody in Miami?"

"No, I tried, but I wasn't successful. I was so upset. Then when I got back here, I was supposed to do something else with this guy, but he flaked on me."

"So you still fucking the masseuse?"

"I was supposed to fuck him when I got back, too, but his schedule didn't line with mine. So I haven't fucked nobody, Kyrie."

"Good."

"Good for you, but not good for me. How often are you having sex with Rittany?"

"We had sex like three days ago."

"Do you make her squirt?"

"Yeah."

"You do? Has she always done that?"

"Not until she got with me. I made her pee on herself."

"How did you do that?"

"I just kept fucking the shit out of her."

"Um."

"I made Big Mamma squirt."

"You did? Do you still talk to her?"

"Does it matter?"

"Yeah, it does."

"Why?"

"You just asked me about the masseuse and everybody else in Miami. I can't ask you questions?"

"Yeah, I still talk to her."

"She still wanna be with you?"

"No, we just have a friendship."

"You sure about that? Does she know that?"

"She knows about Rittany and all this other stuff. It's very complicated."

"Does she know you still talk to me?"

"No."

"Nobody knows you still talk to me."

"No. Except for one of my friends, Karon; you don't know him. He's been my friend since the seventh grade."

"What did he tell you to do about me?"

"It's like unresolved, no closure."

"I'm about to eat breakfast and then work out. I can't be on the phone that much longer."

"I guess I called you at a bad time."

"You asked me what my goal was. What is your goal, Kyrie, for me?"

"I don't know. But I just need to figure out why I care about you so much and why it won't go away."

"I mean do you really care about me? Like honestly or are you trying? I know you are attracted to me, but this is just you wanting to have sex with me or you just wanting to have phone sex with me when you want to?"

"It's more than that. Because I want to see you. I want you in my lap right now. You should be making me cum and not my hand."

"I was really just gonna come to Chicago and call you and be like, 'Hey, I'm here, can you meet me?' but I was scared because you got this restraining order against me."

"You gon' let me eat your pussy?" he asked.

"Yes."

"And your ass?"

"Yes. You gon' let me eat your ass?"

"I am. You gon' put your fingers in it?"

"I'm gonna let you be the one that leads the freaky conversation and what you want to do freaky. Because I don't want you to get offended or be mad at me. Whatever you want to do, we can do it."

"I want you to fuck me, too."

"You do?"

"Yes."

"Like how?" I asked.

"I want you to buy a strap-on and fuck me."

"Ok. I just go to the sex store and get one of those?"

"I guess. I've never done it before, but I want to do it with you."

"So, Kyrie, how are you with all of these other girls if you can't be open and free with them? They judge you, and I'm not gonna judge you."

"I don't know."

"You are so mean to me. All I want to do is accept you for who you are, and I never called you the F-word. I think somebody else called you that or that's how you see yourself, and you don't wanna see yourself as that, but I never called you that."

"You wanna fuck a man with me, don't you?"

"I do. I wanna watch it, yes. I wanna do it, yes."

"You wanna see me take dick?" he asked.

"I want you to be comfortable, and I want you to be able to live your life and live your truth and be ok in that. I want you to love yourself for who you are. It's ok that you are pansexual. You like men, women, and transexuals. You don't have to keep saying that you like women. It's ok."

"What if he makes me cum in front of you?"

"Then I accept that. I don't give a fuck. You don't see that I love your muthafuckin' ass?"

He moaned.

"You don't see that shit?" I repeated myself. "I don't even care. I want to go to the balls with you and see you walk and support you. I ain't never felt like this over no motherfucker. Ever."

"My dick misses you so much. So much. I miss you so much."

Here I am pouring my heart out to Kyrie. I'm literally telling him that I will accept him truly for who he is. Every time I confide in him, he takes it to the sexual realm. This was a clear indication of him manipulating me. Abusing me in a subtle way. I didn't get it though. I had hope in him. I wanted to believe that he was a good person. I didn't get it.

"I can't keep doing this, Kyrie. You cussing me out and throwing me away and then calling me back. I cannot. If you keep talking to me in a crazy way, I'm not meek and mild. I got a mouth, and I got clapback."

"I'm not calling you with that. It's not even necessary."

"I just need you to know that. When you get mad, you can't—"

"I know what fire you got; why you think I like you?"

"I don't know. I'm trying to figure this shit out, like what the fuck is going on here?"

Telling me that he likes me because of my fire was him using "breadcrumbs" to manipulate and gaslight me. This was his tactic to keep me engaged to want more. Each breadcrumb would keep me coming back.

"I was so mad. I wanted to be your birthday dick. I wanted to fuck you after you got off that boat. I should be the one with you in these different countries. Fuck the shit out of you in the jacuzzi."

"So you are looking at my stuff."

"Yes. All I keep thinking about is who you fucking while you are there. Because I know you need to be touched."

Can we please make a promise to each other and be respectful? Whatever this is, don't shut me out."

"Ok."

"Don't not call me." I was concerned.

"Ok."

"Don't not answer my calls. If you are having a moment where you are like, 'Heather, I can't whatever,' just tell me that you are having a morality issue or whatever it is. just say it. But whatever it is, don't shut me out. I can't do it."

"I don't want to be fucking nobody else and to not think about you is not gonna work. I've tried."

"Well, what are you gon' do because you have a whole girlfriend."

"She ain't satisfying me. If she did, I would have never fucked you."

"But you be fucking a lot of people, Kyrie."

"I really do not."

"Not now, but you are stepping out on her a lot."

"I really don't."

"Ok. So why do you stay with her if you are not satisfied?"

"Because it seems like the right thing to do. She's just that type of girl that you should marry, and I don't know."

"I can stay on for five more minutes, and then I gotta go. Did you enjoy having sex with Big Mamma?"

"Yeah."

"When is the next time you are going to see her?"

"Depends."

"I know you tell me that she is just a friend, but I know she thinks it's more than that."

"Are you gonna have sex with somebody else?"

"I don't have anybody to have sex with," I said. "I've been on the apps, but nothing definite. I be horny all the time, and I be trying not to use the Rose because it deactivates my clitoris. I'm so horny, and I don't have anyone to have sex with, so I just masturbate and try to satisfy my craving. But I can't. The only thing that is gonna satisfy it is you. I've tried several times to connect with you to see when we could arrange a meeting. But you say you don't trust me, and all I'm trying to do is make love to you."

"You wanna make love to me?"

"Yes."

Once again, pouring my heart out, professing my love for him. My sheer acceptance of him and nothing but confusion.

"You would have been pregnant by now if we would have been on since December. Can you just sit on me so that I can act right?"

"How can I? You ain't where I'm at. You are not trying to make nothing happen."

"Ok. I'll try. I just said I would let you know about Cleveland. I never said no. But you're literally asking me to leave three days before a ball. Which means I would have to be completely ready. I would have to map out a lot of stuff without me not being here and me being able to fly back in. I hear you, but it's just like you are asking me sometimes to do the impossible. It's not a compromise in a way. It's like give me this right now. I hear you, but it's like you didn't even ask me about my current schedule. We both work crazy."

This point was a clear indication that he wasn't serious about being with me. All of this was a façade for the phone to fill his narcissistic supply. He took pleasure in these conversations. But had no intention on following through in real life.

"I hear what you are saying. I'm just thinking about when I can see you because I have a whole child. I can't leave and go as I please. This is the only time that I can see you when I have a nanny. I asked you to come to Atlanta when I had the nanny, and you didn't come. I even said I would come to Chicago."

"Let's not count that because I didn't even come to the ball, and I got hurt. So that should be excusable. But I hear you."

"I hear you, too. I know you got shit going on."

"I should not be thinking about your mouth on me."

"Do you call Big Mamma to have phone sex?"

"No."

"You don't?"

"Why? I don't think we should ask these questions. Isn't this gonna get both of us frustrated?"

"No, it doesn't get me frustrated; I just need to know what I'm working with. I know you still talk to her, and she's one of your girls. I just want to know what I'm dealing with versus not knowing. It's not gonna hurt me with you saying who you are fucking or not. I want us to be open. I would appreciate it if you didn't lie to me about this. Just keep it one hundred because I will keep it one hundred with you."

"Yes, me and her are fucking."

"Do you love her?"

"I do. She's a good person."

"You tell her you love her all the time?"

"No, we don't say that to each other all the time. That stopped. She's not really a fan of me still being with Rittany, and we really go in and out because of that."

"Oh."

"Do you love the masseuse?"

"No, I'm not really even interested in him like that."

"What do you think my goal is now?"

"Honestly, I don't know. Are you gonna cut me off? Are you gonna answer the phone when I call?"

"What happens if we see each other?"

"I don't care. I just want you to make me feel the way you made me feel before."

"What if it's better?"

"I know it's gonna be better because I don't understand why when I hear your voice, my pussy throbs."

"Even right now?"

"Yes. I don't know if you remember this, but I sent you a video before you came to Atlanta when you were mad at me. I told you don't do this, I need you. There is something about you that lights me up. Lights up my world. There is something about you that I can't release, and I can't let go of."

"You want to release it on me?"

"You always trying to get me to do dirty shit. I told you I can't because my daughter is in the other room. Yeah, I wanna release it on you. I wanna fuck the shit out of you. I want you to fuck my mouth. I want you to eat the shit out of my pussy with guidance from me because I need to show you how to eat my pussy. I don't want you to be offended when I give you pointers."

"What if I know how to do it already?"

"When we did it before, you didn't know how to do it the way I like it. You gotta remember that I am very sexual. I play with my pussy every day, sometimes seven times a day."

"And you be thinking about fucking me, don't you?"

"I do. I try not to think about you. When me and She-Bad have phone sex, it's not the same. I love her."

"You love her?"

"I do."

"When are you going to see her?"

"I don't know."

"Where does she live?"

"Far, far away."

"Like a different country?"

"Close to. It takes like three flights to get to her."

"How did you meet this girl?" he asked.

"On EGO."

"Oh."

"But she has been a comfort to me like no other. And she is fine AF."

"You wanna fuck her, don't you?"

"I do wanna fuck her. And she wants to fuck me, pussy to pussy... Ok, Morgan is calling. I'm gonna start my day."

"Why don't you call me back?"

"Ok, are you gonna answer? How long have you been up?"

"I just woke up when I called you."

"I was the first thing that you thought about?"

"Yeah. Cuz I wanted you since last night."

"That's when you texted me?"

"Yeah."

"I was trying to ignore it."

"I thought you was fucking somebody."

All of this for nothing. No action, no meet up, just fluff. This cycle of manipulation in the end was exhausting, but at the time I was hopeful that he was going to come around and be with me. I was lost in the hope of love and the euphoric feeling from the lovebombing stage that I was desperately trying to get back to.

After this conversation, I thought we were ok. That we could go on and be friends. That we could be civil to one another. For the next two weeks, we spoke on the phone several times. We talked about art and fashion and about what he was working on. He was preparing to walk at a ball and was wearing a custom Gucci suit.

I went to Cleveland to film a reality show, and while there, I talked to Kyrie every day. I thought we were good. I would call him from set and send him videos and pics of me working. His response was to tell me that he was with clients or that he was in meetings.

I had accepted that he was a narcissist and that I was willing to put up with it because I wanted to be in his life. In my messages, I would always be positive and try to compliment him as much as I could. I would say things like, "I can't stop thinking about how much I love you, and I'm gonna keep telling you. And I don't care what your response is. Carry on with being the boss you are! You talented fucker, u!" I knew that he liked this because it would feed his narcissistic supply, and I also liked to pour into him. It made me feel good to do so.

A few days later, I wrote to him to give me the deets on the ball and to send the pics of what he wore. He didn't answer my text messages, videos, or calls.

When he did respond, he said, "You really gotta give me a second to respond. And also respect that I have a whole girl. You call me whatever, any hour, all night."

Wow! The audacity of him. He calls and literally does whatever the fuck he wants, but he wanted me to respect him and the girl that he continued to cheat on with me and every other BBW in the world. This dude was a clown.

After he sent this, I asked if he was free and if he could talk. He told me that he was in therapy. I told him to call me when he left. He didn't call. I called him the next day, and he asked me to text him. I told him that I was driving and that I couldn't text. He asked what was going on? I told him that I needed to talk to him every day, so I would appreciate a returned call.

He told me that was not going to be possible and that I was really doing a lot, and it was making him uncomfortable, so I told him I wouldn't ever call him again. I wanted what I wanted. Goodbye.

"That's not how the world works," he responded.

I expressed to him that he had been consistently getting everything that he wanted. But the thing between us wasn't working for me because he made me uncomfortable when he didn't return my calls or showed me what I needed to see.

"You send me at least twenty-five messages and ten phone calls before I can even look at my phone," he said. "I'm working at 1 p.m. in the middle of the day. You want to see my face? Ok, but calm down. Like you are doing a lot."

"And you never call me the day I send those or even respond. You have called me several times in a day before as well, so let's not get brand new. I'm calling because I want to see you and spend time with you. Obviously, you don't feel the same. I'm not here for it, so I'm tapping out. No love lost or disrespect. I can take a hint from your actions, which are LOUD and CLEAR."

I texted him later that night and asked, "Can you talk now or does that make you uncomfortable that I'm calling you?" What was I doing? Why was I texting him after I said that I was tapping out? I was delusional, too. I felt like I was going in circles.

Whenever he wanted to talk to me, it was ok for him. Whenever I wanted to talk to him, it wasn't ok. It was all about what he wanted when he wanted and if he wanted it. It was only good if it was on his terms.

A week prior, we were talking every day, and it was all good. Now because he has a morality moment or because he was not in control, it wasn't working for him, and he now felt "uncomfortable."

Four days later, I texted him, and he ignored me. I called him, and he ignored me. He then called me back, and I think that he was with his girlfriend, and she was listening to our conversation because he was putting on a show. I told him that he had selective fucking amnesia (toxic amnesia) because it was always about him. Because he was telling me that he didn't want to talk to me and to stop calling him. I told him that I hated him and wished I never met him. I also sent him three voice messages stating, "You kept saying that you didn't want to deal with me, but you kept calling me and reaching out to me! You have a whole girlfriend, and I'm still willing to deal with you silently in spite of that. But then you continue to be wishy-washy when it's not working for you, or you have a morality issue and abruptly cut me off.

"Don't call me anymore saying that you want me to buy strap-ons to fuck you and to see you have sex with a man."

He blocked me on That's That after the exchange. I was ok with that, too. This fool had gone past hitting my last nerve. One day, he's in and then he's out. One minute, he wants to have phone sex and then he doesn't. It's the gaslighting for me.

Yet I continued to engage in conversations with the Devil.

STORY 35
October

Come October, I hadn't spoken to Kyrie for a couple of days. Arriving at my college homecoming, all I could think about was him. I was alone and lonely, and my mind wandered excessively. I wanted desperately to talk with him, but I knew if I tried to call him on That's That App or my Google Voice number, he wouldn't answer.

So I Googled apps that create fake numbers in different states. I found an app called Burner, and it gave me a Chicago number, so I got it and called him. He immediately thought that I was in Chicago. I think he might have gotten a little excited. But the excitement slowly turned to anger. I was just trying to have a regular conversation with him, and he wouldn't let me at all.

"Are you here?" Kyrie said.

"No," I answered.

"Then why the fuck are you calling me?"

From that conversation, I realized that I was dealing with an unstable individual. So much so I didn't know what he was going to do with the upcoming Order of Protection hearing. This really frightened me, so I started looking for an attorney in Chicago. For the next month, I stayed searching for an attorney to help me with my case.

I couldn't take the chance that Kyrie would try to destroy me and everything that I had going for myself. I found out immediately that Chicago lawyers were very expensive, or they were just trying to take your money by fast talking.

One lawyer quoted me fifteen thousand dollars for a retainer. This made me even more scared and fearful of my future and the outcome. I didn't have that kind of money to pay for a lawyer and all for a bunch of lies and bullshit! This was not good. I was so ashamed of myself for getting caught up with Kyrie. I knew that answering those calls would get me in trouble, but I did it anyway. I got played by this manipulative, narcissistic asshole once again.

I hated the fact that I was at my college homecoming, thinking about Kyrie's sorry ass. In need of support, I called my friends, and as soon as they answered, I burst into tears out of disgust with myself. My friend Koko said that everything was going to be ok. She told me that this was a hard thing to go through by myself. She helped me tremendously get through this moment.

When I arrived at the homecoming block party, I found a spot to sit. Not too long after, someone approached me. I knew immediately who the man was—someone who participated in band after I did; however, I remembered him differently because he had taken a total three-sixty turn for the better and was FINE AF! In the band, he was a total nerd: scrawny, glasses, classic definition of a Band Geek. But boy oh boy, did he change.

His name was Montrell, and he played the trumpet in our band. When he came up to me, I had to do a double glance because WHEW! He looked better than Kyrie! His skin was smooth as silk, and his butter pecan skin tone was buttery. If he was food, I would sop him up with a biscuit! His biceps were poppin' out of his shirt, and I knew he worked out because his body was amazing. His legs were sculpted to perfection, and his butt looked like he did a million squats a day. He had beautiful eyes that would pierce the soul of any woman and a smile worth a million dollars. I immediately thought he would be a perfect distraction from what I was going through, and he was.

We talked for a good while at the event, and he asked if we could go get something to eat or get a cup of coffee together. Unfortunately, my stomach started hurting really bad, and I had to leave and go back to my hotel. He asked if I needed a ride. I told him no. He called and texted me on my way home, and when I got back to the hotel, he asked if he could bring me food.

"Sure! Bring me some Waffle House, please!"

He did. The food was delicious, and so was he. I couldn't take my eyes off of him. He worked out, so his body was amazing, and he was so handsome.

We had a night of passionate sex! It was off the hook. He had an amazing member and knew exactly how to use it. He would be the first man to get my mind off of Kyrie.

For the rest of the weekend, we hung out together and enjoyed each other's company at each of the Homecoming events. I was super excited and was eager to get to know him better. I communicated this with him, and he thought the same.

Unfortunately, he lived far away from me and was pretty much a loner. His level of communication differed in mine as well and made it extremely difficult for us to move forward. I eventually had to bid him farewell romantically after we talked for about two months. I was sad about this because I really looked forward to developing a friendship first and then a relationship. He seemed to have his life together and it was great that we had the same collegiate background. I was really hoping that he would be my out with Kyrie.

374

STORY 36
November, Part 1

On November third, we had our virtual hearing for the Order of Protection. I had been consulting with a wonderful attorney out of Chicago, who was actually my frat brother, and his wife was my soror. He helped me tremendously in finding several solutions to my problems with Kyrie.

He told me exactly what to do and what to write to present to the court. I stayed up all night preparing for the hearing. I was so scared that this man was going to ruin my life. A day before the hearing, Kyrie started calling me. He called me twice. I didn't answer. I told my attorney, and he advised me to not engage or talk to him.

"If you do, he can have you arrested," the attorney said. "You are between a rock and a hard place because all of the odds are in his favor."

Because he filed the Order of Protection against me, he could call me whenever and however he wanted. I didn't have an Order against him, so I wasn't protected. I knew this from the very beginning, but lust and hope got in the way and led me to answer and call and talk to him several times.

The day of the trial, he called me twice. I didn't answer. Why was he calling me? I was proud of myself for not answering him. The morning of the virtual hearing, I was so nervous. I woke up early and prepared all of my materials. I also made sure I was professionally dressed. I looked really good. I signed on to the video conference early and was ready. I had my document ready to present to the judge.

When the hearing started, Kyrie did not show up, so they threw the case out! Whoo-Hoo! I was ecstatic and felt like the weight of the world was lifted off of me. I was done with this chapter, and I had survived. Here is what I was going to present to the court.

To: Family Court Judge
From: Heather Moore
Re: Order of Protection

November 3, 2021

Your Honor,

This young man, Kyrie Jenkins Dubois, is perpetuating a fraud against the court. Orders of Protection are serious business and should not be used frivolously.

Your Honor, my name is Heather Moore, and I was in a sexual relationship with Mr. Jenkins Dubois from November 5, 2020, to January 17, 2021.

Our relationship ended December 24, 2020, when I found out that he was a habitual liar who did not want to pay the monies that he owed me. I also found out that he was dating 3-5 other women at the same time as we were dating. He ended the relationship right when I confronted him. Subsequently, I reached out and told all the other women to watch out for him.

I then asked for him to return my money, and he agreed to return it, but he never followed through. During this time from December 25 to January 8, we spoke probably once a week. I got tired of asking for the money and trying to negotiate and work things out with him amicably and filed a Civil Law complaint to retrieve the debt.

I feel this Order of Protection was ordered against me in retaliation.

Kyrie has contacted me over the phone 29 times via Google Voice and 23 times via That's That App. He has sent over 69 text messages from That's That App messaging and 72 messages via Google Voice messaging since this Protective Order was filed.

He has contacted me over 100 times in total via text and via phone since this was filed.

Your Honor, I have an immediate need for an Order of Protection for my safety and peace. I feel that my safety is in jeopardy because he has threatened me and reminded me numerous times that he can always find me due to my public image and entertainment worksite venues. He has harassed me by telephone and electronically after he sought the Order of Protection. He has harassed my circle of people and friends to intimidate and humiliate me. He has referenced my daughter during his rants and too many times has made it clear to me that he can always reach me and ruin me at his choosing. He even called me twice yesterday and this morning! I feel very afraid and don't believe he will stop unless he understands that the court will provide me with the protections he claimed he needed for himself.

<u>Google Voice Calls</u>

That's That App	That's That App Chat
July 6, four times	June 2 to Sep 26, 69 messages
July 29, one time	Apr 30 to July 30, 72 messages
Aug 8, three times	
Aug 15, two times	

That's That App	That's That App Chat
Aug 19, one time	
Aug 30, one time	
Sep 4, 15, one time	
Sep 15, 16, one time	
Sep 17, 26, two times	
Sep 11, three times	

After the hearing, I went on my Instagram to acknowledge what happened to let people know about narcissistic abuse. I received so much positive feedback and comments about my bravery.

The next day, he called again, but I didn't answer. I was trying my best to follow what my attorney said and not to engage with him.

After the court hearing, I felt extremely lonely and depressed. All of the guys that I was trying to get to know were not providing me with the emotional support and affection that I needed. So, in desperation, I called Kyrie a few days later, but he didn't answer. When he did finally call back, it was at 5 a.m.

"Hey. I called you because I thought you were in Chicago," Kyrie said.

"Why did you think that?"

"I had a funny feeling."

"If I came to Chicago and called you, would you answer?"

"Just try. Do you want to fuck me?"

"What do you think?"

"Does he fuck you like me?"

"He fucks me better than you."

"Oh, he does? Why?"

"He's the first person that I've had sex with that makes me forget about you."

"You let him cum in you?"

"I don't let anyone cum in me, Kyrie. I never have; that's not my ministry. What are you doing awake so early?"

"I can't sleep."

"You said try. If I come to Chicago. And I call and you act funny, it's gon' be World War III in this bitch," I said.

"I guess you don't wanna forget about me."

"Just go with the flow, Kyrie. Shit...too many questions."

"Why are you up?"

"Because you just called and woke me up. How do you know I have a boyfriend?"

"I know everything."

"Ummm. Let me tell you something. It's nothing for me to get on a flight. But if I get on a flight, I don't want no fucking shenanigans."

"Just like I don't."

"You are the king of shenanigans. I don't want to even start. I don't want to, and I'm not about to argue with you. I don't want any of that. I'm just saying if I come to Chicago, I don't want no fucking shenanigans or morality, oh I can't do this, etcetera, etcetera. Just tell me now, and I won't come to Chicago."

"What are we doing? Are we fucking?"

"Like rabbits. Ummm. The whole shebang. I wanna see if it's still there."

"Why? Is it because you know my dick is good? That's not the question. If it's the same and then what?"

"Then I can move on with my life. I don't think it's gonna be the same.

"Your pussy still wet when he fucks you?"

"Yes."

"You didn't have that problem when I was in you. I got it all out."

"All what out?"

"All your cum out."

"I just wanna see who the fuck is gonna make me squirt."

"You know it's me, and you are not gonna squirt until you feel my dick."

"You miss my pussy?"

"I'm calling you at five in the morning. What you think?"

"Why do you miss it?"

"I just want to see how I can handle it. You're smaller. With all that ass. And I want all of it. All of it."

"Can I stay with you, or do I need to get a hotel?"

"You should get a hotel because I want to be as loud as I can."

"You can't be loud at your house?"

"Not the way you scream. Not the way that I know I'm gonna make you scream. You need to get fucked the right way."

"How much is an Uber ride from O'Hare?"

"Like thirty dollars, but there are hotels near there. Did Number One Woman tell you that I made her squirt?"

"No. You know me and her are very close. So don't say anything bad about her. I think she told you that."

"I'm just asking you a question, as to why you want me to make you squirt. Because she told you how good the dick was?"

"No, she didn't tell me that."

"So you don't even care about that, you just wanna fuck me?"

"Right. So I can be there on Tuesday."

"How long are you staying?" he asked.

"I can stay until Thursday."

"I mean next Friday I'm off, that could work. Tuesday I'm off ; Friday I'm off."

"Where you work?"

"I don't know if I should tell you."

"You at Bloomingdale's again? Gucci?"

"Naw, but something like that."

"When you start working?"

"It's been about a month."

"So would you be able to get off of work and come stay with me?"

"Yeah."

"So should I stay until Friday?"

"You could."

"Or should I do Wednesday through Friday? Yeah, these flights are cheap."

"You gonna tell your boyfriend?"

"Umm, probably not. I don't think he would want to know that."

"Does he live in Atlanta?"

"No, he doesn't."

"He looks older."

"Why are you looking at my shit, Kyrie?"

"The same reason you look at my shit. Even though there is nothing to look at."

"You look at my EGO?" I asked.

"Yeah."

"He's not my boyfriend."

"You want people to think that he's your boyfriend?"

"Nah, he's someone that I connected with at homecoming. He shot his shot, and we got it in. And it was amazing."

"He didn't make you squirt?"

"No guy has made me squirt."

"Well, he's not better than me."

"You didn't make me squirt, Kyrie."

"I almost did, a couple of times."

"But you didn't."

"It was because you didn't relax. I hope you don't stop me this time. Like you cum and you are done. That made me so upset."

"I know you like to hit it from the back, but I'm not gonna cum that way."

"What if I'm on top?"

"That's better. I will probably cum that way. I can ride you now for a long time."

"I'll grip your fat ass when you do it."

"I rode him, and he came from me riding him. I've never done that before. I wasn't tired because I'm smaller. I was like... this is amazing. His dick is bigger than yours. He has a beautiful dick."

"He doesn't know how to use it."

"Yes, he does, and he has a beautiful body-OMG."

"You sure you want me?"

"I want him, but he's different. He's different. I think he's a little damaged. He's in the Air Force. He doesn't like to talk on the phone."

"So how y'all communicate?"

"That's the problem."

"No phone sex, huh?"

"Nope. He's a loner; he doesn't like to communicate. You sent Number One Woman the text message that I sent you when I was at my homecoming? You know I'm not ashamed of what I do, and I know you still call her."

"I'm gonna fuck y'all together."

"She's not gonna do that."

"But you would."

"You know where I'm at sexually. I'm open."

"I want to have a threesome so bad."

"Who you gon' do that with?"

"I would do that with you," he said.

"Or with another girl? Can I do it with another guy?"

"Is he fucking me, too? What do you think?"

"Yep, I do think you would want him to fuck you, too. You like masculine guys."

"How you know?"

"Because you told me. My guy is not down for that. I asked one of my friends if he would do that for me, and he was like no. He's masculine. But he likes girls, too. You still talk to Big Mamma?"

"Yes."

"She still like you?"

"Yeah, we are still cool."

"Y'all still have phone sex?"

"No, we don't talk like that."

"Why not?"

"No comment. So you saying I can trust you?"

"Yeah."

"I don't know why I think you are gonna record a conversation and send it to somebody. You are making me paranoid. As much as I still want it."

"You paranoid, but you still want it."

"I like the way you sound when I'm fucking you. That shit is addictive," he said.

"You like the way Big Mamma sound when you fucking her, too, huh?"

"Yeah."

"Have you seen her again?"

"I've seen Big Mamma multiple times."

"She doesn't care that you have a girlfriend?"

"Me and Rittany are on and off. Especially since June. We have our own problems."

"Y'all together now?"

"No, we fuckin'. That's it."

"What are you going through when you say you don't want to talk to me, and you push me away and then you block me? What does that mean?"

"I told you. I am paranoid. I just don't trust you now," he said.

"How can you be paranoid when I've told you several times that I don't want to be with you. I accept the situation that you had, and I wasn't going to jeopardize what you had."

"I can't get my mind off of you. I always think about you."

"Has it always been like this, Kyrie? Like since all of the stuff happened with us, you always think about me?"

"Yes."

"You always think about me?"

"Yes. My dick shouldn't be this hard. I was playing with this shit earlier."

"Today, I was very depressed and lonely. Why? I don't know. I just didn't feel good. Hence why I called you back."

"I'm sorry you're going through that."

"I just wish you could have been a regular good person, and none of this would have happened, and we could have been good. I have never had feelings like this for somebody, where all of this shit could happen, and I still wanna fuck with him. I hear you. I know. And like just talking to you, I know what you need, and I know how to pour into you, and I think that's why you keep fucking with me."

"I just want you to sit on me and kiss me."

"I wasn't even talking about sexually, but that, too. When was the last time you had sex?"

"Yesterday."

"Do y'all fuck like over and over again?"

"Just once."

"Does she spend the night, or does she go home?"

"She spends the night."

"Did you get Big Mamma something for her birthday?"

"Why are you asking me that? It doesn't matter. What does that have to do with you and I?"

"It matters because she's the one that took you from me, and she's the one that you love more than me. Am I right? Hello?"

"Yeah."

"That's why it matters. I'm gonna see what my nanny has next week, but I'm coming."

"So are you gonna tell Number One Woman that you are coming?"

"No, I'm not," I replied, "because I'm ashamed, and she is gonna cuss me out. I can't tell anybody that I'm coming."

"Why the fuck is my dick this hard? Are you sure this is what you want?"

"Are you sure? I know what the fuck I want, Kyrie! I been wanting to fuck you since you left in January. And don't put the shit back on me. I'm consistent with my shit. You are the one that's flip floppy. Can you promise me that you are not gonna get into an argument and act crazy?"

"I'm not trying. I'm just paranoid when it comes to you. You wanna come here. I don't know when that will happen. I'm on probation at work."

"So, should I get the ticket?"

"You can do that. You said you're coming Tuesday?"

"Yeah, Tuesday or Wednesday. I can't let no one know I'm coming. Secret trip. I'll just tell my folks that I have an audition. My mom knows about you now."

"What did she say?"

"She's pissed, especially with the court shit. You had papers sent to her house."

"You sure we are doing this?"

"Yeah, I'm sure. In spite of all the shit. I told you how I feel. I can't stop fucking thinking about you. This is some bullshit. I need you to do me a favor. I need you to make me feel the way that I felt a year ago when we were fucking."

"Why?"

"Because that's what I've been trying to get back to all of this time."

"But if I do, what are you gonna do after?"

"If I do, it will show me how I should feel with my next husband. The lesson from all of this with you, Kyrie, has been self-worth and self-love. That's the lesson for me. Showing me how I should be with loving myself. That's the lesson. I know now that the reason that I feel the way that I feel about you is no man even knows you more than you think I do. I know what you think. I really know you.

"You have shown me the reason for being the only person who has made me feel this way. Mind, body, and soul. You are not the right person for me. But what you've shown me is the way I am supposed to feel with the person that I'm gonna be with. You've taught and shown me that, and that's the lesson I am supposed to learn from this. After this, I will be good. I won't need to see you or talk to you anymore. I've been good before. But when you reach out to me, it ignites my feelings again. But I'm not gonna do it anymore. I know what this is. So I'm good. I just wanna have this energy with my real dude. When's the last time you looked at my EGO profile?"

"A few days ago."

"You remember the last picture you saw?"

"I think homecoming."

"You haven't seen the new pics with a new wig on?"

"I don't think so."

"I've lost seventy-five pounds, Kyrie. I wear a size fourteen and large clothes. I can go to regular people's stores now."

"How small are you trying to be?"

"I'm trying to lose one hundred seventeen pounds. My next goal is to lose ninety pounds. I have fifteen more to go. You gon' pay for my hotel room?"

"I get paid Friday."

"So you can pay for my hotel room? Because I can pay for the plane ticket. I have to pay for the nanny. It's a hundred dollars a day."

"Ok."

"You wanna know a fun fact? Tomorrow will be a year since we talked on the phone and started all of this. So can I ask you some personal stuff?"

"What?"

"Do you want me to bring a strap-on?"

"You can."

"Okay, I have to buy one, and I don't know what kind to get. Do you have a size preference?"

"Not a skinny one."

"Okay. I love you, Kyrie."

"You sure about that."

"Yeah, I am. I'm gonna cry."

"You gonna ride me slowly?"

"Yes. We have to use protection."

"Ok."

"Is your dick still hard?"

"Uh huh."

"You playing with it?"

"You want me to?"

"No, I want you to wait until I get there. What we are gonna do, have you done that with anyone else? Me fucking you?"

"No."

"Why you wanna do that with me?" I asked.

"I just do."

"You scared it's gonna hurt?"

"I just want it."

"You'll be patient with me because I don't know what to do."

"Okay."

"So every day you get off work, you gon' come see me and stay with me?"

"Yeah." I was happy about this. I was finally going to get to see him.

After he told me that he was going to stay with me, we started to have phone sex. I lived for this because it excited me so much.

"You stroking it for me?" I asked. "How does it feel? Is it really hard? Is it super hard? Can you put it in my mouth? My nipples are hard. Are you gonna suck my pussy and lick my ass?"

"Yes."

"Can I lick yours?" I asked.

"Yes and put your fingers up there."

"You want me to put my fingers up your booty?"

"Yes. Slowly."

"Ok, I will. I can't wait." I assured him.

"I want that ass. I want that fat ass clapping on me."

"You want my fat ass?"

"Yep. My dick got bigger."

"Really? How big?"

"I don't know. Rittany told me that it got bigger."

"You ever record you and Rittany? With like no faces. Can you send me a video? Of you and her fucking. I think that would really turn me on."

"Yes."

"Tell me what you are gonna do to my pussy? I'm rubbing it right now. I'm gonna make it pulsate and clap on my dick. You gon' manhandle me or are you gonna make love to me? Or are you gonna do both? Kyrie, I'm playing with my clit. I'm thinking about you fucking the shit out of me. Are you gonna fuck the shit out of me, baby?"

"You need it?"

"Yes, I need it so bad. I miss your dick, baby. Oh, baby. I'm gonna fuck the shit out of you, baby." I moaned. "Can you call me, baby? I need you to call me baby, so that I can cum. Am I still your baby, baby?"

"Yes, baby."

"Oh, Kyrie. Oh, baby. I can see you on me. I can feel you, baby. Oh, I miss your dick so much. I have to put my finger in my pussy. My finger is in my pussy now. Oh Kyrie. Oh, baby! My pussy is throbbing. I climax. Oh, God. I came."

"I need to cum. Hold on, let me get some lotion."

"You were supposed to cum with me, fool."

"That was quick."

"Yep, it was."

"You better not stop me when I'm fucking you."

"I'm not gonna play with my pussy when you are fucking me. I'm gonna let you make me squirt like you said you would."

"I want you to ride the fuck out of me until I cum. I want you to ride it slowly and then go faster until I nut in you."

"That sounds good to me, baby."

"Baby, I love it when you call me baby."

"You gon' grab my ass, smack it, and fuck the shit out of me, baby?"

"Yes, baby. You're gonna grab mine? What if I like it? What if I like you fucking me? What if it makes me cum on myself?"

"Then that will be good. It will be even better than you having sex with me if you cum that way. I hope you cum when I'm fucking you. I just want you to be happy. I just want you to cum and feel good."

"My shit is getting so hard. I'm about to bust."

"When you want me to fuck you, do you want me to do it soft or hard?"

"Soft," he said. "And then go faster. Fuck."

"I can do that. I can't wait to do that. I love your big, beautiful dick."

"Do you remember what it feels like?"

"Yes, I remember that; it's amazing."

"Make me cum, baby."

"Can you cum in my mouth, and I swallow it? I can't wait until I suck your dick."

"Did you suck his dick?"

"I did. He didn't cum that way though. He came from me riding him. He's the first person that I fucked where I wasn't thinking about you. I'm gonna ask him to send me a dick pic. You wanna see his dick?"

"No. I wanna see him fuck you."

"You wanna record yourself fucking me?"

"Yes, I may do that."

"So, you can watch it all the time? Watching you blow my back out?"

"Yes, and watching you screaming and hollering. Yep, screaming 'Kyrie, Kyrie.' You still fucking the masseuse?"

"No, we aren't. We are still cool though. I can't wait to lick yo' booty hole. I'm gonna get all sloppy with it."

"You want this dick in your ass?"

"Yes, we can do it all. We can have a fuck fest. This is gonna be the best sex of your life. Banging this pussy and this ass. And I can't wait to get into that booty hole. I can't wait to taste that booty hole. Give me that ass, Kyrie. Give it all to me."

He was moaning uncontrollably.

"I need you to fuck me, Heather."

"I'm gonna fuck the shit out of you."

"I want your dick, Heather."

"It's gonna feel so good, Kyrie. You gon' cum, cuz you gon' be jacking yo' dick at the same time. I'm gonna hit yo' walls, and it's gonna feel so good. It's gonna be the best experience of your life."

"Fuck me, Heather."

"I'm gonna fuck you nice and slow, and then I'm gonna speed it up. You have to make sure I'm not hurting you. It's gonna be so good."

"Then I can sit on it, Heather?"

"Yes, I can lay down, and you can sit on it. That's gonna be fun. I've never seen that. Yes, get all of your rocks off, baby. Yes, all of your fantasies can come true, baby. You want me to get a big one? You want me to bring all of my other dildos, too? I can bring my rose, and we can be fucking like rabbits."

"Fuck me."

"Yes, baby, I'm gonna fuck you, baby."

"I'm about to cum on myself."

"Cum, baby. Cum for momma."

"Are your fingers in my ass?"

"Yes, baby, my fingers are in your ass. I can't wait, baby. I'm gonna put all of my fingers in your ass, one at a time."

"I want some dick so bad," he said.

"Well, I'm gonna give it to you."

"I need to get fucked."

"On Tuesday, I'm gonna fuck the shit out of you. I can't wait, baby. You gonna cum for me, baby?"

"Over and over and over, baby."

"You gon' cry for me baby? Cry for me, baby. Make sure you cry for Mamma."

"Keep going."

"You feel it, baby. I love fucking you, Kyrie. I'm fucking you harder, baby. I'm fucking the shit out of you. Ewwww, you gon cum, baby. Yes, baby. You gotta cum for me."

"Pull it out."

"Ok, I'm gonna pull it out, baby. Cum for momma. Ewwww. I can't wait. It feels so good. You have such a pretty dick."

"Make me cum."

"I say cum for momma and daddy. I'm gonna be momma and daddy when I'm fucking you. Cum on, baby. Release, baby. Release all of that cum in my mouth, baby. Cum for daddy." I was always on cloud nine after phone sex. I was excited mentally and sexually.

He had me caught up once again.

After this phone call, he ghosted me again. But he also told me that he wanted me to come to Chicago. I even told him that if he didn't give me confirmation, then I wouldn't travel there.

He didn't respond back to my text messages. I then started sending him videos of the dildo and the strap-on that I bought for us.

"Oh wow," he responded.

"Can you pick me up from the airport?" I texted, so that I knew that everything was still in order. "So we can get down to business right away?"

He didn't respond.

I then started sending him porno videos of women that looked like me to entice him. That got his attention.

He called me soon after.

STORY 37
November, Part 2

At 5 a.m. on November 15, I sent Kyrie a video of a plus-sized woman masturbating with a dildo attached to a message that read, "are you gonna help me reach my peak?"

"I'm gonna get you on Tuesday," he said. "You should let me cum in you at least once."

"Do you want to do it over and over again like over several days?"

"I want to do it over and over again."

"Ok."

"Are you gonna fuck me until I cum on myself?"

"That's the video that I sent you. I've been watching for pointers."

"Is it turning you on?"

"OMG yes. So much. Did you see the other picture? I got the stuff. I already packed it."

"Yeah. So you wanna put an eight-inch dick in me?" he asked.

"You said you wanted a big dick."

"Oh."

"We can start slow because I'm gonna bring all of my toys. So we can take it slow."

"Why are you trying to open my ass up?"

"I'm just trying to give you whatever you want, baby. Whatever is gonna make you feel good."

"Are you gonna grip my ass when you fucking me?"

"Yes, I'm gonna send you another video. Unfortunately, all they have are white people pegging on here. There aren't a lot of Black people."

"My finger is in my ass right now."

"Your finger is in your ass right now?"

"Yes."

"So do we need to fleet? Have you ever done that before? Or does it matter?"

"Fuck. Uh, baby. Oh God. I need you to fuck me."

"I'm gonna fuck you so good. It's gonna be so good, baby. I'ma start slow with just one finger and work it around. And then I add two and then slowly open you up, so you can be open to this eight-inch cock."

"Wait. We are not calling it a cock."

"Ok dick, that sounds very Caucasian of us. Eight-inch dick, and I'm gonna start slow with my purple vibrator. You want me to send you a video of me playing with my pussy?"

"Yes. What were you thinking about in that video that I sent you?"

"You."

"Fuck. Fuck."

"You are all I think about. You know that, right?"

"Why did you lie? You said that he was the only one that made you not think of me."

"I didn't lie. I made this video in June. I didn't see him until October. You want me to catch the shuttle from the airport?"

"You land at like ten? I'll come and pick you up."

"Thank you."

"I don't wanna use condoms."

"I don't wanna get pregnant, Kyrie."

"Then take a morning-after pill."

"What?" *Morning after pill?* I thought. *He's trippin' if he thinks I would do that.* I already had one child, and I was NOT gonna have another one and especially not with him. *Can you imagine being connected with him for the next 18 years!?*

"Take a morning after pill when you leave. That's gonna make you squirt, feeling all of me. That's what you need. You're a grown ass woman. You need my big, hard dick inside of you. That's what you need. Oh my God."

All of this…TALK. All of it was gaslighting. This was the game that he played. Talk on the phone acting like he really wanted to do all of these things—with no intention of following through on ANYTHING.

"I'm sending you two videos. Do you want both of them?"

"Yes, please send them. You keep playing with me."

"What?"

"I was supposed to fuck you with your girlfriend."

"You were, but she lost her mind, so I had to let her go."

"You ever fucked a girl?"

"I've never had a girl like that. I've had a threesome before though. My friend from college wants me to be a part of his poly family and sleep with his girlfriend. I might do it."

"Are you gonna fuck him?"

"Yes, I am. He's been wanting me since undergrad. I never knew, but he said that he told me."

"Did you send the videos?"

"Yes, I am now. You watching them?"

"No one has been in my ass since Rittany."

"Wow."

"She eats me out and puts her fingers in it."

"She's never strapped on? You can keep the dick and the strap if you want to keep it."

"I want you to fuck me."

I could hear his moans from watching the video.

"Is that me?" I asked.

"Yes, on my big ass TV," he continued to moan and played with himself, while watching me. "You're saying my name. You need my name to cum?"

"Yes."

"The thought of me makes you cum?"

"Yeah."

"Fuck, fuck, fuck."

"Now you got something that you can use for the rest of your life. Does that turn you on?"

"Yes, yes. Fuck, Heather. I'm gonna fuck the shit out of you. I swear to God, Baby."

"Yes, baby."

"Fuck. My ass is getting loose."

"Your ass is getting loose? You got your fingers in your ass?" I asked.

"Yes."

"Eww. Freaky."

"Put it in. You're fucking teasing me and give me that big ass dick. Give me that big dick."

"I will, baby. I'll give it to you, baby."

"Hit my spot. Pull it out."

"Ok, I'm gonna hit your spot."

"Fuck me. Fuck me. Fuck me. Punish me. Punish me. Punish me for the shit I put you through. Punish me. Punish me."

"Okay, I'm gonna punish you, baby. Because you've been a bad boy. I'ma punish you and fuck the shit out of you."

"Make me cum on myself. Make it shoot out. Oh my God, make it shoot everywhere."

"Get that nut, baby. Come for momma."

"Give me that dick."

"I'm fucking the shit out of you. I'm punishing you. Take that dick."

"Grab my ass. Grip it."

"Ok, baby."

"Give me, give me, give me that dick."

"Yes, I'm giving it to you. You taking that dick, baby."

"Get me ready. Cuz, if you fuck another man, he has to fuck me, too."

"Ok."

"He gotta fuck me, too."

"You never letting me go, that's what you saying?"

"No, keep going."

"I'ma fuck the shit out of you."

"I know you are."

"I've been waiting for this for so long," I said.

"Come on, come on. Heather, Heather, I'm about to cum on myself. That dick is gonna make me cum. Oh, um, yes. Fuck me harder."

"Yes I'm fucking the shit out of you. Cum, baby, cum."

"Fuck." He moaned hard and was about to cum.

"I'll be there tomorrow night, baby. You ready for all of this?"

"Yes, fuck."

"You cum, baby?"

"I'm 'bout to get in the shower."

"Was it good for you?" I asked.

"Em hm."

You gotta work today?"

"Yes?"

"What time?"

"Eleven to seven."

"Ok. You good?"

"Yeah."

"Anything else I need to bring? You got lube, or do I need to bring it?"

"Yeah, we need that. Bring it. I'll call you in the morning, or I'll call you later on."

"Ok so I don't have to worry about a shuttle? You are gonna come get me?"

"Yeah."

"Ok."

"Alright, I'll call you."

After we got off the phone, I felt confident that everything was a go for my trip to Chicago. I organized for Morgan to stay with her Nanny. I packed all of my things and Morgan's. I also consulted with my friends Natalie and Deeran about how to strategize, so that I would get what I wanted… to see him one more time and have sex.

The next morning, the day that I was scheduled to leave, I texted Kyrie a video of a man getting "pegged."

"I'm sorry I can't do this right now," he texted back.

"Is everything ok?"

He didn't answer.

I had a lot on my plate that day, so I really didn't have time to investigate what he was talking about. Maybe he didn't want me to send the video, or he changed his mind about me "pegging" him.

I went on about my day and prepared for the trip. I picked Morgan up from daycare and took her to her Nanny and went to the airport.

At the airport, I called Kyrie from a private number, and I asked him what he meant by he couldn't do this right now?

He said that he was cleaning his house, and he would have to call me back. He hung up the phone. I called back.

"Does this mean that you aren't picking me up from the airport?"

"Read the room!" He hung up again.

I knew at that moment that he was going to ghost me in Chicago, and there was nothing I could do to stop him. I called my friends to see what I could do to get him to see me. Natalie told me to text him, so I did.

"I'm on the plane, and my pussy is wet knowing that I'm about to be so close to you. I hope I can see you. You'll probably ghost me, and I probably deserve it."

Natalie felt that if I showed a self-deprecating spirit that it might lead him in the right direction. It didn't work. When I landed, I took a picture and texted, "I've landed at O'Hare, and I'm on my way to my hotel."

He didn't respond. The feeling in my heart at that moment was one of despair, pain, and disappointment.

Then it turned into rage!

When I got to the hotel, I went to the bar and got a cocktail, which enabled my liquid courage. I sent him a video message on That's That. I told him that "I can't believe that you had me come all the way to Chicago to ghost me. But it's cool. I'm gonna be in these Chi-

Town streets by myself doing the damn thang. I look good AF, too. I'm Gucci down to my socks. Check it, Niggah!"

After that, I met a flight attendant in the lobby, and we talked for a couple of hours. I went to my room after that.

With four days until I would leave Chicago, I called my friend who lived there and asked if we could hang out. I told her what happened. She was pissed just like me. She had come to visit Atlanta a few months prior, and I told her all about what was happening. She also had an experience with a narcissist.

She told me that the best way to get rid of them is by going no contact. I knew this as well, but I wasn't ready to do that. We hung out for the next day or so, and she showed me around town. We had an opportunity to catch up, but unfortunately, I wasn't good company. I was in a shitty mood because of Kyrie ghosting me. After we hung out, I went back to my room. I didn't cry. I was very calm about the situation. I was hurt, but I remained calm.

The next couple of days, I called him from different numbers because I was pissed.

Conversation Number 1 in Chicago

"I hate your motherfucking ass," I said.

"First off, I told you not to come because my aunt died. I told you not to come."

"You did not tell me that your aunt died. No, you did not. You didn't tell me not to come. You told me that you were picking me up from the airport."

Conversation Number 2 in Chicago

"I'm really not in the mood," Kyrie said.

"I'm really not in the mood. You made me come here, and then you ghost me."

"I told you not to come."

"You didn't tell me not to come. I thought you were picking me up from the airport."

"That day, I told you not to come."

"You texted me that you couldn't do this right now. And when I called you—"

"Exactly."

"If you didn't want me to come, my niggah, you should of fucking told me, bitch!"

"I don't have time."

"I don't have time either. I hope you burn in hell, you narcissistic ass bitch. Fuck you!"

"You done?"

"No, I'm not done. I wasted all this fucking time, and I'm calling Rittany and telling her everything. I'm calling the church and telling them everything. You gon' reap the benefits of this wrath. You gon' try to embarrass me, bitch? I'm gon' embarrass you. Get ready. You better tell your folks I'm coming."

"You want me to call the cops? I already had a restraining order against you. You really wanna try me."

"I do want to try you. I'm gonna go home, and I'm gonna make some calls to Rittany, the pastor, the church, her sister, to her brother, to her whole family. To let them know about all of your masquerades."

"Are you done? What masquerades? Nobody cares."

"All of your lies, all of your deceit."

"Because I didn't meet up with you? You're tired."

Conversation Number 3 in Chicago

"I already told Rittany and her mother. Me and her are not together, but I told her anyway. You're not gonna threaten me because I don't have an obligation to you or nothing. I never said that I would pay for a ticket. I don't owe you shit. So what do you really have? The same allegations that you made before? So you are gonna look stupid again, for what? All I have to do is call the cops and say that you contacted me, and I have a case. You really want to do this back and forth? Leave me the hell alone. I'm gonna leave you alone. I told you I'm not in the mood for this. What the fuck do you want from me? You're not gonna get anything that you want with no threat. So what do you want from me?

"Fuck you, Kyrie."

Conversation Number 4 in Chicago

"I just don't understand. Did you miss the whole part when I said I was not in Chicago? You thought I was lying?" he asked.

"You never told me that you weren't in Chicago."

"I'm gonna break this down again, and you are not gonna tell me what you thought you heard. I told you I cannot do this right now. And in the process of you talking over me, that's when I was trying to tell you that I had a death in my family.

"What do you want me to do to stop somebody from dying? Then you proceeded to do exactly what I thought you would do. Oh, I'm gonna contact Rittany. First off, that's stupid because me and her don't speak no more. So you proved why I didn't want to deal with you. That's why I go in and out with you because of that exact reason. It's like you have an arsenal waiting. I'm good. This ain't worth it. It's not."

"First of all, you didn't tell me that someone died in your family."

"I did. You didn't listen. No matter how you try to shape it, that's what I'm dealing with right now. What are you gonna make this into?"

"Make it into what? You literally acted like you wanted me to come here."

"To be honest with you, I really didn't. It goes to show that you are still on whatever type of tip that you are on, and I'm good."

"So you're trying to tell me that you had nothing to do with both of us wanting me to come here?"

"No, I'm trying to tell you that I played the game, and you fell for it."

"So you were trying to play me the entire time?"

"You think I want you to fuck me with a strap-on? You must be out of your mind. You shouldn't have come. I told you not to come."

"No, you didn't."

"I said that I can't do this right now."

"But what did that mean? You didn't say that over the phone. You texted it."

"You didn't listen. You couldn't fucking hear. What are you not understanding? Whatever you are trying to make this into, it's not gonna be. Nobody is gonna pay attention to you. Nobody is gonna give you life. I don't owe you shit. You paid your money, you got on a plane. That was your decision. I didn't force you to do nothing."

"You know what? You're right. You didn't force me to do anything. It's all my fault. It's all my fault for believing in someone that I shouldn't have believed in."

"I don't need you to believe in me. Believe in Jesus. Just leave me alone. Is this the last time that we are gonna talk on the phone because I only called you back because you called me."

"It is. This is the last time that we are gonna talk on the phone."

"Enjoy your day."

"I will."

"Enjoy," he repeated.

"You do the same."

He ghosted me. He set me up to humiliate me and ghost me. He was the epitome of a narcissist. He ruined my life for a year, and this was the pinnacle event that led me to reach my breaking point.

STORY 38
Last Story

After I was ghosted, I tried my best to be okay with the results. But I wasn't. I was hurt and felt disrespected and betrayed. But as I recollected, I believed it was all my fault. Time and time again, Kyrie showed me exactly who he was; I just chose not to believe what I saw. Being an empath, I thought there was a good side to him, and I hoped that side would show up for me because it was the least that he could do.

But that wasn't in the mindset of a narcissist. They only care about themselves. He didn't care about me; he didn't love me. He didn't care that he would crush me with what he did. It didn't matter to him. Just like all of the other times that he disrespected me or treated me bad, this was no different. He only cared about Kyrie. Kyrie wanted to hurt Heather for good. To sign, seal, and deliver the ultimate pain that he could produce…and that's exactly what he did.

As I walked through O'Hare Airport, I felt dead on the inside. I felt like a walking zombie. I felt no depth in my soul, in my heart. My eyes were tearful, and I was trying my best to contain myself from crying my eyes out and falling on the middle of the floor in the airport. I wanted to sob uncontrollably. I wanted to release all of this negative energy. I wanted to never feel this pain again.

I hated Kyrie Jenkins Dubois for what he had done to me. This was beyond repair, and this could never be forgiven. He had gone past the point of no return. He was a despicable, horrid, low class, piece of shit. It had been an entire year, and this was the finale. This was my final breaking point. This was the last chapter of the story. What I was about to write was very disturbing to write and retell. This person singlehandedly played, preyed, and manipulated me and every other woman that he came in contact with.

What you are going to read was a session in his deceitful, demonic obsession with himself and filling his narcissistic supply.

Most men would never do this for fear of retaliation, karma, repercussion, consequences, and how things might affect you. But that is if you are dealing with someone who is normal or sane. This person was in the same vein as R. Kelly, Harvey Weinstein, Woody Allen, Jeffrey Epstein, and others.

They play with someone's emotions with the intent of destroying their soul. He was playing a very deadly and dangerous game.

Unfortunately, this wasn't the first time that I thought that I was writing the last story.

Today is July 28, 2021.

I am on my way back to Atlanta from Cincinnati, Ohio. I felt very much so inclined to get this off of my chest because I have to be done with this chapter in my life. I have been communicating with Kyrie for the past month off and on. He has given me broken promises only to keep me on his narcissistic supply. I kept falling for it over and over again because there was some type of void that I was trying to fill. I wanted desperately to be in his life and be his friend, but that was not possible. It would only be on his terms, and because I was finding new boundaries for myself, I couldn't allow that to happen. When I call someone, I expect them to return my call in a timely manner. When I call Kyrie, he didn't answer and didn't respond. I was not gonna deal with that anymore.

Also, I was bringing all of this to a screeching halt because I had a horrible argument with my dad yesterday. I now understand that I had problems with accepting the verbal abuse and mental abuse from Kyrie because of him.

For many years, I endured slurs and negative words from my father because I had no other choice. I listened to him call me out of my name and degrade me because of my size and weight.

No daughter should have to endure this type of abuse from anyone, let alone their father.

We had this argument yesterday because I told my father that I would no longer allow him to speak to me in a disrespectful manner. Well, he didn't like that, and we got into a full drag out cussing match and almost went to blows. I told him that he will not talk to me crazy and will only talk to me with respect. He will also not have the opportunity to say crazy things to my daughter. He will never see her if he does that.

Because of this fight, I called and texted Kyrie one more time, and he didn't answer.

I was done.

I have closed that trauma with my Dad, which was freeing me from taking it from Kyrie any longer.

I was very proud of myself. But it wasn't over. What I realized is that I had issues. I talked to my spiritual advisor, and she told me that the current Heather wasn't the one contacting Kyrie. That it was my childhood self. She was the one that would engage with him because of all of the trauma and abuse that she endured. This was the behavior that she was used to, and that was the direction that she would go into.

My advisor told me that in order to heal my current self, I would have to heal my childhood self. In one of our sessions, she showed me how to start. She told me to give my childhood self a name. I called her

Maya. She told me to talk to Maya. To let her know that she didn't have to go through this kind of pain any longer. I had to let her know that I was going to take the driver's seat moving forward and that I had her back. I would not let anyone else hurt her anymore. I would help make her whole. This exercise only instantly helped to heal me. I knew that the reason I asked so many questions was because of Maya. Maya wanted to know. Maya expected the hurt, and it was time to set her free.

When I returned back home and as the week progressed, I found myself checking his Instagram and his girlfriend's. He told me that he wasn't talking to her, which was a bold-faced lie.

That week, I was home in Cincinnati, and it was Thanksgiving, which meant that it had been a year since this all started, and he visited me.

In fact, on my Facebook stories, our pictures came up from last year when we went on a sound bowl meditation. This was triggering for me. I still couldn't believe for the life of me why I had such heavy feelings for this disgusting individual. I wanted to move on. I wanted to let go, but it was still pulling on me heavily.

All of the pain, hurt, and disrespectful things that he had done. This spoke to the level of trauma that I was under and needed to deal with. No one should have this much power and control over your mind. This was not good.

I contacted Ron, my therapist, to see if we could start again. He told me that he would get back to me. I really wanted to work to get over this and move the fuck on.

I also started looking for another therapist to help me. The only way to heal from this was to get help. Every day, I was taking strides toward healing. I journaled daily, prayed, meditated, and I spoke to my ancestors. They were rooting for me to live in my greatness. I often thought of Kyrie, and several things reminded me of him. The one comforting thing that kept me going was knowing that he would never change and if I engaged, the cycle would repeat. Kyrie tried to contact me three times via That's That App, but I didn't respond. I couldn't. If I touched that fire, I would get burned.

This entire experience was the lowest part of my life. If that was hell, I was there. I wouldn't wish that kind of hurt or pain on my worst enemy. Going through that taught me all of the signs of narcissism and how to deal with one.

I hope that my story of desperation and wanting love will resonate with you to not make the same mistakes that I have made.

The lesson in all of this is that we all need to heal our past traumas. Our mental health is very important. Sometimes, we think we can just talk to friends or go to church to heal, but that's totally not the case. We need to be healthy spiritually, emotionally, and physically in mind, body, and soul.

January 17, 2022, a year later after operation Fuck you and Fuck you.

I went out the night before, so Morgan was with the nanny. I slept in because she wasn't home, and it felt great.

When I woke up, I checked my phone, and all of a sudden, the doorbell rings. I wasn't expecting anyone; maybe it was the mailman.

I went to the door and opened it.

"Hello, Heather."

"Hello, Kyrie."

STORY 39
Lessons Learned

The lessons that I learned and point of reference that I took away from this whole experience were invaluable. I learned all of the traits and characteristics of dealing with a narcissist.

The most important being, paying attention to the red flags. There were several. With a narcissist, they come with various traits and appear to be someone totally different than who they really are.

The first thing that Kyrie did to me was infused his charm on me and used lovebombing to hook and reel me in. At the beginning, he seemed very friendly, confident, kind, compassionate, and totally interested in me. He used his charm to size me up and worked very quickly on what made me tick and told me exactly what I needed to hear. He pretended to be the one whom I was looking for or who had a specific skill set that I didn't have myself but felt that I needed in my private or public life.

He was very creative. I thought that his creativity would add to mine, and we could be a muse for each other. Because of his sexuality, he served as a girlfriend and a boyfriend. So it was like I had the best of both worlds. With all of these wonderful qualities that he exhibited, the thoughts of "this is too good to be true" were ignored by me because it felt right. All of the comments from my friends that this was moving too fast were disregarded because I didn't want to ruin the idea that "this is exactly the person I've been waiting for."

Kyrie exhibited character traits that were questionable. The way that he spoke of his friends and so-called ex-girlfriend. Red flag! If this person was your good friend (Temi), and you were calling him everything but a child of God, none of that adds up. When he also said that his ex-girlfriend Rittany was stealing his career and spat such horrible things about her, these were also signs, truly eye-opening signs—that I ignored.

When everything hit the fan, and I tried to pour into him, he said a lot of troubling statements: He was hurt, so he could hurt other people. This is what a narcissist does. They hurt and destroy whoever is in their way, no matter who they are. There were also times when I would have solutions to the problems at hand, and we could never come to a resolution. He always had to be right. All of these instances were there for me to see, but I ignored them again.

I was suffering from cognitive dissonance, which is when you make up stories to logically convince yourself of a reality that is totally in opposition to what your emotional true self is telling you. Kyrie was abusing me little by little. Destroying me emotionally, mentally, physically, spiritually, and financially. After figuring this out, I lied to myself and tried to maintain something rather than valuing my soul, which was screaming, "Abort!"

When Kyrie showed me the Dr. Jekyll-Mr. Hyde side of him by losing his temper and yelling at me uncontrollably, I should have left. My first mind told me to do so, but I fell for his gaslighting and lovebombing. I had no idea what was going on. Because I am an empath, I saw the good in him, not knowing that I was dealing with a sociopath. After he showed this side of himself, he immediately went into a quiet smear campaign to his friends that we shared on the app, saying that I called him homophobic slurs, which was not true. This immediately made these people think that I was the one who was unstable, which was far from the truth.

This experience with Kyrie was very powerful and emotionally binding and draining. When I would share what was going on, most people could not understand why I would endure such pain. Hell, I couldn't either. The reason that this was so traumatic was because of what's called trauma bonding. Trauma bonding is whatever unhealed traumas we have inside us regarding our love/relationship code and are exactly the people and situations we seek out, are attracted to, attractive to and make excuses for.

Narcissists are a spiritual phenomenon entering our life to reflect back to us the unhealed parts of ourselves that get smashed up to the surface. These are our unhealed parts which were once unconscious. Narcissistic relationships are not ho-hum or light in nature. They are seriously impactful and excruciatingly emotionally intense. If they were not, then they would not generate the serious awakening in our life that needed self-reflection and healing.

Kyrie connected with my unhealed love code dealing with my father. Because he was verbally abusive to me, I accepted this and looked for this in Kyrie. I literally ignored what he would say because I was used to this kind of trauma and pain. The subconscious Heather, the little girl who was verbally abused throughout her life, gravitated toward this abuse because it was what was normal for her. This connection created extremely powerful bonding chemicals, which led me to be in supreme anguish when my narcissistic relationship deteriorated. The abuse that I was enduring continued, and in my head, I was not going to leave Kyrie and stay away no matter how bad he treated me. When I was trauma bonded with Kyrie, my body controlled my head. My head was following the programs of my body. When the red flags came at the start, they were ignored because of the bond. Then when they became a little more obvious, and I would second guess, doubt myself, and even explain them away to myself.

Basically at the heart of all of this, self-healing is paramount. It is important to take the necessary time needed to heal old wounds and childhood trauma. I found a mental health professional to help me do the "root work," getting down to the nitty gritty of the why. This all takes development, inner healing, and consciousness. It's also important to take the time to get to know people and have those hard conversations and ask for verification, especially if they are pushing for a fast connection. Doing the investigative work is hard, but if there are signs that present pause, look into it more and ask questions. If it looks like a duck and quacks like a duck, it's a duck.

During this entire process, I realized that Kyrie had severe mental issues and struggled with his sexuality because he was molested and abused as a child. He used titles and deflected from his truth because he had not come to grips with what he wanted and who he truly was inside. I know that he opened up to me because I was the first person who truly accepted him and loved him for who he was: gay, bisexual, or pansexual. He had to learn how to accept that and only allow people in his space that accepted that as well.

As long as he continues to live double and triple lives, he will continue to suffer and not truly be at peace. I can only hope that he will seek out the proper help and guidance to truly be free. There has to be a large amount of mental turmoil that he endures daily. A never-ending hell on earth that he experiences subconsciously. I also realized that he is hurting on the inside, and hurt people hurt people. I know that I am not the first person and won't be the last that he has done this to.

I forgive him of all of the pain that he made me feel, but I will never forget.

I wrote this book to heal myself and also try to help others in their mission to heal. I hope that this story has inspired or helped you on your path for discovery and recovery. I am a work-in-progress every day because of the turmoil that I experienced with Kyrie. I work toward being the best person I can be mind, body, and soul. During the whole process, it was important that I showed myself grace. Show grace to yourself, too.

Thank you for going on this journey with me.

Narcissist Help Guide

Narcissist Meaning

Aside from being tricky to live with, those who suffer from Narcissistic Personality Disorder (NPD) will follow familiar narcissistic behavior. Most notably, they're identifiable by their:

- Lack of empathy for others
- Inflated sense of importance
- The deep need for excessive attention and admiration
- Perpetually troubled relationships

Official Narcissist Definition for NPD

The Diagnostic and Statistical Manual of Mental Disorders has outlined nine key criteria for Narcissistic Personality Disorder. The official narcissist definition for NPD includes:

1. Grandiose sense of self-importance
2. Preoccupation with fantasies of unlimited success, power, brilliance, beauty, or ideal love
3. The belief they are special and unique and can only be understood by, or should associate with, other special or high-status people or institutions
4. Need for excessive admiration
5. Sense of entitlement
6. Interpersonally exploitative behavior
7. Lack of empathy
8. Envy of others or a belief that others are envious of them
9. Demonstration of arrogant and haughty behaviors or attitudes

What Causes Narcissistic Behavior?

For those with NPD, the traits they possess are ingrained. While it's not fully understood how a person becomes a narcissist, there are some common background issues, many of which can be observed from early puberty. Usually, a parent gives excessive pampering in childhood years. They might have come from a broken home, having abandonment issues that forced them to rely only on themselves. These people have substituted the lack of love and support from a parent by overemphasizing their own self-worth.

NPD seems to affect more males than females. But even though the list of famous narcissists is headlined by dictators and cult leaders, not all those who exhibit the common traits are motivated by fame or money. It's important to make this distinction in the dating arena. If you focus too much on the stereotype, you'll often miss the red flags that aren't directly related to vanity or greed. Some narcissists may be of the communal variety and actually devote their lives to helping others. They are grandiosity, altruistic martyrs, self-sacrificing and big-noting themselves at all times. And they are highly introverted or vulnerable individuals. They feel they are more temperamentally sensitive than others. They react poorly to gentle criticism and need constant reassurance, and they feel superior to others, and they are not necessarily satisfied with themselves as a person.

Signs You Are Dating a Narcissist

It's an interesting disorder that can be altruistically confusing. On one hand, they can be magnetic and highly skilled at attracting people. Their charm can be seductive, their charisma can light up a room, and their confidence can be comforting, which is why so many people fall into the trap of dating them. Narcissists are smart, which is why they are so skilled at getting what they want. These traits draw us in for good reason. The seductive traits are the ones that block our ability to detect red flags. They play into our vulnerabilities and egos, and we end up being pulled so deep in.

9 Traits of a Narcissist & Behavior to Watch For

1 | Lack of Empathy

A lack of empathy may be the key-defining characteristic of a narcissistic person. It is the inability to identify with or recognize the experiences and feelings of other people. Everything is about them and belongs to them. They smoothly overstep the personal boundaries of others, mistreating, devaluing, and humiliating to bend others to their desires. From a basic perspective, a narcissist does not care or understand how other people feel and rarely considers other people's feelings in their actions or words. This can manifest itself in physical or verbal ways. For example, a narcissist will often say cruel things in an offhand manner, remaining oblivious to the pain they cause with their words. It is not unusual for them to launch into a one-way discussion about what they are doing, without any regard or even inquiring about how the other person feels. They become highly impatient or even annoyed when other people share their problems.

2 | Manipulation

Another weapon in the arsenal, manipulation is a major sign that you could be dating a narcissist. The ability to twist the situation to better suit their narrative is a poignant personality trait that all egotistical people possess. It can be exhausting for those in the relationship. When a person is so skillfully manipulative, you may find yourself falling into their trap and remaining relatively unaware it is happening. Years later, you will connect the dots and see the manipulation is clear as day. But we often miss it. Narcissists are masters at getting what they want, and because they have no empathy, they may not care what it costs to someone else. They deviously use manipulation as a tool to get their most essential needs met, which are typically attention, validation, and status.

3 | Projection

A clear-cut sign you are dating someone with NPD is the psychological trick known as projection. A self-absorbed person will accuse someone else of doing what they are doing or will call out their flaws and fears in someone else; more often than not, the person who is cheating accuses his partner of cheating. Projection is a defense or an unconscious pattern that occurs when the person feels psychologically threatened. The narcissistic ego is always monitoring the world for threats and often finds them. Then they quickly blame other people for their deficits.

Projecting is frustrating because your partner is actually accusing you of doing things you aren't actually doing. These projections are not just about cheating and betrayal; they can be about the narcissist's own vulnerabilities and weaknesses. They are likely to be accusing you of what they are doing or feeling.

4 | Emotionally Cold

It's not a huge surprise, but those with NPD are continually shallow with their emotions, meaning they don't do well with emotions. To be with an emotionally cold partner often means not being comforted, sometimes during the most difficult days in our lives, the relationships expert explains. The emotionally cold or distant trait rears its head during arguments when one person is experiencing and expressing significant emotion and the narcissistic person just checks out and does not respond—or does in a cold manner. The emotional coldness can be confusing for you and may result in attempts to jump through hoops to generate warmth and connection with your partner.

5 | Gaslighting

This is a term that has been gathering pace over the past few years, and people are suddenly realizing the link to narcissism. From a historical perspective, the term arose from the 1930s' play *Gas Light*, where a husband, in an attempt to drive his wife crazy, keeps turning down the gas-powered lights in the house. When the wife asks why he is dimming the lights, he denies it and says there is no dimmer. Over time, she finds herself going mad. Gaslighting qualifies as a form of emotional abuse that involves denying a person's experience and making statements, such as "That never happened" or "You are too sensitive." The gaslighter uses techniques, such as withholding or stonewalling, contradicting, or diversion. An example would be you bringing up something that concerns you, and your partner turns it into something you said years before or deflects it and describes it as a conspiracy. They also minimize your feelings and deny events that definitely occurred. The damage of gaslighting is that it is confusing, isolating, and often results in you questioning your own reality. You may find yourself constantly apologizing and no longer as relaxed and joyful as you once were.

6 | Never Takes Responsibility

Being in a relationship is a partnership; there should be give and take in every aspect. Part of this means accepting when you are wrong and taking things as they come: two things narcissists generally struggle with. They are master deflectors and try to avoid the blame with lying, cheating, and everything in-between. They will make up complex excuses and rationalize anything. When someone never takes responsibility for anything, words, actions, feelings—it is challenging, if not an impossible way to maintain a relationship. Even preschool aged children are asked to take responsibility for a broken crayon or toys left out. It is not too much to ask a person to take ownership. Since they are unable to distinguish the boundary between responsibility and blame, narcissists attempt to avoid both. Genuine acceptance of responsibility is very unlikely to be issued by someone with NPD, and you can wear yourself out by waiting for it.

7 | Controlling

The term "control freak" gets thrown around a lot, but it's a key trait. What makes the situation even more frustrating is that often the narcissist is controlling you while remaining completely disinterested in the other aspects of your life. Like many other traits, the other person in a relationship can mistake control for affection. It's natural to want to be involved in your partner's life, but it's not healthy to dictate it. Control is often a part of abuse dynamics in relationships. The control culminates to the point where a person feels like they cannot move without asking for permission, and the narcissist uses control to isolate the person. The most common manifestations of this relationship control are a partner monitoring your whereabouts at all times, checking your emails and text messages, criticizing your appearance, and making nearly all-important decisions, with little regard for your opinion.

8 | Grandiosity

Grandiosity is a pattern in which a person tends to exaggerate accomplishments, talents, connections, and experiences. They do not have to be real experiences. Grandiose people tend to maintain over-the-top fantasy worlds. Grandiosity can also be manifested by a sense of self-importance—a belief that their existence is bigger and more important than anyone else's and certainly more important than yours.

9 | Infidelity

Sadly, the culmination of the previous eight signs will inevitably lead to a final or habitual act of betrayal; they will cheat. Their need for admiration and novelty is so vast that they are wired to be unfaithful. Affairs are typically characterized by excitement, flattery, and superficial grandiosity. They may keep a steady relationship with you, and cultivate other needs outside the relationship.

<u>How to Prepare for a Breakup with a Narcissist</u>

- Constantly remind yourself that you deserve better.
- Strengthen your relationships with your empathetic friends.
- Build a support network with friends and family who can help remind you what is reality.
- Urge your partner to go to therapy.
- Get a therapist yourself.

About the Author

Mara Hall is an actress and new author from Detroit, MI. She is the mother of a beautiful daughter Marley Nicole. Learn more about Mara at her website: www.marahall.com.

www.ingramcontent.com/pod-product-compliance
Lightning Source LLC
Chambersburg PA
CBHW060606300726
48975CB00005B/1468